DARE TO CALL ME VAMPIRE

DARE TO CALL ME VAMPIRE

TAMARA GRANTHAM

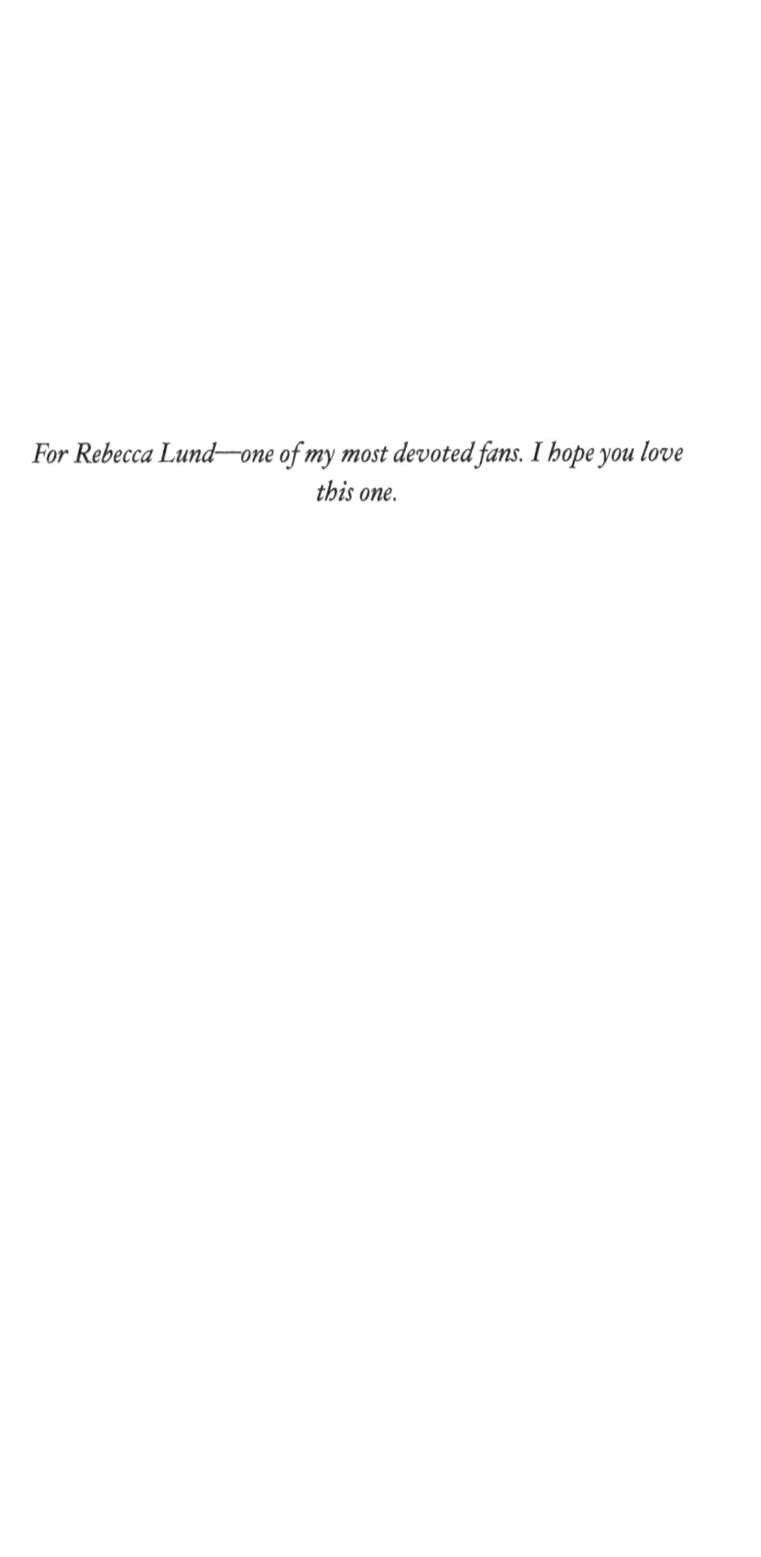

For Rebecca Lund—one of my most devoted fans. I hope you love this one.

Tyger Tyger, burning bright,
In the forests of the night;
What immortal hand or eye,
Could frame thy fearful symmetry?

William Blake

1

AMAYA

Shadows chased me. Autumn leaves muffled my horse Pharaoh's hoofbeats as I led him through the forest. His black coat disappeared in patches of mist. Although the trail behind remained empty, the fog enshrouded tall pines and hawthorn bushes. A brisk wind brought a chill that burrowed under my skin. My wolf-Husky, Kahn, paced silently alongside, his ears pricked forward, as if he too sensed the ghosts of the woods wandering just a hair's breadth away.

When we entered the clearing by the stream, Khan bounded to the water. My horse gingerly picked his way over leaves and sticks until he reached the shore. Afternoon sunlight broke free from a layer of thick clouds, dappling the forest floor with its rays.

I sat on a nearby boulder and clasped my hands. Electricity buzzed under my fingertips. I exhaled a pent-up breath. Worries crowded my mind, and it was only in places like this—out in nature, away from people—where I felt I could finally think. Yet why did today feel so different? I glanced over my shoulder, though saw nothing but an empty forest half-hidden in the mist and deepening shadows.

Shaking my head, I attempted to put the worries out of my mind. Since returning from Romania last fall, my life had been a whirlwind of transformations. I'd begun to use my ability, I'd helped Lucian recreate the facility, and I'd learned more about the aftereffects of viridae sangre than could possibly be necessary. Pretty impressive resume for a college dropout.

Still, despite these accomplishments, an empty hole had opened inside me, and I wasn't sure how I would ever fill it. The chasm had cracked open after my parents' deaths, and although being with Lucian had seemed to help for a time, he'd grown distant, reopening those old wounds that had never properly healed.

A flock of ravens called from overhead. My eyes trailed to the horizon. Above the treetops rose the towers of Crimson Hollow. The place was all but abandoned since we'd started work on the new facility. Still, Crimson Hollow was an imposing structure that refused to blend into the landscape. Its granite gray stones seemed to puncture the sky. It stood as a grave marker to the thousands of lives that had died inside its walls.

I didn't go inside much anymore.

Call me a coward, but the place terrified me.

Twisting my fingers, a burst of static zapped from knuckle to knuckle, so I unclenched my hands and held them in front of me. I still had trouble comprehending my *powers* when I thought of them. This sort of thing happened to people in movies, not regular twenty-one-year-old girls from Miami.

When I snapped my fingers, a burst of blue flame flickered, wavered in the gusting wind, and I focused on holding it steady. The heat warmed my face, but my fingers had turned strangely cold, as if the fire were using my own heat for fuel. How the process worked exactly, I couldn't be sure. Scientists had only speculated how those with viridae sangre controlled fire, since no one had experimented on us. Not that I'd want them to.

Khan trotted to me, sniffing the fire as he always did, curiosity in his wolfish yellow eyes.

After extinguishing the flame, I patted his head. I still hadn't found much use for the talent, unless one counted making tacky internet videos, which I refused to do. The facility had already started getting bad press after we'd released the cure. The public was more afraid of us now than when we'd been supposed vampires. Could I blame them? People who wielded fire were dangerous. There was no denying it. Before, we'd just been a bunch of sick people who drank blood. Now, we were a threat. No. I wouldn't advertise my ability.

Lucian had enough trouble on his hands.

Since his transformation, he'd only become more popular. We'd resorted to building fences and posting a dozen more guards, but that was only a temporary fix. I couldn't blame Lucian for worrying about me and everyone else at the facility, but it seemed his worries had consumed him, and I rarely saw the man I fell in love with.

Khan's ears pricked, and his gaze darted to the trail.

I turned and saw a dark-clad figure moving toward me.

A trickle of fear went through me before I realized who it was. Lucian moved soundlessly through the underbrush, as if he were part of the forest, as if he belonged here.

"You scared me," I called to him as he emerged from the shadows.

His smile held a hint of humor. He kept his hands tucked into his hoodie's pockets. While he'd ditched the sunglasses and gloves, his hood still shaded his face, leaving him half-clad in mystery.

I still had to catch my breath at his magnetic presence. There was something about being a vampire transformed, coupled with being one-hundred-and-sixty-something, that made a person so much greater than a simple human. He was tall and corded in muscle, and he had an angular face that resembled a Roman statue, but there was more to Lucian Vidraru's immensely overwhelming charisma than looks alone. It was the feeling of standing on the edge of a cliff and looking out at miles of vast earth, enormous and breathtaking and frightening all at the same time. His presence made my breathing stutter and heart race faster, feelings that could overwhelm me if I let them. Instead, I took a deep breath to steady my nerves.

Lucian sat beside me and nudged my shoulder. "I thought I'd find you out here." He leaned in and gave me a kiss, and in that one moment, my worries melted away.

His lips were soft and inviting, and I never wanted him to leave my side again. But he pulled away, then grabbed my hand, his skin soft on mine.

"You've got to warn me next time," I said with a wink. "Yell my name or something." My lips quirked into a half-smile, and I squeezed his hand. Being near him was a breath of fresh air, and a heavy weight on my chest lifted. With his nearness, my insecurities faded.

He ran the pad of his thumb over my cheek. A tingle went straight to my toes, and I couldn't help smiling.

"You're blushing," he said quietly, his voice deep, as he leaned toward my ear.

Tail wagging, Khan jumped up and propped his front paws on Lucian's lap. Lucian laughed, patting my dog's head.

"Hey, you," he said to Khan. "What's Amaya doing out here?" He gave me a quick glance.

I shrugged, then picked up a leaf and twirled it in my fingers. "Just wanted some time to think."

He nodded. His gaze wandered to the horizon, where the towers of Crimson Hollow dominated the sky, and his eyes darkened. "I need to go inside and find a book. Want to come with me?"

Go inside? Was I ready for that? "I don't know." I hesitated. "Doesn't the place bring back bad memories? It's super creepy in there, especially since it's abandoned now."

"I know, but it's adventurous, too."

I frowned. "That's one word for it."

A smile tugged at his lips. "You need more adventure in your life. Admit it."

"I've got plenty, thanks." I nudged his shoulder, and he grabbed my hand, then kissed my knuckles.

"Let's go," he said. "I want to get this over with."

"Okay, just let me take care of Pharoah first."

We stood and made it back to the barn, where I unsaddled Pharoah and let him out to graze in the pasture. As we hiked to the main building, we took a path through the woods. Twigs snapped under our shoes, and the cawing of crows sounded in the distance. The air smelled of autumn leaves, and patches of sunlight burned off some of the fog and warmed my skin. Funny I hadn't noticed the warmth until now.

When we entered the clearing leading to the building, the towering structure overshadowed us. My skin bristled with chills, and it was hard to fight off the fear trickling through my blood. Snapshots from Crimson Hollow's past surfaced in my memory. The sickness and death had left an imprint on the walls and lingered in the passageways. In the past, especially when I'd been alone, I'd felt as if I were being watched, as if the dead were still lingering. I still felt that way at times.

We hiked over the lawn and to the gravel pathway, and I couldn't help but notice the eyes of the stone-carved angels seeming to follow us. I'd gotten that feeling since the first day I'd entered this place, and the uneasiness hadn't lifted.

I gripped Lucian's hand, and Khan trotted silently beside us, his ghostly white body standing out against the oranges and reds of fall leaves. When we reached the entrance, the oaken doors loomed before us. Lucian pulled a ring of jangling keys from his pocket and stuck one of them into the lock. He turned the key, and the door swung open on rusty hinges.

Afternoon sunlight only illuminated a small area of the

entrance. Dust covered the marble floor. Beyond that, darkness swallowed the foyer, and my spine tingled with fear. When we stepped inside, our footsteps echoed through the immense empty room. The ceiling spanned up to a dome thirty feet above.

The scent of char still lingered from last year's fire. Yellow police tape blocked a staircase. Soot covered one of the walls and dusted the ceiling. The place sat in a state of half-repair, in limbo, waiting to rot, but never actually dying.

"They never could repair it properly," he motioned, as if sensing my thoughts.

"I never understood why. They did all that work to fix everything, then just stopped and said it wasn't repairable. It doesn't make sense. What happened, exactly?"

His eyes wandered, as if he were revisiting the past. "The fire revealed a whole host of problems. Faulty wiring, tons of fire hazards, asbestos, you name it."

"You've told me that before, but I never understood why we didn't just get everything replaced?" I'd asked Lucian before, but he'd always dodged the questions. Made me wonder what he was hiding.

"Too expensive," was his only answer.

"Too expensive?" I raised an eyebrow.

He cast a sidelong glance at me.

"What are you not telling me?" I asked.

He frowned, still not answering.

"Lucian," I prodded.

He smiled. "Amaya," he mimicked my tone. "Everything's okay. At least, it will be."

I pulled my hands from his. We stood near the windows overlooking the graveyard. The soot and grime on the glass made it hard to see the headstones, which loomed as shadowy outlines against the forest.

Dad was buried out there, somewhere. My heart clenched at the thought of his body decomposing underground. I remembered the way he laughed at his own jokes that were never very funny, the way he made Mom roll her eyes, the sound of his voice as he called me *My Amaya*. He would waggle his eyebrows and speak so fast, it sounded as if he were calling me *Maya Maya*. It all felt like a different lifetime now, and I wondered if that was how Lucian felt, having seen so much, lived with so many different families, as if he were a spectator watching life pass by over and over again.

I glanced at the man standing beside me, his profile barely illuminated by the sunlight managing to seep through the window, as he stared out over the graveyard.

"What did you mean just then?" I asked, my tone serious. "Everything will be okay? What's wrong? You'll have to tell me someday. Might as well be now."

He sighed, standing to face me. "I suppose you're right. I can't keep secrets from you. I've been so closed off all my life, talking openly about my problems doesn't come easy, to say the least."

I rested my hand on his arm. "But things are different now. I'm here for you. I always will be. Lucian, what's troubling you? You've been closed off for months now."

He ran his hand down his face, and it was only then I noticed the circles under his eyes. In the past, he'd worn sunglasses to hide the strange appearance of his red, reptilian eyes. But now, even with his eyes humanlike—a rich brown, the color of teakwood—it seemed he still needed something to hide behind. "I don't know how to put this."

I gently squeezed his arm. "Just try your best."

When he looked me in the eyes, his jaw locked, anger simmering in his irises, I had to make a conscious effort to breathe. "Amaya... when Dr. Warren left, he took everything."

I tilted my head, confused. "What do you mean *everything*?"

"Everything. Every cent I earned in my life. He had access to my bank accounts. He knew one day I would figure out what he was doing, so he made sure he had access to all the wealth I'd accumulated. We don't even have insurance, Amaya. Worse, he defaulted on taxes, and now we owe thirty-four thousand to the government. If I can't pay it in three months, we lose everything. The new facility is gone. Everyone who lives here to get treatment will have no place to go." He sighed and glanced away. "Anyway, now you know why I didn't want to tell you."

Shock rooted me to the spot as I tried to process his words. "And you didn't bother to share this with me? What can we do?"

He locked eyes with me. "There's only one thing we can do. We need investors. Sadly, there aren't many people willing to put money into the facility. Call it superstition or fear, but people like us have gotten a bad reputation. We scare people. No one wants to touch us. Well... no one, except for one corporation."

"One corporation?" I tilted my head. "Who?"

"They're called Zen-Viro. Ever heard of them?"

"No. Should I have?"

He shrugged. "Maybe. They're a research development firm creating pharmaceuticals from naturally derived sources. Botanicals and organics from the rainforest. That sort of thing. Some of their developments have been groundbreaking."

"Then that's good news for us, right?"

"Yeah, sort of, but they're controversial. Some of their methods and treatments are questionable, and they haven't gotten approval from the government. They're about as well-liked as us. Even so, we could use their help. They have the funds to pull us out of this mess, but they haven't committed to anything yet."

"So, we set up a meeting with them," I suggested. "Tell them what we're up against and why we need them."

"I tried. But they want to make sure they know what they're getting into before financing us. They're sending two of their top reps out here tomorrow."

"Tomorrow?" I gasped. "Why didn't you tell me this sooner?"

He took my hand again. "Maybe it's a lousy reason, but I

couldn't. You've got enough to worry about without me adding to it. Plus, this is my problem, not yours."

I squeezed his hand. "You're wrong. We're in this together. You need to stop taking all the burdens on yourself. Let me help you. It's what I'm here for. What time is the meeting tomorrow?"

"Amaya, you don't have to be there for that."

I ground my teeth in frustration. "But I want to. Haven't you heard a word I've said? Please. Let me help."

"All right," he conceded with a sigh, glancing at the windows where the empty graveyard waited. His eyes seemed to track past the graves, past the forest, past the horizon, to a time only he knew.

"Lucian," I said quietly, placing my hand on his shoulder. "You still with me?"

He gave a single nod. "Yes," he said, then took a deep breath. "Sorry." He gave me a quick smile, one meant to put me at ease. I wasn't buying it.

"Is something else bothering you?" I asked.

He frowned, then opened his mouth to speak when a bang echoed behind us.

We spun around to face the stairwell.

"This place is empty, right?" I asked.

"Yeah. No one has a key but me."

"Then what made that sound?" I asked.

His eyes widened. "I don't know. Squatters, maybe? We should probably find out."

He took my hand, and we hiked to the staircase, then ducked under the yellow tape. Our footsteps reverberated over the marble steps as we climbed. When we reached the top, we followed the hallway.

Another thud echoed, this time closer.

I pointed to a door at the end of the hall. "Dr. Warren's old office."

He nodded. His clenched jaw revealed his pensive mood. "Let's check it out."

I hesitated. "Are you sure? If there's a vagrant or someone living here, it could be dangerous."

He lifted an eyebrow, curiosity written on his face. "By now, you should know people like us don't fear danger." His smile revealed the edge of his teeth, and a bit of humor reflected in the hue of his slightly red-tinted irises. "We welcome it."

2

From the editorial section of the New York Daily
by Brandon Bowman

The untapped resources of fire wielders, or phoenixes, or whatever you prefer to call them, is glaringly obvious. Call them whatever you like, they're power. Why? Simple. Imagine a homegrown John Doe enlisting in our US army. How much of our taxpayer money goes to arming this person? Would it surprise you to learn that the number is in the tens of thousands of dollars? That's right. We're shelling out some serious cash to afford arming just one member of our military. Crazy, right? Now imagine a fire wielder joining. Same army, same rank, same everything except for one thing—this person already possesses their own weapon. Now how much of our taxpayer dollars are being spent on arming this soldier? None.

Do the math yourself. We're better off recruiting fire wielders to fight our battles. They are literally a powder keg awaiting a lit fuse, primed for the annihilation of our enemies.

LUCIAN

Dust tickled my nose as we entered Dr. Warren's old office. With only a little light seeping through the windows, Amaya and I turned on our phone's flashlights. Most of the shelves sat empty, which was a stark reminder of what had happened in this place.

Dr. Warren now sat in a prison cell. The government had confiscated his research. Although the doctor was gone, a chill still prickled the back of my neck, as if he knew we were here, as if he could sense us wandering through his once-private office. The room looked skeletal in the light, the shelves covered in dust and seeming to stretch forever into the darkness.

"No squatters," I said, running my hand over the imposing wooden desk hulking at the center of the room. The wood grain was smooth and cold. It elicited memories of the man who'd once sat there, his eyes secretly calculating as he'd manipulated my fame to accumulate a fortune for himself, one that he'd taken with him once he was gone, and I quickly yanked my hand back.

"I hate this room," Amaya said.

We wandered toward the staircase.

"I do too," I answered. "But I don't want to leave anything behind. The information Dr. Warren collected could be dangerous in the wrong hands."

Amaya shot me a questioning glance. "What do you mean by that?"

"All those myths and legends," I explained. "All the research. There's a little truth to every story, and like my father, Victor Warren was interested in finding those creatures of myth and using them for his own purposes. Creatures like me." I ran my hand over the staircase banister, stirring the dust, as if rousing the ghosts of this place. "Unlike my dad, Dr. Warren wanted to use them for his own selfish reasons."

"But he can't hurt anyone anymore. So we've got nothing to worry about, right?"

"Maybe."

Amaya raised an eyebrow. "Maybe?" she questioned. "You don't sound convinced."

"Victor Warren's a conman, Amaya. He managed to evade the authorities for more than two decades. I don't think a prison cell can keep him from manipulating people. He still has power. Even in prison."

"Do you think he'd come after you?"

My gaze wandered to the top of the staircase, where a little sunlight seeped through a stained-glass window, painting the banister railing in shades of copper and crimson. "I wouldn't put it past him."

Footsteps thudded from the room above us. "There's someone here," I said quietly.

Amaya nodded. "Unless it's a ghost."

Or Sally, I almost added, but didn't. Saying her name out loud felt as if it might conjure her. She'd escaped after our confrontation in Romania. We hadn't heard from her since. Was it possible she had returned? If we caught her, she'd go to prison for aiding Dr. Warren in his scams, but still, I wouldn't put it past her to come back to this place. It had been her home, after all.

We took the staircase leading up to the room once known as Archive Five. Now, the door had been removed, revealing an open space filled with scattered books and overturned shelves.

"What happened in here?" Amaya asked as we entered the space.

"Looters broke inside, most likely," I answered, my tone dark. I bent and picked up a book. *Vampire Myths Through the Ages.* "Victor loved collecting books on vampire lore. He probably owned every book on the subject. No wonder he was so fascinated with me."

"But you weren't a vampire. Not really."

"Yes. That must've bugged him. He tried so hard to perpetuate the myth of me being a vampire." I sighed and tossed the book on the floor with a thud. "Never succeeded in making me one."

We wandered through the open space, past overturned bookshelves, and empty cans of food. In a room at the back, we found a blanket and pillow, along with open candy wrappers and other garbage.

Amaya nudged a banana peel with her toe. "This hasn't even turned brown. Someone's been here recently."

I nodded, considering who might have been hiding in here, when scurrying came from behind us. Spinning around, I spotted the form of a skinny teenage boy, and I recognized him. Jayden Black. Stains spotted his ripped jeans and T-shirt. His hair was a disheveled mess, with sticks and leaves knotted in the dark strands. He stood staring at us with wide, surprised eyes.

"Hello," Amaya said calmly.

Tilting his head, he gave us a look of confusion. A glint of madness reflected from his irises.

"Leave," he growled before he turned and sprinted away.

We chased after him. When we entered the main room, clattering came from a hallway, and we followed the sound until we reached a dead end.

"Where'd he go?" Amaya asked.

"I don't know."

We paced the hallway when a breeze wafted. Amaya and I stepped to the paneled wall. Fresh air drifted inside. Amaya grabbed one of the panels and it slid aside, revealing a narrow metal ladder bolted to the stones of the building's exterior. I caught my breath as I looked down at the drop nearly three stories down. A shadow darted off the ladder, to the ground, and out of sight behind the building. When I tried to see where he'd gone, Amaya slipped as she also glanced over the edge, and I grabbed her slim waist, pulling her to my chest.

"Steady," I said calmly in her ear, the scent of lavender enveloping me.

"Yeah." She spoke with breathlessness, then placed her hand over mine.

We stood at the opening, staring out over the horizon past Crimson Hollow and into the heart of the forest.

One of her delicate eyebrows lifted. "Did you know this exit was here?"

"No." My gaze wandered to the mountains. "I suppose there are a few secrets Crimson Hollow is holding onto. At least the mystery of where Jayden gets in and out is solved."

She tilted her head, glancing up to stare me in the eyes, as I stood holding her against my chest. "Jayden?"

"Jayden Black," I explained. "He's the boy who went missing a few years ago. You may not remember me telling you about him, but he didn't respond well to treatment. He went missing for a while, until we realized he was still here."

I drew her back, away from the edge, and kept my hands protectively around her waist. Holding her to my chest, I brushed a kiss over her temple.

Her warmth filled me with a peace I hadn't experienced in ages—and certainly not in this lifetime. We stood together, overlooking the view of the forest, of fiery reds contrasting undertones of gold.

Resting her head against my chest, I listened to the steady sound of her breathing, of the life that filled her lungs, a sound I dared not hope for only a year ago when she'd been infected with the virus. Now, was it still dangerous for me to hope we would have a future together?

I knew we needed to go. We had things to do and dozens of people who depended on us, but for the moment, I simply stood with her, her head pressed to my chest, and I had never felt more complete than in this moment.

A flock of ravens cawed overhead, and I finally found the motivation to pull the panel closed, plunging us into darkness.

By the time we made it out of the facility, I had collected a few of Dr. Warren's books and documents. We hiked the path to the new facility as I carried them under my arms. Khan trotted at Amaya's heels, and we took the path to the new facility, although I had come to refer to it as home.

The two-story structure resembled an oversized log cabin. Amaya had poured her heart and soul into designing the place. She'd picked natural stone and wood. Soft beiges and greens decorated most of the interior spaces. She'd had a vision of creating a place of solitude, somewhere our patients could find peace during their transitions from human to something else—something we still didn't have a name for. Fire wielders was the best term we'd thought of, but that didn't seem to suit everyone.

The place smelled of new lumber and paint, and a smile spread across my face as we took the porch to the front door. Unlike the old place, the new facility had a homey, cheerful feeling, one that put me at ease and made me want to sit by the big fireplace and breathe in the scents of cinnamon rolls coming from the kitchen. This place, more than any other in my life, was home.

We wandered through the front foyer until we reached the great room. A few former patients sat on bean bags or couches. Near the fireplace, I spotted a girl with bright blonde hair and a glittery pink T-shirt.

"Amaya, Lucian." Chloe waved us toward her. Every eye in the place went to me as we crossed to where Chloe sat. Even though I wasn't nearly as reclusive as I'd been in the past, my presence still seemed to draw an undue amount of attention. I would always be an enigma to people, even to those who shared the same abilities as me, and with that thought, I left Amaya to chat with her friend, keeping Dr. Warren's books—and his secrets—tucked under my arms as I left her behind.

———

AMAYA

I SAT on an ottoman across from Chloe. Lucian had squeezed my shoulder and gave me a smile before leaving the room. As I watched him go, a knot formed in my chest—that old familiar pang of loneliness making its grand return anytime he left me.

Although I felt I knew Lucian better than most, there was still a side to him I would never know. He'd lived too long and seen too many things. Even if I spent the rest of my life with him, I'd never know everything.

Rest of my life with him...

That thought scared and excited me at the same time. Deep down, I knew I wanted to be with him more than anything, but there was still too much distance between us, and I didn't know if we'd ever span the gap.

I sighed and turned my attention to Chloe. Enough worrying about my own problems for once.

"How are you?" I asked, attempting a smile.

She shrugged and returned the smile, although her eyes were rimmed in red, and her face was abnormally pale.

"Is something wrong?" I asked.

"I'm okay, Amaya," she answered, but hesitated. "For the most part," she added.

I raised an eyebrow. "You don't sound okay. What's going on?"

She fidgeted with her fingers. "Damian's gone, you know. He has a girlfriend now. He's dealing with this fire power thing like a champ, and I'm..." she trailed off.

"You're not dealing with it so well," I finished for her.

"Yeah." Her eyes didn't meet mine. She bit her lip and stared at the fireplace instead. The flames flickered and reflected in her eyes. "I guess I've never had to deal with being different like this. When we were considered sick, people treated us with compassion. They felt sorry for us, which wasn't great, but this. It's different. Everyone's afraid of us."

"I think that's because they are," I said. "And I'm not sure I can blame them."

"Well." Chloe crossed her arms. "I hate it."

I eyed her. "Do you want to leave?"

"No," she answered resolutely. "But sometimes, I just wish things could go back to the way they used to be. Before the virus. Back when life was normal with regular problems to worry about."

"Yeah. I understand."

"Do you?" she asked, her tone sharp.

"Chloe," I said calmly. "Yes, I understand."

"Hmm..." She crossed her arms. "It seems like you are doing fine. At least you've got someone here who cares about you. I've got no one."

I was tempted to tell her that just because I had Lucian didn't mean I escaped the same sort of problems she had. But I held my tongue. Right now, what Chloe needed was a friend.

Leaning forward, I placed my hand on hers. Her eyes widened, but she didn't push me away. "Chloe, you're not alone. That's why you're here. We're a family. Remember that."

She didn't answer at first. But after a moment, she nodded, then swiped a tear from her cheek. "Yeah, you're right." She sat up tall and took a deep breath. "It's just crazy how things are right now. Who would have ever thought people with fire powers would exist?"

She pressed her hands together. A glow emanated from her skin, lighting her face, illuminating the loneliness in her eyes.

"We'll get through this," I said. "One day, society will realize we're normal people with something a little extra special."

Khan nudged Chloe's knee and gave a playful yelp. His wide yellow eyes held a hint of humor.

"See? You've already made a friend."

"Yeah." She smiled for the first time—a genuine smile that lit up her face, and she patted my Husky's head. "He's a good boy, isn't he? Maybe I should get a dog."

"I highly recommend Husky-wolf hybrids," I said with a wink. "They're the best."

She laughed, then scratched behind Khan's ear. "Thanks for cheering me up, Amaya. I don't know why I feel so lousy. Guess I'm just not myself today."

"It's okay, Chloe. I totally get it. Being who we are isn't always easy. We'll get through this together, okay? I'm always here whenever you need me. So is Khan."

He wagged his tail when I said his name, and Chloe hugged him to her chest. "Can I keep him?"

"Sure," I said teasingly. "You can have him as long as you need him."

"Thanks." She stroked his fur.

"Why don't you come horseback riding with me sometime?" I offered. "It's helped a lot of other people here."

She bit her lip. "It's not really for me. But... I guess I could give it a try."

"Good," I said, sitting tall. "Tomorrow?"

"Okay." She took a deep breath. "Tomorrow."

3

***Horses on the campus of the new Crimson Hollow facility.
VS survivors use horseback riding to overcome the trauma
caused by the disease. Horseback riding is known to relieve
stress, depression, anxiety, and a host of other conditions.***

AMAYA

Chloe and I rode our horses near the riverbed. Hooves shifted over smooth pebbles. The air tasted of the crispness of autumn, and the musical trickling of the water blended with the soft hum of the wind. Chloe rode stiffly beside me, her hands clenched tightly around the reins until her knuckles turned white. Her horse snorted and shook his head, and she jumped.

"Remind me why I'm doing this again?" Chloe asked.

"It's good for you."

"Right," she said without much conviction. "It's also terrifying."

"You've got to relax. Horses can sense when you're nervous."

"Wonderful," she answered with sarcasm.

We rode up a riverbank and onto a hill overlooking the valley where green grass stretched to the horizon. The towers of Crimson Hollow shone in the afternoon sunlight, a black mark against the pristine blue sky. The path continued through the open field. Tall grass grew on either side of the trail. Wildflowers and butterflies dotted the area. A warm breeze stirred the tall stalks of daisies and black-eyed Susans.

"I guess it is sort of pretty out here, isn't it?" Chloe admitted.

"Yes. I've always found it peaceful. It's a good place to think."

Chloe nodded, her eyes wide as she stared out over the field. Khan trotted ahead of us, his ears perked and on the alert. We rode to a sprawling oak tree with an ornate stonework bench underneath, and we stopped our horses on top of the hill.

After allowing our horses to graze, Chloe and I sat on the bench. The unyielding stone seat felt cold despite the sunlight. I ran my hands over the worn granite. How old was this bench? It looked to be carved from the same material as the angel statues surrounding Crimson Hollow.

"Amaya," Chloe said tenuously, her eyes flicking to mine for half-a-second. "I need to ask you something. It's sort of personal."

"Sure," I answered. "What is it?"

"I want to know if you can take away my powers. I don't want to be this way anymore."

I studied her. "Why?"

She glanced away and didn't answer. Chloe was one of those people who lit up a room. She'd always been popular and likable. She'd never worried about not fitting in. Now, with her newfound powers, she was faced with the very real possibility of never being a part of the popular crowd again, and perhaps that was why she no longer wanted them.

"Is it because you think they make you too different?" I prodded. "Because if so, then you should reconsider keeping them. They make you different, yes, but is that such a bad thing?"

"No, that's not the reason." Her gaze met mine, her blue eyes clouded with fear. "It's hard to describe, but I feel like these powers are trying to control me, like they're a piece of me that doesn't fit. It feels like they're making me into someone else, someone I don't know, someone who scares me." She looked at her hands clasped in her lap. "Someone dangerous," she said in a quiet voice.

Her answer surprised me. I'd assumed she wanted her powers removed for shallower reasons—to fit into a crowd, to be normal and likable, to stay the status quo.

"I'll see what I can do," I admitted. "If you truly feel that way, then you shouldn't have to keep your powers."

"Thank you." Tears brimmed in her eyes. "I can't keep living this way. It's not right and it's not natural. I just want to feel like I'm me again."

"I understand." I patted her shoulder. "But I want you to remember that you're strong. *You* control your powers, not the other way around. The Chloe I know would never hurt anyone." I gave her a half- smile. "I doubt you could kill a spider without feeling awful."

She gave me a tiny smile back, then wiped the tears from her eyes with the back of her hand. "You're right, Amaya. One time I hit a squirrel with my car, and I cried the rest of the day." She threw her arms out, self-conscious. "It *still* bothers me!"

"See?" I patted her knee. "You're too compassionate to ever become a dangerous person."

"Yeah." She sighed, her gaze lingering on the trees above us. "You're right."

I didn't admit it to her, but her admission bothered me. What if this *cure* we had found wasn't a cure at all? Perhaps the serum was only morphing us into something we didn't under-stand? Something dangerous and uncontrollable? I had no proof of that happening, but there were too many unknowns, and until we knew more about the serum, I had no answers.

The rumbling of car engines came from the valley below. A

trail of dust followed two white SUVs. The road wound through the old oaks and willows, ending at the overshadowing towers of Crimson Hollow.

"Who's that?" Chloe asked.

"I'm not sure." I stood to get a better look.

Lucian, wearing a black duster, paced near the entrance of the facility. What was he doing there?

"The investors? Why would they go to the old facility?" I questioned. "Shouldn't we show them the new place first?"

"What investors?" Chloe asked.

I pursed my lips, realizing too late I'd let it slip that we were in financial straits. "Just some people Lucian was meeting with. He said they wouldn't be here until this evening. Guess they got here earlier than expected." I paused. "And they're going to the wrong facility."

I pushed a strand of hair into my sloppy ponytail. I smelled of horse, and I was half-drenched in sweat. Had Lucian purposely invited them earlier to keep me out of the loop? No. He wouldn't do that. Would he?

"Are you going down there?" Chloe asked.

"Yeah. I probably should." I turned to her. "Let's get the horses unsaddled. Sorry I have to go so soon."

Chloe shrugged. "Doesn't bother me. You know I'm not super fond of riding anyway."

"Fair enough," I said with a smile.

We took our horses' reins and walked them down to the barn. After getting them unsaddled and put back into the field, I gave Chloe a brief goodbye and rushed to the old facility.

Gravel crunched under my riding boots as I jogged down the road. Two white Range Rovers were parked between the overgrown weeds in the driveway. The facility's main doors were opened, revealing the dark foyer inside. I wiped beads of sweat from my forehead and tucked in my mud-splattered shirt. My blue blouse, lace skirt, and strappy sandals were currently arranged neatly on my bed covers, ready to be worn promptly at six PM. Instead, I wore boots caked with mud. Holes had worn through the knees of my jeans, and any sort of makeup was a lost cause. I loosened my ponytail and attempted to tie my hair into a bun, but my hair had grown nearly to my waist, and I did a poor job of smoothing the tangled strands with my fingers. What I really needed was a shower and ample amounts of hair product, but I didn't have the luxury of time, which meant I looked like a hot, sweaty mess.

If I was hoping to make any kind of professional impression on our potential investors, it was ruined now.

But why had they shown up so early? Worse, why had they come to the old building? Crimson Hollow was the stuff of nightmares, certainly not fit for the eyes of investors. Why hadn't Lucian warned them away? I was eager to hear his explanation.

My footsteps echoed over the expanse of marble floor as I rushed inside. Voices echoed from the back room, and I slowed.

Glancing through the open doorway, I spotted a man and a woman standing with Lucian near the windows. A little sunlight managed to seep through the grime-covered glass, illuminating Lucian's dark-clad form, and a man and woman wearing business suits. The man had a neatly trimmed beard and rimless glasses, and he stood with a straight posture. His suit molded perfectly to his toned frame. He was in his mid-forties, maybe?

The woman's deep red lipstick contrasted her pale skin and raven-black hair. Razor-straight bangs accentuated her striking blue eyes. Taking a deep breath, I smoothed my shirt once again, and I stepped inside.

The investors turned to look my way. I forced a smile and crossed to stand by Lucian. His eyes lit with surprise for only half-a-second. Maybe he hadn't expected me here so soon, but as he took my hand in his, I doubted he'd deliberately kept me out of the meeting.

"Hi there," the woman said with a silken voice. "You must be Amaya de la Vega."

"Yes, that's me," I answered.

"I'm Yasira Emmerson." She stretched her hand toward me, and we shook. Her skin was so cold, it came as a shock, and I quickly pulled away. "I'm so happy to finally meet you. Umber and I have heard so much about you and Lucian. We're you're biggest fans."

The man, Umber, only nodded, giving me a half-smile that didn't seem to touch his eyes. He placed his hand behind the woman's back in a possessive gesture.

"Yasira isn't exaggerating," he said. "My wife has read every tabloid published about you. Although I assume half of what she reads can't be true, you're still a fascinating couple all the same."

"Thanks," I said awkwardly, not sure how else to respond, as I pushed a wayward strand of hair behind my ear. If the Emmersons minded my appearance, they didn't show it.

"Amaya," Lucian said. "Mr. and Mrs. Emmerson were interested in touring the old facility."

"We would like to restore it to its former glory," Mrs. Emmerson's eyes scanned the darkened hallways. "This place has such a fascinating history. It would be a shame to lose it."

"Perhaps," I said. "But Lucian and I have been focusing on creating a new place with more light and an open atmosphere. It seems to be helping the patients better than a facility like this."

"Yes," Mr. Emmerson said. "We look forward to touring the new addition. I've heard you're making some great progress. Helping the patients deal with their newfound powers can't be an easy task, but it seems you've got it under control."

"We've had a little success," Lucian admitted. "Some of our patients respond better than others."

"And some don't respond well at all," Mr. Emmerson said. "At least, that's what I've heard."

Mrs. Emmerson cleared her throat. "Would it be possible to see upstairs?"

"Well..." Lucian hedged. "It's actually been condemned. It's not exactly safe up there."

"I'm sure we'll be fine," she said with a smile meant to put us at ease, though something about the iciness in her piercing eyes set me on edge. "Trust me when I say Umber and I have seen worse."

Lucian raised an eyebrow. "You're sure?"

"Positive," Umber answered, his hand held protectively at his wife's back. His gaze wandered to the balcony. "This place is steeped in so much mystery. It was a world-renowned mental hospital during its prime. Did you know they housed over three-thousand patients here at one point? Incredible. I would have loved to have seen it."

Lucian nodded, and we walked to the staircase. Dust coated the banister and covered the floors. We took the flight of stairs up to the balcony overlooking the entryway. Mrs. Emmerson ran her fingers over the banister railing. Her eyes roved the ballroom below, past the dusty chandelier, and down to the cloth-covered furniture, as if she could see past the peeling paint and soot-covered portraits, and envision the structure how it was meant to be.

"So beautiful," she said, her voice nearly a whisper.

"They certainly don't build places like this anymore," her husband added.

I wasn't sure I shared their awe. Maybe it had been architecturally impressive, but the amount of death and disease inside these walls made it hard for me to see it as anything but a tomb.

We continued through the facility with quiet conversations. The Emmersons walked ahead of us and into a room, and Lucian took my hand. I peered up at him.

"What do you think of them?" he whispered, squeezing my hand.

"I'm not sure yet," I admitted. "But they seem interested in the facility, which I count as a good thing."

"I agree."

"Lucian." I cast a quick glance up at him, though the hallway was dimly lit, and it was hard to see anything but the silhouette of his profile. "Why didn't you tell me they'd be here so early?"

"I didn't know. They called half an hour ago and said they were on their way. I guess they were anxious to see the place. The first thing they wanted to do was come here to Crimson Hollow, although I can't understand why."

"Neither can I. Why do they want to restore this old place? What do they plan to do with it?"

Lucian shook his head. "They haven't said."

We watched as the Emmersons stood by a window, talking quietly to one another.

"If they become our investors," I asked quietly, "what do they want from us in return?"

He locked his jaw. Worry creased his brow. "I'm hoping we'll discuss that. They want to meet us for dinner tomorrow night."

I nodded, and we continued the tour. They stopped in Dr. Warren's office, the old cafeteria, and wandered to the graveyard in the back. The fog returned, wrapping and coiling around the headstones. Evening fell by the time they left, and I had to rush to feed the horses, who were impatiently snorting and pawing by the time I arrived.

———

THE NEXT DAY, Lucian and I spent our time with the other patients. I sat in the family room on a couch with a girl named Hannah, a nine-year-old who'd arrived only a week ago. Unlike the old place, the new facility filled me with a sense of peace, and I could only hope Hannah and the others felt the same. Sunlight spilled from the wall of windows behind us, and I let the warmth settle inside me, allowing the light to melt the chills I'd had since I'd met the Emmersons.

Through a window across the room, I could just see the towers of Crimson Hollow peeking above a hilltop. Why hadn't I thought to sit with the towers behind me? Even better, why hadn't we thought to build the new facility so far away, we'd never have to look at them again? Shaking away my unease, I focused on Hannah. A glow emanated from her palm.

"Trust it," I said to her. "Don't be afraid. Try to keep the heat steady. You're using the energy from your own body to fuel it. Can you feel the warmth increasing?"

She nodded but pouted as impatiently as any small child. "But how do I make fire?"

"Give it some time," I answered. "It doesn't come easily for everyone. It can take some practice. Concentrate."

She knit her brow. Her tongue peeked from her mouth as she fixated on her cupped hand.

"Nice job," I said. "Now, try to increase the warmth. Can you feel it flowing into your fingers? You'll use that heat to create a flame."

The glow brightened, then faded.

She took a deep breath. "That's all I can do." She frowned. "Why is this so hard?"

I patted her knee. "Don't stress too much. Like I said, it takes practice. We'll keep working on it."

She bit her lip and glanced away. "Why do I have to do this anyway?"

"Because it's better to learn how to control your powers than to let them control you. You wouldn't want to catch your school desk on fire, would you?"

She laughed. "Sometimes maybe. If I could burn up my math worksheets, I wouldn't mind that so much."

"Okay, bad example." I tapped my chin. "You wouldn't want to accidentally set your boyfriend on fire when he's trying to kiss you, would you?"

She giggled.

"Or your cat when you're trying to pet him, or your phone when you're trying to text someone… I could go on, Hannah."

"Fine." She huffed. "But I don't want to practice anymore. It makes my head hurt." She rubbed her forehead, then her face brightened, as if she'd had a brilliant idea, and she grabbed my hands. "Show me the butterfly again."

I gave her a stern look. "If I do, will you give your flame one more try?"

She nodded vigorously.

"Promise?" I questioned.

"Yes." Her smile showed her dimples. "Promise." How could anyone say no to a face like that?

"Okay. Here goes." I cupped my hands. Closing my eyes, I relaxed, and allowed warmth to flow from my heart, and into my hands. A flame formed just above my flesh, burning as if on a wick, though the chemically modified oils in my skin kept it from burning me. I channeled more heat into it, then allowed it to blossom. The flames coalesced into the shape of a butterfly. Wings fanned the air. The creation lifted an inch off my palms. Amber and cobalt flickered, combining in swirling patterns.

"It's so pretty," Hannah whispered in awe. "How do you do it?"

"Practice." I left the creation to flutter above my hands until the warmth drained away, and the fire flickered, then disappeared, leaving a cold spot inside me, one that demanded to be filled with my own energy once again.

Worry nagged me, and Chloe's words returned to me. Was I becoming too dependent on my fire power? If so, how would I know if it were controlling me?

Hannah clapped. "Can I make a butterfly someday?"

"Sure." I winked, attempting to smile, trying to ignore the lingering icy emptiness left inside me after using my fire power.

"Except I'll become the butterfly," Hannah laughed under her breath.

"Are you sure that's a good idea?" I asked.

"It's a great idea!" She beamed. "Think of all the things I could do—and places I could go. All over the world. I could do anything I wanted or be anything I wanted."

"Anything you wanted, huh?" My gaze snagged on the towers outside once again, and I gave up trying to ignore them.

———

AFTER WORKING with more than a dozen more patients, the day waned. Exhaustion tried to overwhelm me as I made my way back to my room. After showering, I sat on my bed combing through the wet strands of my hair. Khan lay sleeping by my feet, his ears twitching every now and then. With the quiet, my thoughts turned back to the Emmersons.

The couple confused me. Why did they have such a fascination with Crimson Hollow? And what did they plan to do with it? Turn it into another rehab? Surely, they could see how problematic that would be. The place was falling apart. Plus, it should have never been a treatment facility in the first place. There was too much death there. Its stains left an imprint that lingered.

I rubbed my eyes. Lucian should have told me about the financial problems sooner. But would it have done any good? I stood and paced my room, Khan's eyes tracking me, then I sighed.

"Just stay focused," I told myself, deciding it would be best to go to dinner and get more information from the Emmersons. No need to let my worries overcomplicate things.

After putting on my blouse and skirt, plus a little mascara and lip gloss, I grabbed a pearl necklace from my armoire.

The jewelry had been Mom's, and I rarely wore it except for special occasions. After fastening the necklace, I fingered the long strand. I remembered sitting on Mom's lap and playing with the beads, the pearls so smooth I could see my reflection in them.

I took a deep breath as I studied my image in the mirror. People who knew Mom said I looked just like her, and I wondered what she'd think of me now. Would she be proud of me? Or disappointed? Had I ever measured up to her?

She'd been a successful scientist with a doctorate in biochemistry. I was a college dropout, my life devoted to helping people rehabilitate from the vampire virus. I did it mostly on my own, and the world feared me for it. Maybe if we could get the Emmersons involved in investing, we could afford more professional help for those patients who needed it.

And maybe we could start to make a difference.

With a sigh, I turned away from the mirror. I made my way downstairs, then wandered through the hallways until I reached the patio. Strings of lights wrapped the cedar posts supporting the wood-beamed ceiling, giving the place the feeling of a mountain lodge. The foothills stretched in the distance. As the fog returned, it quietly settled over the peaks, shrouding them in silence.

The screened-in area kept out the bugs while still allowing a gentle breeze that smelled of spruce. A long table took up the center of the room. Lucian sat chatting with Mr. Emmerson, their voices nearly drowned out by the rush of wind.

I quietly crossed the room and took the seat next to Lucian. He gave me a smile—one that lit up his whole face—and I hoped he reserved such a smile only for me. He grasped my hand under the table, and I squeezed it gently, happy to feel his bare flesh not covered in gloves.

Mr. Emmerson nodded in my direction. "I'm glad you've joined us, Amaya." He spoke with a gentle, quiet voice, though his piercing blue eyes seemed too shrewd for such a soft-spoken person. Everything about him spoke of calculation. The angular lines of his face looked perfectly geometric, as if someone had drawn a grid on his skin and measured every angle to produce the straightest possible lines. His tie was pristinely straight, his suit jacket was without a wrinkle, the strands of his hair were neatly combed, and his beard was trimmed at precise degrees.

I fingered my pearls, fidgeting under his gaze, hoping he didn't notice any tangles left in my hair.

"Is your wife coming?" I asked, hoping to put an end to the awkward silence.

He took a sip of water, then placed the glass on the table. "I'm afraid Yasira won't be joining us. Headache. Nothing to worry about. But traveling always does that to her. I hope you don't mind."

"Not at all," I answered. "Is there anything we can do to help her?"

"No." He tapped the table in a nervous gesture, and his gaze darted from mine. "She needs rest more than anything. I'm sure she'd want us to enjoy our dinner."

"I see."

A few servers entered the room. They carried steaming plates that smelled of the heavenly scents of pork chops and fried potatoes. Soon we enjoyed a meal together, our conversation light and easygoing.

"Originally from LA?" Lucian asked.

"Yes," Mr. Emmerson answered. "Born and raised. Yasira was also born in the LA area, although she and her mother moved around quite a bit."

"How did you meet?" I asked.

"In college," he answered. "She was a Bio-chem major. I was more interested in the arts. Theater major."

"How did you get involved in pharma?" Lucian asked.

"My wife," he answered. "It was her business, and I became a partner. We started out as a small gig selling herbal remedies and that sort of thing. People loved our products because they actually worked. Business exploded, and ten years after opening, we became a Fortune Five-hundred company."

"That's impressive," Lucian said.

"Yes, Yasira works hard at what she does, which is why she's interested in expanding her business to studying the aftereffects of viridae sangre."

I raised an eyebrow at his remark. "How does she plan to study it?"

"Taking samples, for one." Mr. Emmerson leaned forward. Shrewd calculation flashed in his eyes. "I hear your strain of the virus is quite interesting."

"Mine?" His comment caught me off guard. "What do you mean by that?"

He waved his fork. "You were the only person to be injected with the actual serum found in Constatin Vidraru's tomb. Everyone else received a derivative of it. Such a strong dose of the serum must give you unique abilities."

I tapped my fingers on the table. I wasn't sure I was comfortable with our conversation. Should I tell him I'd already learned to manipulate fire into the shapes of various creatures? No. That didn't seem like something I wanted to volunteer.

He took a sip of water. "You may not have noticed anything. Not yet anyway. It's just a theory, mind you, but I believe the mutations in your blood could be a breakthrough for treating others like you."

"Treating them?" I raised an eyebrow. "How?"

He waved his hand. "Increasing their powers... or possibly reversing them."

"Reversing them?" His revelation caught my attention. If that were possible, how? I'd promised Chloe to research the subject, but until now, I had no idea if it was even possible. "You think you could do that?"

He shrugged. "I can't say for sure, but there is a possibility. It all depends on the gene mutations and how they work. It would be an interesting concept to study nonetheless."

I flinched at the word *study*. Did he mean to study me? "How do you plan to learn more about my gene mutations? You'd have to take blood and possible bone and tissue samples, wouldn't you?"

"Perhaps. Our research will require tissue samples and such. I'm fascinated to know more about your blood and its possibilities. We could learn a lot from you both. You're intriguing people to study, but what excites me even more is learning what you harbor inside your cells. Could your blood be used in healing? Not just viridae sangre, but cancer? Diabetes and Alzheimer's?" His smile was a look of calculation, a gesture that reflected the coldness in his eyes. "But that will all be sorted out in the future. Of course, we would never operate on anyone without their consent."

Now we were talking about tissue samples and operating on people? This conversation just kept getting better and better. Next, he'd be talking about cracking open our skulls so he could study our brains. But maybe I was overreacting. Too much time spent with Dr. Warren had left me suspicious of everyone.

"The pork chops are delicious." Mr. Emmerson smiled, turning his attention to Lucian. "I hear you prefer your meat rare. It that true? Or just another rumor?"

"It was true for a time," Lucian answered. "But the more therapy we go through, the more we're able to eat a normal diet." He speared a potato. "I can even choke down a few of these every now and then."

Mr. Emmerson chuckled. "Does that mean you've eaten French fries?"

"I have." Lucian nodded. "Although I'm probably the only person living in America who doesn't like them."

"Give it some time," Mr. Emmerson suggested. "Everyone comes around eventually."

Despite his carefree demeanor, his earlier talk of studying us left a bitter taste in my mouth, and I placed my fork aside.

Lucian and Mr. Emmerson chatted about the old facility's intended renovations, and I excused myself to get a breath of fresh air. I passed a few people in the hallways and gave them a brief smile, then, taking the path toward the barn, I allowed the evening air to help me straighten out my thoughts. I stood with my hands propped on the wooden-beamed fence overlooking the horse pasture. The air carried the scent of hay, and I rested my chin on my hands.

Why had Mr. Emmerson's suggestions bugged me so much?

Maybe it had nothing to do with him, but with Lucian. Shouldn't he have jumped to our defense? Lucian, more than anyone, knew the horrors of becoming a lab experiment. Why hadn't he said anything?

I rubbed my temples. Then again, shouldn't I be happy the Emmersons were willing to take their time and money to invest in our facility and in our treatments?

"Nice evening out," a female voice said behind me.

I spun around to face Yasira Emmerson. She smiled, revealing perfectly white teeth that contrasted with her dark red, almost black lipstick. Smoothing strands of hair away from her face, she stepped toward me.

"Oh," I stammered. "Hi. Yes... I suppose it is."

"I forget how beautiful Upstate New York can be."

"You've been here before?" I asked.

"Oh yes," she said, her voice musical. For some reason, she reminded me of winter, her skin so white it could've been snow, and her eyes icy blue. "It's been a while though. Funny how you forget little things." She stepped to the fence post and rested her arms on the rail in the same way I'd been standing. "Tell me honestly, Amaya, how do you like it here?"

Her question caught me off guard. Wasn't she supposed to be back in her room with a headache?

"I love it here. It's peaceful and it feels like home. But..."

"But?" She raised an eyebrow.

"But... I guess I don't feel like we're doing enough. I feel like we're not really helping anyone."

"What do you mean?"

"We don't understand the virus and its aftereffects," I explained. "We don't really know what it's doing to our brains or how it's changing our biology and chemical makeup..." I stopped, realizing I may have gone too far and said too much.

"And you don't have the funding to do the research you need?"

"Yes," I admitted. "Lucian only recently told me how bad it

was. Apparently, Dr. Warren made sure he had control over all the money... and now..." I took a deep breath. I hadn't meant to open up to Yasira Emmerson, but if she was going to be an investor, she needed to know everything. The good, and the ugly, and everything in between.

"I hope that can change," she said, her voice quiet, yet intense. "I've been interested in alternative forms of medicine my entire life. I guess you could call it an obsession. I was diagnosed with a rare disease when I was a child. My mom took me to every doctor and specialist she could find. Nothing helped. But Mom was persistent. She found a healer in Argentina who claimed to have an antidote. It was hard to believe his claims at first. But we were desperate, and Mom had decided she would try anything to find a treatment for me. So, we went to Argentina. A week later, I was cured."

"Really?" I said. "That's impressive."

"Yes. It's also how I got into alternative medicine. I realized the current medical community dismisses things they view as superstitious. We need to have open minds. It's the only way we'll progress."

"I agree," I said. The wind rushed past, carrying a torrent of leaves across the field.

"It's so peaceful here," Yasira said. "I see why you love it so much."

I nodded. Yasira rubbed her forehead and winced, and I raised my eyebrows. "Are you okay? Mr. Emmerson said you had a headache."

"I'm all right. It comes and goes. Side effect from working too much." She gave me a strained smile that didn't touch her eyes. "I hope we can reach an agreement for funding the facility here. It would be a shame to see it go under."

Go under? The words scared me more than I cared to admit. Until now, I hadn't really believed losing the facility was a possibility. Maybe we'd have to cut back on the staff or take out a few loans, but go under? If that happened, what would become of everyone here? Where would they go? A hospital? Or what if they failed to control their powers? Then the most likely place would be prison.

"I agree," I said to Yasira. "A shame." Which was the biggest understatement of all time.

She absentmindedly rubbed her forehead again, as if it were a nervous habit. While the idea of funding from the Emmersons was tempting, I still couldn't shake the feeling that something was off.

For one thing, my conversation with Mr. Emmerson still bugged me. I was torn between learning more about the aftereffects of the virus and proceeding with caution. How could I be sure those were the Emmerson's same motivations? Yasira believed in non-traditional medicine, but we didn't need medicine here at the facility, we needed training, and I wasn't sure there was a person on the planet qualified to give it—other than perhaps Lucian. I also wasn't sure the Emmersons agreed.

But did it matter if they agreed? If we needed the money, we didn't have the luxury of being picky about where it came from.

4

Dear Athena,

As you can guess, this is my diary, and I've named it after you. Mother says you were smart and good at war. I want to be like you someday.

AMAYA

A conversation echoed behind me and Yasira. Lucian and Mr. Emmerson walked down the path toward us. Lucian walked with his hands in his pockets, chatting and smiling occasionally. His laidback attitude sent alarm bells ringing in my head. We'd already had our necks in a noose when Dr. Warren controlled everything. Who could say anything would be different now?

But rationally speaking, I knew I was reading too much into it. My heart was too involved in Crimson Hollow, and that made business decisions difficult.

Mr. Emmerson's mouth gaped when he looked at his wife.

For a half second, fear flashed though his eyes. A moment later, he smiled, all composure once again.

"Yasira," he said. "I'm surprised to see you out here. What about your headache?"

Her red lips stretched into a smile that revealed her perfect white teeth. "It's gone, dear. You know how it comes and goes."

When he came near, she looped her arm through his. He gave her a peck on her cheek and wrapped his arm possessively around her waist. Down the road came the soft rumble of car engines. Two Range Rovers moved down the gravel drive toward us, their tires crunching loose rocks.

"Is that our cue?" Mrs. Emmerson asked her husband.

"Unfortunately, yes." He turned to us. "It was a pleasure to meet you both. I'm sorry we couldn't stay longer. You have an amazing place here."

"Thank you," Lucian said.

The Range Rovers parked nearby, stirring a cloud of dust, and a security guard exited each of the vehicles. Mr. Emmerson escorted his wife to a SUV and helped her inside, then he closed the door behind her, and he took the car in the front.

With a brief wave, he smiled, then shut the door, and the vehicles rolled away.

The cloud of dirt rose like smoke, obscuring the cars until they disappeared, reminding me of a magician I'd seen as a kid— one who'd relied heavily on theatrical fog.

I glanced up. "Do you think it's weird they took separate vehicles?"

He shrugged. "Not that weird. It's a security thing. If one of the cars got in a wreck, at least one of them would survive."

"Hmm..." I creased my forehead, not completely sold by his answer. "I still think it's weird. It seems ultra-paranoid."

"Maybe," he admitted, then kissed my forehead. He took my hand, and we walked on the gravel path back toward the new building. "What did you think of them?"

I gave him a sideways glance. "Do you want my honest opinion?"

"Of course."

"All right then." I took a deep breath. "I like them. They seem friendly and want to help us. But I don't trust them."

"Don't trust them?" He raised an eyebrow.

The setting sun turned the sky fiery rose gold, reminding me of the glow of Lucian's wings when he took the form of a phoenix. It happened rarely, but every time he transformed, he took away my breath and left me speechless, making me realize all the things we believed in this world were constructs, and there were some things out there we didn't understand.

I pondered what to say. "I don't get a good vibe from them. It's hard to say why. Mrs. Emmerson seems nice. They're gracious and polite. But how can we be sure they have our best interests at heart? Plus, I don't like the way Mr. Emmerson talked about studying us. We're not lab rats." I shrugged. "I don't know. Maybe it's silly, but I don't feel comfortable giving them so much control over the facility."

"Do you think you feel that way because of what Dr. Warren did? Maybe you feel they'll take advantage of us in some way?"

I chewed my lip. "Yes. Maybe so. And perhaps that's not a good reason to mistrust them."

The sun sank lower, leaving a fading sky in its wake. The air turned chill. Goosebumps prickled my skin. I couldn't shake the image of Yasira Emmerson's strained smile, as if she were trying hard to hide something.

"Well, I've got some good news for you." Lucian flashed a bemused grin.

"Good news?" I asked, casting him a wary glance.

"In a way." He sighed, looking out at the setting sun, and his smile faded. "I told Mr. Emmerson no."

"Already? Why?"

"Mr. Emmerson asked to have a lab and surgical unit built exclusively to study you. You should have seen his plans! He already had blueprints drawn up for how they plan to reconstruct Crimson Hollow. It won't be focused on treatment, but study. We would become, exactly as you say, lab experiments."

I locked my jaw.

He smoothed his hand over his head. "He wasn't happy. Argued with me. Said he would pay off all our debts, even back taxes. Promised to renovate Crimson Hollow to its former glory. He seemed pretty desperate to take control of this place, which was one reason why I could never agree to something like that."

I sighed, one part relieved, another part anxious at still having the trouble of finding investors. "What do we do now?"

"I don't know, but we'll figure something out. Maybe I just need to do more research, find some more people to beg."

I frowned. "You hate doing that."

"Says who?" he said with a teasing tone, then looked behind us at the looming structure of Crimson Hollow. "Sometimes I feel like it won't let me go, you know?"

"Yeah," I answered. "I know."

He was referring to the facility, but I knew he meant more than just stones and lumber. Victor Warren's presence still lingered. So did Sally Anderson's. I couldn't discount the former wife of the doctor as being gone forever. She'd escaped Romania. Where she was now was a mystery, but I didn't doubt if she got the chance, she would be close by. This had been her home for so long, I couldn't imagine her going anyplace else.

Still, if she were here, she was doing a good job hiding.

I took a deep breath and focused on the present situation. "So, where do we go next?"

"Keep searching. I refuse to give up hope. There's got to be someone out there willing to help us out, who doesn't want to experiment on us in the process."

"I agree, but we're running out of time." I ran my fingers through my hair. The ends had tangled again in the wind, and my fingers caught on a knot.

"I'll head back to the house. Then I'll start researching who we can ask next. I might be pulling an all-nighter trying to find someone else. Time isn't on our side right now."

I nodded. "I can help you, but I need to feed the horses first."

"Meet me in the library?" he asked.

"Sure."

He leaned in and gave me a kiss. A tingle went through me, its warmth going straight to my toes. I kissed him back, and all my fears for our relationship disappeared in that instant. It was as if we were the only two people in the world, as if none of our worries mattered, like he could make me happy for the rest of my life if I would only let him.

He squeezed my hand before turning away and walking toward the new building. I stared after him until the sunlight faded, and he blended with the shadows. The wind brought a biting chill, and I shivered as I turned toward the gate leading to the barn.

A few horses pricked their ears as they stood in their stalls waiting for their evening meal. One of them whickered as I scooped a can of oats from the barrel. I poured the feed into a trough, then repeated the process, my mind straying from the familiar sounds of oats being poured, and the sweet scent of hay and grain.

The routine had become so repetitive, I worked as if on autopilot. When I filled the last trough, I took the path out of the barn and toward the new facility. Night had fallen with a freezing bite to the air. I ran my hands over my arms where goosebumps formed. A few stars twinkled overhead, though there was no moon, making the familiar path nearly impossible to see. Still, I knew my way back well enough.

Something about walking through the dark of night unnerved me. It was a primal fear that settled deep inside. The idea that anything could be out there, that I wasn't alone.

The fear intensified. It was the feeling of being hunted. If I had some light, maybe I would feel less terrified. Flexing my fingers, I remembered I'd left my phone in my room. But I didn't need an electronic device for light.

I snapped my fingers. A flame formed above my fingertips. I allowed the fire to grow until it became the size of a baseball, lighting the path ahead. An owl hooted somewhere in the distance, though the rest of the world remained in silence. My footsteps sounded too loud, as if I were intruding on the hushed symphony of night. I hugged my arm around me. Shivers racked my body, and a tingle went down my spine.

Something whispered behind me.

I spun around, staring into the inky blackness. In the distance, the only light came from a bulb hanging in the barn.

Heart racing, my flame flickered. I willed more energy into creating the fire, until the chemical reaction burned hotter, creating a brighter aura around me.

A pair of footsteps crunched over gravel in the distance.

"Is someone there?" I shouted.

Nothing but the wind answered.

"Hello?" I asked.

Maybe my mind was playing tricks on me. Or if Sally had returned... No. I shook my head. If she returned, she would have no power over me or anyone here. Not anymore. Not ever.

I spun around and slammed into a brick wall of a man, at least six and a half feet tall. My flame sputtered out. I started to scream when a gag was shoved inside my mouth.

Flailing, my survival instincts took over.

I kicked the man's shins. He grunted and staggered back when a pair of strong arms grabbed me from behind. I slammed my head backward, catching the edge of a person's jaw. His grip loosened. I ripped the gag from my mouth.

Forming a flame in my hand, I struck out at the nearest person. The world lit up in an intense shock of bright white, blinding me.

Screaming came from somewhere. Had I hit someone?

Voices shouted. At least half a dozen. How many people were

out there? Something slammed into me. My necklace ripped, spilling pearls. I fell back so suddenly, my skull slammed the ground, and the world spun overhead. Stars whirled in my vision. Warm blood pooled in my mouth. The back of my head ached as if I'd been stabbed. I tried to sit up, but my body wouldn't cooperate, like I was made of concrete.

Someone loomed over me. I could barely make out the person's features.

My vision blurred.

"We'll take care of you now, Amaya..." were the last words I heard before the world went black.

5

———

———

LUCIAN

I'd fallen asleep at the computer, still looking for potential investors. Amaya had never come in. What time was it? Rubbing my temples, I stared around the library. A clock ticked on the wall. Half past three AM. My computer screen had gone blank long ago. My cup of coffee had gone cold too, and I pushed them both away.

A spark of fear sped my heart. Had I had a nightmare? I couldn't remember anything since I'd passed out a little after midnight. I'd been looking through a list of investors as I'd waited for Amaya to get back.

Maybe she'd been too tired and gone straight to bed?

I couldn't blame her. Maybe I'd be smart to do the same thing.

I stumbled away from the table and made my way out of the library. The scent of freshly painted walls smarted as I entered the foyer. The new place was such a contrast to the old. Here, the light-colored walls, plentiful windows, and open spaces gave the feeling of freedom. Amaya had been the inspiration behind the new décor choices. She'd wanted this to be a place of warmth and light, an area where healing was a priority. A haven. But we weren't there yet.

I rubbed the knot in my neck as I took the hallway to my room. The passageways were unusually quiet, and a shiver went down my spine. That same fear I'd felt when I'd woken persisted. What was wrong?

I was tempted to stop by Amaya's room and make sure everything was okay, but she hated when I acted overprotective. Plus, she was a grown woman and could take care of herself, as she reminded me daily.

My headache pounded behind my eyes, and I took the stairs to my room, then stopped at my door. I grabbed the knob, but I hesitated before opening it. Glancing down the hall, I strained my eyes to see the end of the hallway where Amaya's room was. My night vision didn't illuminate much, but there wasn't much heat to see in the wood and sheetrock anyway.

Maybe I should just check quickly before she got a chance to wake up?

No.

I clenched my jaw and turned the doorknob.

Amaya trusted me to let her be on her own, and I would respect her wishes.

I entered my room and shut the door behind me.

6

———

Dear Athena,

***I think Mother is very smart, but it makes me mad when she
says I'm not good enough. She says our problems are
because of me, and if I had been born smart like her, we
would have money. I don't think that's true. I think I'm
smart. I made the honor roll and I won the spelling bee. But
she won't look at my school papers anymore. Sometimes she
cries a lot. When I ask her why, she gets mad and goes away.
I don't think I'll ask again.***

———

AMAYA

Screaming startled me awake.

I tried to sit up, but metal bands around my arms and legs kept me pinned to a table.

Where was I?

An IV line protruded from my arm to a bag hanging beside me. Clear liquid filled the bag, and I vaguely wondered what I was being injected with. The screaming stopped, then started again. It was a muffled howling that echoed as if from a few rooms away.

Glancing around, I realized cement walls and floor surrounded me. Metal slats covered the room's only window, which was little more than a rectangular slit near the ceiling. I couldn't see much through the window, as the glass was covered with grime.

The room held the sterile scent of rubbing alcohol, reminding me of a hospital.

Grogginess fogged my head, and the overwhelming fear I might've felt in such a situation was muffled by a faint sense of confusion.

I tried to recall how I'd gotten here. The last thing I remembered, I'd been ambushed outside the barn. But who had attacked me? Fragmented memories came as if in bursts of a shattered mirror, and I couldn't make sense of the image in the glass.

Closing my eyes, I focused on breathing.

Who had attacked me?

The thought swam through my head until dizziness overwhelmed me. I felt as if I were falling. Frustrated, I opened my eyes to stare around the room once again, trying to remain grounded in the here and now.

Maybe some clue in the room would give me an idea of where I was? I looked from the window to the bag of liquid, to the barren walls.

I noticed a chair in the room's corner I hadn't seen before.

A black cat laid curled in a ball on the cracked plastic. It was so dark in the room, no wonder I hadn't spotted it before.

"Kitty..." I started, my throat hoarse, forcing me to clear my throat and try again. "Kitty, kitty..." I whispered.

The cat shifted, but it didn't look at me. Still, I felt a sense of comfort knowing at least something else was in the room with me, even if it was just a cat.

Footsteps came from outside.

I turned my head as best as I could. A man wearing a white coat walked toward me. He was around fifty years old, with a salt-and-pepper beard that covered half of his pockmarked face. His eyes widened for a fraction of a second as he noticed me staring at him.

He mumbled something, then turned and marched out of the room, leaving me alone. Minutes later, several nurses entered.

One of the women pressed a stethoscope to my chest.

"Where... where am I?" I attempted.

The nurses spoke to one another in Spanish, but I had trouble making sense of their words, and they ignored my question.

My vision blurred, and a clammy sweat broke out over my skin. The room seemed to grow darker.

Breathing deeply, I tried to keep focused. One of the nurses pressed a button on a machine by the bag of fluid.

"That should do it." Her voice came as if from a dream, and my world went black once again.

7

———

Interview with Lucian Vidraru for Lifelong magazine

Stacey: You believe you had something to do with your wife Barb's death?
Lucian: Indirectly, yes.
Stacey: How so?
Lucian: My genetics. Once she conceived the baby is when I first noticed it. She wasn't herself. Whatever is in my blood keeping me alive did the opposite for her and our unborn child. It killed the baby first. Then it killed her.
Stacey: You sound certain about that.
Lucian: Yes.
Stacey: Why?
Lucian: It's more than just a gut feeling, Stacey. Her autopsy confirmed it. My blood is toxic for ordinary people. We all know that.
Stacey: How did you deal with such a heartbreaking loss?
Lucian: Time. It's been ten years, and I learned not to blame myself for something my father did to me.
Stacey: Do you blame your father for what happened?
Lucian: Who else could I blame but him?

Stacey: *Will you ever marry again?*
Lucian: *No. Never. I would never put another person*
through that again.

LUCIAN

Storm clouds loomed on the horizon. I stood on the front porch looking out at the sunrise. The wind gusted, and the air held the scent of rain. Amaya wasn't planning to meet me for breakfast for another half hour, and I'd decided to spend a little time outside before she arrived.

A flock of geese soared in V-formation overhead. Their calls echoed with an eerie wail that filled the valley. I rubbed my eyes, sleep still making me groggy. I'd spent half the night researching investors and gotten nowhere. The vampire virus had become a taboo subject since most of our patients now displayed powers. Finding anyone willing to help us out wasn't going to be an easy task.

Unease pulsed through my blood. I gripped the porch railing and inhaled the scent of spruce and crisp morning air. I would get through this, just like I'd gotten through every other trial in my life. One way or another, we would find the funding we needed. Pondering what would happen otherwise was a useless waste of time.

Footsteps came from behind me, and I spun around to face Chole. She wore baggy pants and a wrinkled top, and her usually styled hair hung in limp strands down her face. Her skin was sallow, her face drawn, and I hadn't seen anyone so pale since we'd cured the virus.

"Morning," she said weakly.

"Hi, Chloe. You're awake early."

She shrugged. "Couldn't sleep."

I tilted my head. "Is everything okay?"

She sighed and stood beside me, looking out over the valley highlighted in wisps of white fog. "I guess."

"You don't look okay."

She fiddled with the frayed edge of her shirt sleeve. "It's just... I haven't been myself ever since I received the serum. These powers..." she said the word mockingly... "feel so foreign. Unnatural. Like they're warping me into some kind of monster. I don't know." She glanced at me quickly, then darted her gaze back to the forest.

Monster. The word echoed in my head, leaving a sour taste in my mouth. I'd been called the name for so long, it shouldn't bother me now. But the way Chloe said it was so personal, as if I'd betrayed her by being who I was—a vampire, some called me. And now? What was I? A phoenix? Amaya had called me that, and I liked it. But everyone's powers varied.

"You really believe that? You're becoming a monster?"

She picked at the splinters of wood on the porch railing. "I'm not sure. But I just feel so torn all the time." She gave me a point-blank stare, her blue eyes intense and accusatory. "There's something wrong with me. I don't know what, but I don't feel like I'm me anymore."

"What exactly makes you feel that way?" I asked.

She only shook her head and glanced away. "I can't say for sure," she mumbled.

The sun rose higher, and the fog dissipated. As birds chirped from the nearby spruces, I pondered Chloe's words. What if her reaction to the serum was warping her in a way we didn't understand? Truthfully, she was most likely fine, and needed more time to adjust to her new life. Amaya could help with that. Speaking of...

"Has Amaya woken up yet?" I asked.

"I don't know," she answered, her voice quiet, and her gaze gone distant once again. "I haven't seen her today."

I nodded. "I'll go look for her. You might think about

spending more time with her. She has a gift for helping people heal."

"I've already been out riding with her. But…I'll keep that in mind."

With a nod, I stepped away and back into the house. Chloe's troubles only compounded the problems of finding a new investor. She needed help adjusting, as did the other seventy-plus patients still here.

I entered the dining room and searched for Amaya. Withered sprigs of lavender sat in the vases on the tables. Didn't Amaya usually change out the lavender every morning?

I rubbed at the sore knot in my neck. She must've slept in. I couldn't blame her. Maybe she needed the extra rest.

Turning around, I left the room and entered the hallway. Maybe a walk outside would help me clear my head.

As I left the building, I flexed my hands, letting the cool morning air rush over my skin. For so long, my hands had been encased in gloves. Scales had covered my hands, making it impossible for me to feel wind or cold, hot or dry, the way any normal human would.

Now, I reveled of the feel of the crisp air biting at my skin. I didn't mind the cold so much now. In fact, I welcomed the feeling of being alive. I owed that emotion to Amaya. She made me feel alive in a way I'd never experienced before. She could brighten the world around her with just a smile. I owed my life to her, in more ways than one.

My sandals crunched over gravel as I walked toward the stables. I could usually find Amaya here, tending the horses, which had become her favorite hobby.

The scent of fresh hay carried through the air. A horse neighed from the barn, and I thought it odd they were still stabled. Didn't Amaya usually let them out by now?

I walked to the barn and found the stalls closed, so I went to each one and opened them. The horses snorted and stamped, as if annoyed they'd had to stay inside for so long. I patted the neck of the one nearby.

"Hey, Buddy," I said. "What's going on in here?"

He only swished his tail, then lumbered away. I left the barn and followed the path back to the house.

A glimmer on the ground caught my attention. As I neared it, I noticed a spray of pearls glittering from the dirt. After kneeling, I picked one up, the small sphere cold in the morning air, and pinched it between my fingers.

Amaya had worn a pearl necklace from time to time. Her mother had given it to her. And she'd been wearing it last night, hadn't she?

A drop of fear trickled through my blood.

Was this Amaya's necklace? If so, why was it broken and scattered across the ground?

Standing, I paced to the house.

Amaya was fine. She had to be. She always got so annoyed when I worried about her. Still, I quickened my pace until I reached the steps and took them by two. After entering, I jogged down the hall and stopped at her room.

The thudding of my knuckles on wood echoed down the empty corridor.

"Amaya?" I called. "Are you in there?"

I waited only a second before cracking open her door. Sunlight streamed from her window, rays falling over her already made bed. The patchwork quilt had been smoothed and tucked around the mattress edges. Had she already made up her bed and left? Or had she slept in it at all?

A headache throbbed, and I massaged my temples. Where was she? Bathroom, maybe?

"Amaya?" I called again. "Are you here?"

I knocked on the bathroom door, then peeked inside to find it empty. As I turned around, Khan trotted to me from his spot on the couch.

"Hey there, big boy." I scratched his head. "Where's Amaya?"

He barked, then wagged his tail, which thumped the wood-planked floor. "Why don't you help me find her?"

Khan barked again, as if agreeing, and trotted outside the room alongside me. "Where do you think she went?" I asked the dog, as if he could hear me or answer. But Khan was usually with Amaya all the time. I couldn't imagine where she might've gone without him.

My heart pounded with every footstep. Sweat beaded on my neck. I didn't know why, but I felt something terrible had happened.

I prayed I was wrong.

8

____

Dear Athena,

When Mother took us to Greece, it was the most fun I ever had in my life. We saw the Parthenon ruins, and I even saw your statue! The ocean water was perfect and blue. I think I could live there and be happy forever. And the food! I've never eaten so much food! Mother bought gyros and hummus and baklava and grape leaves and a lot of wine for us. I got so full I puked, but Mother said I should drink more because I would never get such fine wine again. So, I drank some more, but it tasted so gross after I puked! I couldn't sleep all night because my stomach hurt so bad. I don't think I'll ever drink wine again.

____

AMAYA

I woke with a dry mouth. My head pounded so badly, my vision blurred, and I had to blink to focus on the room around me. Howling carried through the hallway. Human or animal? It was hard to tell. Footsteps thudded behind me. I tried to shift to see who entered the room, but my neck was so stiff, I could barely move an inch. Plus, the bands holding me in place kept me pinned to the metal table.

A man dressed in a black suit stood to inspect me. His neatly trimmed beard, angular face, and cold blue eyes seemed familiar. Where had I seen him?

"I'm glad to see you're awake, Amaya." Though he spoke softly, his voice was deep, and a hint of a warning glinted in his calculating eyes.

A dull ache pounded through my head, and my eyes burned. The fog in my brain made it hard to focus on the man standing over me.

"Where..." I attempted to speak, but my throat was so dry, my voice cracked.

"You're at my research facility," he answered, then smiled. His gloating grin made my empty stomach roil. "We're going to take care of you, Amaya. Unlike Crimson Hollow, here, we'll see fit you get the treatment you need."

He patted my arm.

His touch jolted my memory. Through the fog in my head, I remembered who he was.

I would have jerked away when his skin contacted mine, but I could only remain where I was, a wave of revulsion rolling through me.

"Emmerson..." I managed.

"You remember me?" His eyes lit up. "That's impressive. The medication we gave you should've impaired your memory, but perhaps we didn't give you enough. Ah well...that's an easy fix." He laughed, as if amused by his outburst. But his laugher faded quickly, and he sighed, his gaze going to the room's only window, where a hint of jungle greenery appeared behind the grimy glass. "We'll start your treatments when you're properly subdued. It seems like we still have a little while before that happens. In the meantime, you can relax. Sleep as much as you can. Your treatments won't be easy, but I'm hopeful we'll unleash the full potential of your powers."

My mind reeled.

How could this be happening?

The last coherent memory I had was of being outside the barn. I'd heard footsteps... then. Nothing. I had no memories until I'd woken here. But where was I? And more importantly, where was Lucian? How much time had passed? Did he know I was missing?

A knot formed in my chest, and tears burned my eyes, but I blinked them back. I locked my gaze on Mr. Emmerson.

"You... can't do this," I managed.

"No?" He raised an eyebrow. "I never cared much for people who told me I couldn't do something. Always had the opposite effect on me. Tell me I can't do something, and it gives me even more reason to do it. Do you know what I'll do with you, Amaya?" He patted my cheek, his hands cold, sending a spark of anger shooting through me. "I'll make you a greater person than Lucian ever was. He was never really a vampire, was he? He was a fraud. No. For you, we'll make you what he could never be." His leering grin made my insides coil with revulsion. His words struck me as if he'd slapped me. Make me what Lucian could never be?

Escape was my only coherent thought. I flexed my arms against the metal bands, and I kicked as much as I could, but the steel cords were unrelenting, and all I could do was fight against an impossible enemy.

Mr. Emmerson took a syringe from a metal tray and inserted a clear liquid into my IV. Its chill seeped through my veins, and my body relaxed. Its numbness swept through me. "This will help you relax, Amaya. Have a nice nap." He took a step away from me, then stopped. "I advise against trying to escape. This facility is monitored twenty-four seven. We've got armed guards posted around the clock." He took another step away. "And don't try to hurt yourself. You wouldn't want to spoil the fun before it starts."

He smirked, then turned and marched out of sight. Footsteps echoed, then faded, until all I could hear was the pounding of my own heart, the proof of my fear.

I jerked against my restraints again and again, but the steel shackles were unrelenting, and the numbness from the drug had weakened me. Taking a deep breath, I closed my eyes.

This had to be a nightmare.

I'd gone into a strange coma, one where nightmares seemed real.

If so, then I would force myself to wake up.

But I knew that no matter how much I wished it, this was not a nightmare. I'd been abducted and taken to an unknown place. I could've been on the other side of the world, for all I knew.

I swallowed the heavy lump that blocked my throat.

I didn't know how, but I would escape. I had to.

As I opened my eyes, the sound of whimpering came from down the hallway. I'd heard the voice before, meaning I wasn't the only prisoner here. Who else had they captured?

"Hello?" I whispered weakly.

The whimpering stopped.

"Can you hear me?" I asked.

Silence.

"Is anyone there?" I asked, but I got nothing in response.

Taking a deep breath, weariness tugged at me. My eyelids felt heavy, and I was forced to close them.

I will escape... was the last thought I had before the blackness took me.

9

Dear Athena,

I ate three crackers plus all the crumbs, a can of tuna fish, and the last of the ketchup. Mother said she would bring me a sandwich, but she's been gone for two days now. I'm so starving I think I might pass out. I don't know what to do.

LUCIAN

I gripped the loose pearls in my hand. I'd found seventeen of the beads strewn over the ground near the barn. They'd been tossed away, as if forcefully removed, and when I'd found the scuffled footprints and tire tracks, it was at that moment I knew something was horribly wrong.

Pacing in my office, I held the ringing phone to my ear. The incessant sound was enough to drive me crazy, and I wanted nothing more than to toss the cell across the room and march after Amaya myself.

But there wasn't a chance I could find her without help, which was why I was stuck here, in my office, pacing and cursing under my breath. I'd already contacted the police and given my information twice, but no one had followed up, which left me chasing after any help I could find.

"Sergeant Butler," a man said on the other end. He spoke with a gruff, no-nonsense voice.

"Hi, yes, this is Lucian—"

"Vidraru," he cut me off. "Calling to report the missing girl?"

"Yes." I paused to gather my thoughts. "I need your help."

"I've read the report. Sorry to say, I can't help at this point. It's been what—two hours? The truth is, she probably got mad about something and took off. Give it a few hours. She'll be back in time for lunch."

My head spun. How could I make him understand I needed help now? "Pardon me, Sergeant Butler, but I disagree. Amaya wouldn't do something like this. She wouldn't just take off without telling me. Plus, I found her broken necklace near the barn. Sergeant, I think someone took her."

"I understand your concern. But ninety-nine percent of the time, they come back. Trust me. Believe it or not, I do have a little expertise in missing persons cases. Been on the force going on forty years now."

"Forty years?" I ground my teeth. "Do you know who you are talking to? Forty years to me is a blink. A drop in the bucket."

Maybe living too long had jaded me, but I knew enough about the world to understand the evil out there. Someone had taken Amaya, and the cold dread hollowing out my insides told me she was in danger.

I could hear by his huffing breath that he was about to hang up on me. "Sergeant," I spoke as calmly as possible. "Something is wrong. Please, I can't wait a few hours. She needs help now."

The sergeant sighed.

"Please," I repeated, hoping he heard the desperation in my

voice. "Amaya wouldn't have left without saying anything. Something is seriously wrong. We never fought. She wasn't mad. She didn't just take off. She went out to feed the horses last night. This morning, I found her broken necklace near the barn, and I suspect she never slept in her bed overnight, which means someone must've taken her last night. Things aren't adding up. Can't you see?"

The line remained silent, as if he were considering what to say. "All right, Vidraru. I'll free up my schedule and come out. Show me the necklace and anything else important. I'll do what I can on my end."

"Thank you, Sergeant."

He grunted, then hung up.

I collapsed into my chair and slid the phone across the marble tabletop.

Weariness sank straight through my bones, threatening to drown me. I rested my head in my hands. Old feelings of fear and loneliness gripped me, and I was reminded of being twelve, lying in the dungeon in Bran Castle, listening to the sounds of dripping water echoing through the cold, empty space.

I'd thought Father had abandoned me there.

She probably got mad and took off.

It couldn't be true, could it?

Would Amaya just leave me like that?

Others had left the facility. But that usually only happened when treatment wasn't going well. Amaya had seemed perfectly fine. Then again, I knew enough about the world and the people in it to realize that some were better at hiding emotions than others.

Was Amaya hiding her pain? Had she truly been so unhappy that she'd left?

Chloe had been unhappy, and perhaps Amaya had felt the same and never told me.

I laid my head on the desk, the marble cold and unyielding.

These thoughts would do nothing but drown me in a sea of bitterness, and I couldn't afford to think that way.

I would find Amaya, and if it were her choice not to return, I would make peace with it.

Although I would suffer a fate worse than death if I had to let her go.

10

Dear Athena,

We went to the opera, Madame Butterfly. Then we ate dinner at a restaurant that served oysters and lobster and chocolate cake with cream that I thought would taste good. But Mother laughed when I took a bite, and it burned my tongue because it had alcohol. And I laughed too but it wasn't so funny to me. Mother said we had no money left after that, so we slept on a bench in the park. It started to snow, and it was hard to sleep when I was shivering so hard. She said New York was beautiful and that the snow was magical, and if I had my fire powers like I was supposed to, then we wouldn't have been cold.

AMAYA

I woke in a cold sweat and opened my eyes to a room lit only by moonlight. The room's window taunted me. The wind howled outside, and the leaves of the jungle greenery tapped the glass, as if reminding me that freedom was just a pane of glass away.

I sat up as best as I could, which wasn't much. With the restraints pinning me down, I was only able to lift my head.

Sleep lingered, and the daze caused by the drugs made my head feel as if it were stuffed with cotton. Hunger pinched my stomach, and I realized I hadn't eaten anything since I'd arrived. Were they trying to starve me?

I tried to think through my situation. Despite Mr. Emmerson's warning, I wouldn't stop until I'd escaped this place. There had to be a way to get free, but how?

Flexing my hands, I felt a tiny flicker of warmth coursing through my fingertips. Rubbing my thumb and pointer finger, I willed a whisper of heat to flare to life. A tiny flame sparked, then faded.

Still, for the first time since I'd arrived, I smiled. If I could create a flame, I could also create enough heat to melt through metal. At least, I hoped so.

I only had to concentrate and be smart about using my energy.

Focusing, I allowed a bit of heat to form in my fingertips, but this time, I sent enough energy into the flame to allow it to burn bright.

I paused, listening, although the presence of footsteps or voices were absent, so I burned the fire brighter, until I cupped a fireball in my hand.

The fire mesmerized me, and I nearly forgot my purpose as the amber and cobalt flames flickered from my own body, as if fueled by magic.

Opening my other clenched fist, I let the fire consume my

hand, although only warmth enveloped me, as the flames didn't touch my skin.

With fire in both hands, I poured out my energy until the fire blazed.

The bands around my wrists heated, then glowed dull red.

"More," I whispered, allowing an abundance of my energy into the flames until they sparkled and danced.

My retinas burned, but my skin remained warm and unscorched, as the metal finally began to drip to the floor.

My heart leapt with excitement.

Patches of molten steel broke from the cuffs and splattered to the ground, hitting the floor with quiet hisses. Smoke burned my nose and stung my eyes, but I didn't stop until enough metal had burned away.

When I finally extinguished the fires burning in my hands, I breathed heavily. Sweat coated my skin, and my heart pounded with adrenaline and excitement.

Weakened muscles protested as I moved my arms. I was shaky and stiff, and it took me a minute to stretch until the blood began to flow. I picked dried lumps of metal from my wrists. With a deep breath, I pulled out the tubes taped to my arms, then pushed to a sitting position.

I half-expected sirens to alarm once I removed the tubes, but I heard nothing except the frantic beating of my own heart.

My head spun, and I nearly collapsed back onto the table. But I steadied my hands on the tabletop, breathed deeply, and focused on the rings around my ankles. The loops were fastened, but were they locked?

I pried at one of the clasps, but it remained sealed, so I grabbed it with both hands and pried at it until it released with a click. Repeating the process on my other ankle, I managed to wrench it open. My legs ached when I moved, and they were so stiff, I could barely swing them over the side of the table.

Resting on the side of the bed, I clamped my hands to the metal edge and waited for the room to stop spinning. Cold concrete chilled my bare feet as I stood. Where had they put my shoes? I held to the table for a moment, then took in my surroundings, gauging my possibilities for escape.

The window was set high in the wall, and I didn't see any way to open it. The only other exit was the door, which was shut, and I made my way to it. Listening with my ear pressed to the steel, I heard nothing but silence.

I glanced back at the window, then at the door again. Squaring my shoulders, I tried to turn the knob, but it wouldn't budge. Locked.

I could burn through the metal, but I wasn't sure that was in my best interest. Not yet. Especially if they really did have guards posted.

Running my hands down my face, the lingering fog made it hard for me to concentrate, but I knew I had to do something about this drug they were giving me. I could never plan an escape while my mind was being controlled. Pacing the room, I spotted a cabinet. I knelt and opened one of the doors, where I found several plastic bags filled with clear liquid.

They were labeled *saline*, while in another cabinet, others were labeled *zicanthodine*. Was this the drug they were giving me? I wasn't familiar with the name. I'd spent enough time in Mom's lab to be familiar with all the sedatives out there, but this was a new one.

Something surfaced in my memory.

The Emmersons. Creating their own pharmaceuticals. Maybe this was one of their creations.

My stomach soured as I looked at the bag. I wanted nothing more than to rip it to shreds. But soon my thoughts faded. I shook my head, but I couldn't remember anything.

At one point, I found myself sitting on the cement floor, staring blankly at the bags filled with solution, not remembering how I got there. The cold concrete chilled me, which was the only thing bringing me back to the present.

Think, Amaya, I told myself. *You have to concentrate.*

The bags. The drugs. Could I throw them away? Rip them open and dump them all out?

But if I did that, the Emmersons would only replace them with more. It would solve nothing.

What if I switched the labels?

I took one of the saline bags and picked at the label's edge. It lifted without a hitch, and I pulled it off.

A drop of excitement blossomed in my chest. It may have been the first time I'd felt anything but terror since I'd entered this nightmare.

I placed the label aside, removed the sticker from the bag of *zicanthodine*, and placed the saline label on the opposite bag. I repeated the process until I'd traded labels on twelve bags.

By the time I finished, my head pounded. The metal bed looked much too far away. Still, I couldn't pass out right here. If someone found me lying by the bags, they would get suspicious.

Breathing heavily, I rested my head in my hands.

I'd already broken my restraints. I couldn't go back to the bed now. This may be my only chance to explore the facility. With a deep inhale, I pushed to my feet and stumbled to the door.

Gripping the cold knob, I let it chill me, helping sort out my thoughts.

Deep breaths. Think. You can do this.

I snapped twice before forming a spark. Fire ignited. I let the flames engulf my hand like a glove, then I gripped the doorknob.

Metal warmed, then grew hot. The scent of singed steel burned my nose, but I held my grip until the metal turned molten and dripped like hot wax to the floor.

I pushed the door open.

A dark hallway loomed.

No guards. No cameras that I could see. Emmerson had been bluffing.

I took a steadying step, then another. Only a little light seeped from windows, giving the cinder block walls a bluish glow. A few doors punctuated the hall. One was ajar, and a muffled moan came from it.

My bare feet slapped cold cement as I walked to the door, then peeked through it. A bed and window like mine filled the space. From this angle, I couldn't see if anyone was on the metal bed, so I craned my head to get a better look.

A shock of black hair stuck up, and the moaning started again.

I tiptoed inside, just enough to see who was there. A young man about my age lay on the bed. His eyes were closed, and metal bands encased his arms and legs in the same way I'd been held captive.

He wore a loose-fitting white gown, a match to the clothing I wore. The thin fabric covered a frame so malnourished, his collar bones protruded. With a second glance, I noticed wrinkles lining his eyes and dark circles shading his skin, and I couldn't be sure of his age. I'd first thought he must've been younger, but perhaps he was much older.

Whatever the case, my gaze snagged on the tubes protruding from his hands and arms. How long had he been here?

His head lolled, and he moaned weakly.

Questions swam through my head.

Who was he? Why was he here? Did he have some sort of powers like me?

On closer examination, I noticed faint white scars running the length of his arms and crisscrossing over his hands. One of the bones in his leg was bent, and a raised scab formed over the protrusion.

My throat tightened, and I took a step away from him.

He moaned louder, and his eyelids fluttered. I backed toward the door, leaving him behind, and stepped into the hallway before he saw me.

I gripped the door handle with a sweaty palm, my heart beating too quickly.

He must've been here for months, possibly years. Would I look like him if I stayed here?

I released the door handle and squared my shoulders to face the hallway.

No.

I would escape before that happened to me.

As I took a step forward, regret weighed on me at the thought of leaving him behind. But how could I possibly take him with me? With the wound on his leg, he didn't look capable of walking. And how would I keep him quiet?

Although a twinge of regret tugged at me, I paced to the end of the hallway and glanced in either direction.

One hallway ended at a door, another stopped at a T-intersection.

I took the hallway leading to the door, moving quietly as I stepped lightly on the balls of my feet until I stopped, listening with my ear pressed to the metal door. The hooting of an owl came as a distant echo. I tried the handle, and it opened with a click.

I smiled inwardly. Freedom was just a footstep away.

11

———

Dear Athena,

I told Mother I was hungry, and she said she couldn't afford to feed me, then she cried all day and wouldn't stop.

———

LUCIAN

Cold wind bit through my jacket and sank its teeth into my skin. Sergeant Butler, his shoulders stooped against the stiff breeze, and a younger officer followed me across the field. The sergeant had only spoken a few words since he'd arrived, and most of his communication had been in the form of grunts. I didn't hold out much hope for finding Amaya in a timely manner. But I needed their help. I would never be able to find Amaya alone.

Frost crunched under our boots as we neared the barn. I pointed to a muddy spot on the ground.

"I found the beads there," I said.

Butler frowned and rubbed his white mustache. The skin

around his eyes crinkled, and he frowned. Deep wrinkles etched his skin damaged with a multitude of age spots. The man had to be at least eighty years old. He wasn't kidding when he said he'd been working at his job for more than forty years.

"Foster, what do you make of it?" He nodded at the younger officer.

Foster, a man with a buzzed haircut and a hooked nose, knelt by the muddy spot in the ground. "There are some tracks here." He glanced up at the sergeant. "Several pairs of prints from what I can tell. A smaller set. Maybe a young woman's? And two larger prints. Military boots from the looks of it. See the treads here?" He pointed to a deep print in the mud. "These are standard issue combat boots."

Butler rubbed his chin. "Vidraru, does anyone at the facility have a military background?"

I shook my head. "I can check our records."

"They lead this direction." Foster pointed to the road. "Only one print goes this way." He looked up at us. "The military boots."

Behind Butler's black-rimmed glasses, his eyes narrowed. "Took her to a car parked on the road, most likely."

"Yes, right before they subdued her."

Subdued her. The word sent an uncontrollable shiver down my spine. "Can you tell how long ago it happened?"

"No," Foster answered. "But my guess is that it happened sometime last night."

"Meaning they could be halfway across the country by now," I added.

Butler tapped his fingers on his belt. "We'll send out an alert. See what we can come up with. Do you have any security cameras posted anywhere?"

I scanned the area. The new facility had a few cameras, but none faced this direction. The old building sat on the hill above us. I pointed to it. "No cameras. But there's a chance someone saw something."

"At the old place?"

"Yes," I answered without further explanation. Telling him we had a vagrant living on the grounds didn't seem like a great idea at the moment.

"It's worth checking out," Butler said.

The two officers followed as I trekked up the hill. Grass wet with dew slipped under my shoes. I tucked my hands protectively in my hoodie's pockets, wishing I had my gloves for protection.

Sunrays beat down on us as we crested the hill, and vines grew up the outer stone walls. Their yellowing leaves stood in such contrast to the darkened gray stones, as if the stones were pushing them away, not allowing anything with color to intrude on its muted solitude.

I paused to stare at the structure.

A thousand voices seemed to scream at me all at once, those of the departed, the ones who were jealous that I remained alive while they slept.

With a deep breath, I pushed the voices away.

The ghosts of Crimson Hollow held no power over me now.

"This way?" Foster questioned, taking the gravel path to the entrance.

"Yes. It should be unlocked."

We made our way down the drive until we reached the steps. Wide granite stairs led up to the ornate double doors. Stone angels overshadowed us as I opened the doors, then led the two officers inside the rotting remains of Crimson Hollow.

12

Lidar has revealed that some 60,000 Mayan structures have yet to be discovered.

AMAYA

I breathed in the humid nighttime air. The damp scent of jungle greenery filled the world. Floodlights shone from the back of the building. I crouched along the wall to stay out of their glare and keep to the shadows.

Boots echoed in the distance. I tensed. My heartbeat betrayed my anxiety, and I flexed my fingers, readying to use my fire.

Two men armed with rifles strode past. My throat tightened. Sweat beaded in my palms. My fingers burned so hot, I feared flames would ignite. The two shadowy forms drew closer. Berets shaded their eyes. They spoke in hushed voices. Beams of light shone from their flashlights, cutting through the thick darkness of the jungle beyond.

As they passed by me only a few yards away, I held my

breath, my back pressed to the wall. I feared my heart would pound out of my chest if they stepped any closer.

Something rustled in the bushes. The guards stopped, peering into the jungle, their lights piercing through the immense darkness. After several heartbeats, they continued along their path, around the edge of the building until they disappeared from sight.

I dared to let out my pent-up breath, then relaxed my fingers, which were cramping from clenching so tightly.

Bare feet squished over cold mud as I moved away from the building and into the shelter of the trees. Jungle greenery brushed against my thighs and arms. A narrow path wound through the forest.

It occurred to me then that I had no idea where I was. I had no survival equipment, not even a pair of shoes. And my thin nightgown would be no protection against the weather. I had no food or water.

But I had fire.

Briars tugged at my clothes, and one scraped my exposed skin. I pulled away from it, only to step on something that cut my foot. Pain shot through my heel and up my calf muscle. Leaning against a tree, I plied at the flesh on my foot where a woody thorn lodged. Blood oozed onto my fingers. Gritting my teeth, I pulled at the thorn until it came free. In the little bit of light glowing from the facility, I held the thorn up for inspection, at least an inch long and dripping red with my own blood. After tossing the thing aside, I hobbled forward.

If I were going to step on more of those things for the rest of my hike, I wasn't sure how much longer I'd be able to walk. I'd be crawling in a matter of hours.

The light from the facility faded so quickly, I wondered if I'd been swallowed in a black hole.

A well of terror opened inside me. Without light, how could I possibly see my way through the jungle? I could create a flame, but wouldn't that give away my position? With my hands out for balance, and to keep from running into anything, I continued forward.

A click resounded behind me.

I froze.

My heartrate spiked.

I spun around, and a light blinded me.

A guard stood with a gun's laser pointed at my chest.

My stomach bottomed out, and I had to swallow the fear rising in my throat. Shouts echoed around me. More than half a dozen guards appeared. Lights flashed and created a halo around me. Emmerson hadn't been bluffing, after all.

I took a step backward. Heat burned in my palms. Fear dominated my thoughts, and my only hope of escape was to burn my way out. But could I do it? Could I set fire to a living, breathing person?

No.

The single word came with clarity.

Although freedom was just a breath away, I couldn't set fire to a person, no matter how desperate I might be.

One of the men grabbed my arms, jerking me forward toward the building. Another grabbed my other arm until we entered the clearing leading to the building. It was little more than a squat concrete structure that could've been used a nuclear bomb silo.

Through the doorway ahead, a man's silhouette filled the frame. As he neared me, his hawkish features came into view, and disgust made my blood boil at the sight of Mr. Emmerson. His eyes laughed with mirth, and a smug grin curved his mouth. He clapped slowly.

"A nice attempt, Amaya. Not the best I've seen, but you're young. Try a little harder next time and maybe you'll make it off the property." He laughed.

Anger boiled in my chest, and I wanted nothing more than to spit in his face.

"Take her inside," he said with an edge of contempt in his voice. "Use the titanium bands this time."

He turned around. Rough hands tightened around my arms, but I shoved them back.

"No," I said with steel in my voice. My fists flared with blue flames. Maybe I didn't have the heart to burn anyone alive, but they didn't need to know that.

"I'll burn you." I spoke with such contempt, I surprised myself. "All of you. If you make me take one step inside that place, I swear on my father's grave, I'll burn you all."

The fire streamed up my arms, the flames turning purple as they licked at the humid jungle air.

Mr. Emmerson turned to face me. His eyebrows rose.

The guards backed away with mouths open, though the barrels of their gun still pointed at my chest.

"Put your weapons down," I shouted. "Now!"

Mr. Emmerson's jaw locked. Flames reflected in the fury of his eyes. "If they put their weapons down, then you extinguish your weapon as well." He smiled darkly. "De la Vega," he said my name with venom. "Let me give you a word of advice before you set off on your own." He pointed to the velvet inkiness of the forest looming behind me. "You won't survive out there. It's three-hundred square miles of nothing but jungle. There are jaguars and snakes. Toxic plants. If they don't kill you, drinking the water swimming with parasites will do it. And trust me, that's a painful way to go. You'll die within a week, and no one will find your body. Is that what you want? To die alone in a remote jungle? Where your corpse will rot within a matter of months, and not even your remains will survive to tell your story?"

I stood defiantly with my hands clenched. My fingers tingled with numbness. Heat radiated from the flames burning up to my shoulders and lighting my face.

Deep inside, I knew he was right. Going it alone in a jungle by myself would kill me. I had no choice but to remain here.

Something broke inside me as I realized the truth.

I controlled fire.

But Mr. Emmerson controlled me.

And he had everything he needed.

With a bitter sigh of defeat, I released my clenched fists. The fire extinguished, leaving an empty hole in my chest. I felt hollow inside. Cold. As if someone had taken a vital part of me and shattered it.

The guards lowered their guns, then grabbed my arms so tightly, I swore they'd leave bruises.

I limped on my injured foot until we made it onto the cold concrete slab flooring.

My head spun. I had trouble processing my situation. I'd been so close to freedom, but I'd been wholly unprepared for what was out there. How far were we from civilization, from anyone who could help me? The guards shoved me through the door.

Revulsion welled inside me as we entered the facility. Harsh fluorescent lights stabbed my vision. My injured foot stung, though my anger masked the pain, until all I felt was dull throbbing.

Instead of throwing me inside my room, the guards led me down another hallway. I felt like an ant in an ant hill, one with no exit. An eternal maze where the only escape would be in losing my own sanity.

We stopped when we entered a lab.

The familiarity of the room caught me off guard. It could've been any of the labs Mom had worked in. The acrid scent of ammonia tickled my nose. I could hardly believe how much equipment filled the room. Stirrers, hot plates, glass vials, mortar and pestles, droppers, and countless other supplies cluttered the tables and shelves. It was enough to make my head spin. What on earth were they doing here?

What disturbed me most were the small mammals and reptiles floating in jars of formaldehyde. A shiver went down my spine as we passed an oversized glass filled with a coiled black snake, its milky dead eyes peering at me.

Some of the mammals lay splayed and pinned to boards. Others were in various stages of being dissected, their hearts and livers splayed in neat rows. I even spotted larger mammals on the far side of the room—dogs, cats, and something larger with golden fur, though I couldn't tell what sort of creature it was.

The guards placed me on a chair, then slapped a pair of cuffs on my wrists that they chained through a metal loop welded to the table.

"Try burning through those," one of the men said smugly, chuckling to himself before backing away.

I shot him a sharp glare, but he turned and left with the other guard, leaving me alone. A few moments later, a woman entered. She walked with a humped back, and her hair hung in matted gray strands.

Wrinkled scrubs hung off her emaciated frame, and her sallow skin was pocked with age spots. She lumbered toward me, but when she looked at me, her eyes gave me pause. They were cat's eyes, with long slits for pupils—wild and animalistic—and tapered to points.

An uncontrolled shiver spiked like an ice pick straight through me. They had to be contacts, right?

Yet what made them shaped as a cat's?

She sat across from me. Her fingers were so bent with arthritis, she had trouble picking up a tube and inserting it into the port of a machine that sat on wheels behind her.

"Who are you?" I asked, my voice hushed and laced with suspicion.

"Flora," she answered curtly, then pressed a button on the machine.

"What are you doing?"

She shot me a dark glare. "No questions," she snapped, her words clipped. "When you're here, you obey him. Nothing else matters."

"You won't even answer a simple question?" I asked.

She frowned, then shook her head. Beeping filled the room as she pressed a button. After opening several packages of alcohol wipes, she took my arm and swabbed my skin. Cold wetness chilled me. The sharp scent of rubbing alcohol filled the room.

"Sting," she said before shoving a needle into my arm.

Blood filled the tube and streamed up the line until it entered a bag.

"I didn't agree to any of this," I said. "I didn't give you permission to take my blood."

Her cat's eyes narrowed. As I got a better look at them, I felt as if I stared into the eyes of an animal. She studied my blood as it streamed through the tube.

"Are you hungry?" she asked.

"What?" I questioned. That had come from nowhere. "Hungry?" I hadn't thought of it. I'd felt hungry earlier, but since my attempted escape, food had been the last thing on my mind. Still, shouldn't I have been starving? I hadn't eaten or drunk anything since I'd been captured. How long ago had that been? "Not really," I answered.

She nodded. "Good."

"Good?" I raised an eyebrow. "How is that a good thing? I should be starving, shouldn't I? And I'm not, which proves they've already been altering me."

"Good," she repeated. "The treatment is working."

"Treatment?" I leaned forward, pressing her with my most scrutinizing gaze. Besides Mr. Emmerson, she was the first person I'd gotten a chance to talk to. Maybe I'd get some answers. "Flora," I said her name softly. "Please. Tell me what's going on here. Where are we? What are they doing to me?"

Apprehension flashed in her eyes, then she glanced at the door.

"Flora," I repeated with desperation. "Please. I need to know."

With a sigh, she nodded. Her wild animal eyes met mine, and I felt as if I were looking not at a person, but a demon housed in a person's body. "You become someone else in this place." She spoke in a fearful whisper. "It's what they do. They take these." She pointed to the animal's corpses behind her. "And they put them into you."

"What do you mean? How is that possible?"

Gray hair swished as she shook her head.

"Gene splicing?" I asked.

She remained speechless. My heart sank as I watched my blood draining into the bag. They were turning me into some animal hybrid—or perhaps, something much worse.

I wanted to rip my arm away from her and run until I couldn't breathe, until my feet bled from getting stabbed by a thousand thorns. Until I died in the jungle. Wouldn't that be a better fate than this?

But maybe I wasn't thinking straight. It wouldn't be the first time.

My thoughts turned to Lucian. Had he discovered I was missing? Or did he suppose I ran away? Maybe he was already searching for me, but if so, I had no idea how he would find me. I didn't know my location, but I knew one thing. I was nowhere near upstate New York.

A giant hole gaped inside me. Being torn away from Lucian, and from the new home I'd created, made me choke back tears. I'd lost my first home when I lost my parents, and now, after finally finding it again, home had been robbed from me.

Flora placed a cotton ball on my arm and removed the needle.

"Still won't tell me what you're doing with that, huh?" I asked.

She ignored more, stoppering the vial, and turning away.

The door swung open.

Two guards led a young man between them. The shock of black hair told me he was the same person I'd seen in the room by mine. He limped, barely able to hold himself upright as the guards led him to a metal chair.

When he sat, his vacant gaze peered at nothing. His eyes were so bloodshot, the whites looked almost completely red. Sunken cheeks and sallow skin gave him a zombie-like appearance. Flora shuffled over to him, moving stiffly, her movements jerky and uncoordinated, as if her bones weren't aligned properly.

He didn't react as she stabbed a needle into his shoulder.

I opened and closed my hands, creating fists, then relaxing my fingers. Warmth stirred, starting in the palms of my hands, then traveling through my joints and to my fingertips. I didn't let the flames escape. Not just yet. But sometime soon, I would test Mr. Emmerson's theory on the titanium cuffs.

If they could be melted, then I would take my chance to escape again. And next time, I would be prepared for whatever lay out there. And I would conquer it.

13

LUCIAN

The two officers followed me inside Crimson Hollow. Unease pulsed through my blood as I stood in the foyer looking up. Shards of sunlight drifted through cracks in the ceiling and walls. Broken glass littered the floor in places. I almost felt as if I could hear the voices of the patients who'd been here a hundred years ago. Hear the squeak of the wheelchairs, the laughter and crying. The pleas for help.

I laughed under my breath. I would've been in my thirties when the patients had been alive. Maybe my age had something to do with my nearness to this location. I'd been alive when they'd been walking these halls, and the connection I felt was almost uncanny. Like Crimson Hollow knew I belonged here.

"Look at this," Officer Foster said. He pointed to a dusty area near the corner. "It's a footprint. An actual print. Not a shoe print. Look." He knelt to be closer. "You can see the toes and heel here." He glanced up at me. "Any idea who made this?"

I nodded. "Jayden Black."

"Who?" Foster asked.

"He was a patient here a few years ago. Didn't respond to treatment, so he ran away. At least, we thought so."

"Yes." Butler scrubbed his hands down his face. "I remember him. We searched for months trying to find him after he escaped. After he turned eighteen, as a legal adult, and with no family, there wasn't much more we could do except keep searching whenever we could. That always bugged me that we couldn't find a trace of where that boy went."

"That's the thing," I said. "He never escaped. He's still living here."

Butler arched a bushy eyebrow. "You sure about that?"

"Yes. We've seen him. At least, someone who looks uncannily like him."

"If that's so, then we need to bring him in." He frowned. "Why didn't you call us about him sooner?"

"Because..." I answered. "I don't think he'll leave."

Foster stood and faced us. "It looks like he went that way." He pointed. "Up the stairs."

"Think we can find him?" Butler asked.

"If we can, then there's a chance he saw something," I answered. "And maybe he saw who took Amaya."

"Where did you see him last?" Foster asked.

"We spotted him on the third floor," I said. "We may be able to find him there. But I'll warn you, he's fast. And he escaped quickly when we noticed him. We'll need to approach him carefully. Don't startle him, whatever you do."

The two officers nodded, and we marched to the stairs. After ducking under the yellow tape, we climbed to the third floor.

Morning sunlight drifted through the windows. Dust motes floated on the stagnant air. The hallway branched, and I led the others down the corridor to the left until we reached the room where we'd last seen Jayden.

Scuffling came from the hallway behind us. The sound was so faint, I doubted the officers heard it, but my enhanced hearing magnified the sound. I held a finger to my lips, then treaded out of the room and to the passage where we heard the sound. Footsteps echoed ahead. The others followed as I walked. Scraping emanated from inside a space to our left, and I hurried to open the door.

A single bed and some dressers filled the space. Dust motes floated on the air, and a pair of outdated curtains partially covered the window.

Movement behind one of the chests of drawers caught my eye. I nodded toward it.

Back there, I mouthed.

Sergeant Butler nodded, and Officer Foster followed.

A knocking sound came from behind the bureau, followed by a muffled scream.

We darted to the dresser and peeked behind. An ashen faced young man tugged on a sealed window, trying to pry it open. His eyes widened, and he squatted in the corner, holding his hands over head. His ratty clothes and unkempt hair gave him the appearance of a rabid dog.

"Jayden..." I said softly.

"Leave me alone," he snapped.

"We're not going to hurt you. We just want to ask a few questions."

He scooted closer to the wall and cast a frightened glance up at the window.

"Have you been living here all this time?" Officer Foster asked.

Jayden barred his teeth, wolflike. "Don't come any closer."

"Jayden," I said softly. "Please. We're not here to hurt you. I need to ask you some questions."

He cast a terrified glance at the officers, then looked at me.

"Do you know who may have taken Amaya?" I asked. "You must have had a good view of the field from here, if you were up here last night. Did you see anything?"

His eyes widened, and he tilted his head. "The girl?"

"Yes. She was with me when we were here last. Do you remember her?"

He thrust his finger at the officers. "Make them go away."

I peeked back at the officers. They traded glances, then nodded, and slowly backed out of the room, leaving me alone with the boy.

"You're Lucian," he said in a hushed tone, almost too quiet to hear.

I nodded.

"The vampire," he added.

"Some people call me that. But not so much anymore."

He nodded. A spark of intelligence flashed in his eyes. Although he lived as a vagrant, his mind didn't seem to be affected.

"You're looking for the girl," he stated.

"Yes. Amaya. Do you know what might have happened to her?" I pointed to the window. "You might have seen something or heard something out there. Did you?"

He bit his lip, as if pondering what to say. "Two men," he finally answered.

My heart leapt with excitement. Maybe we were finally getting somewhere. "Two men?" I repeated, to clarify.

He nodded.

"What did they look like?"

He shook his head. "Too dark."

"Ah." My excitement faded. "Did you see anything else? Any detail will help me, even something that might have seemed insignificant."

He shook his head again and pressed his back to the wall. "N —no... Nothing..."

"Jayden, please," I pleaded. "They took Amaya. She could be hurt. Do you remember anything else?"

He tilted his head and blinked slowly. "A car," he whispered.

"A car? Yes?" I questioned, tension in my voice. "Could you tell what kind?"

"No."

"Could you tell anything else about it? Where it went after it took her?"

He glanced at the window. It was a brief motion, but I'd seen it. "Can you show me which way it went?" I asked.

Jayden clapped his hands to his ears. "No. Don't talk." He grimaced. "Don't talk to me anymore."

I ground my teeth. I'd been so close to getting more answers, I couldn't let him push me away now.

"Jayden." I rested my hand on his. He flinched and opened his eyes. Then his gaze tracked to my hands.

"You're not wearing gloves?" he asked.

"No. I don't need them anymore."

He pulled his hands out of his pockets and threaded his fingers together. Scales sloughed from his skin.

"Jayden…" I pointed to his hands. "How long have you been that way?"

He hung his head.

"We could help you," I explained. "We have a serum now."

"No." He vehemently shook his head.

"Why?"

He tensed. Tears sparkled in his eyes. "No," he repeated.

"Okay," I said softly, pulling away from him. "I understand. You want to be left alone."

With a sigh of defeat, I stood and backed away from the boy. His eyes tracked my movements. When I reached the door, he stood.

"Wait."

I paused from taking another step, and he pointed to the window. "There," he said. "They took her that way."

I crossed back to where he stood, and I looked in the direction he pointed.

"Down that road," he said, then his eyes met mine. "Then… I heard the helicopter."

My eyebrows rose. "You heard a helicopter? Do you know

which direction it came from?"

He pursed his lips as he thought. "That way." I followed his line of sight. A sea of trees spanned around us. A helicopter? Where would it have landed?

My heart hammered, imagining what Amaya must have felt like as she'd been taken. How terrified she must have been. I stood at the glass looking out over the forest, wishing I could reach out to her and pull her away from whatever horror she was going through. The terror nearly overwhelmed me. I took a deep breath to steady my breathing.

When I opened my eyes, I spotted a treeless hill jutting just beyond the mist.

"Did it come from that direction?" I asked Jayden.

Looking through the window, he bit his lip, then nodded. He pressed his hand to the glass, then quickly yanked it away, as if it had burned him. I gave him a sidelong glance. Was it painful for him to touch things?

I frowned. It wasn't right for him to be living as a recluse, alone and in pain. "Jayden, you're hurting. Please. Come to the new facility. We can help you."

"No." He took a step backward. "I don't want you. I don't want anyone."

He turned to stare out the window, turning his back on me, as if putting an end to our conversation.

In some ways, he reminded me of myself. Had I been so different from him not so long ago? If so, then I should've known how to help him. But there was only one problem—he didn't want help.

Still, he'd given me more information than what I'd come with.

Amaya had been taken by car, then possibly a helicopter. A tremor as frigid as ice coursed through me. She could be anywhere in the world right now. But all I knew was that she wasn't with me. And in that loneliness, I wasn't so different from Jayden after all.

14

AMAYA

I lay staring at the ceiling. The incessant chirping of crickets, and the occasional howls from monkeys, kept me awake. That, and the images playing through my head. The look in Flora's eyes had left a lingering chill. After spending time at Crimson Hollow with Lucian and the other survivors, I should've realized someone like her could've existed, yet why did it feel so wholly unnatural?

The young man also bothered me. He was being warped into something inhuman. He hadn't even looked at me when we'd been in the same room, as if I didn't exist. Who was he? Where did he come from? I didn't even know his name.

Voices echoed down the hall. I couldn't make out what they said. Sounds of shuffling feet came from behind me. Someone walked inside. Coarse, unkept hair stuck up in patches around balding spots where red, puss-filled lumps formed on his scalp. More lumps bulged from his forehead and cheeks. His beady eyes shifted from the walls to the floor, and finally to me. Like Flora, his movements were jerky and uncoordinated.

He held something. As I got a better look, I realized it was a vial filled with orange-tinged liquid.

He didn't speak as he placed the liquid on a tray and inspected the port taped to my arm.

"What's in the vial?" I asked.

The man's face stretched into a too-wide smile, revealing teeth sharpened to points. "Food," he answered, his voice raspy, then he picked up the vial and held it close to me.

I wanted to swat it away. "Get that away from me."

"I can't do that. This is for your own good, you know. The sooner you get used to your... treatments, the better." He spoke haltingly, as if he had trouble remembering the words.

"I don't need treatments," I said through clenched teeth. "I'm fine the way I am."

"Are y—you sure?" He leered, his too-wide smile and sharpened teeth making revulsion well inside me. "They make you something better. Like me. You'll become stronger, a better hunter, you won't feel hunger or pain..."

"What?" I demanded. "I don't want any of those things."

"Maybe not now, but you will." He smirked, then stuck the vial into the port taped to my arm. Cold liquid flowed through my veins. As the coldness went through my arms and into my chest, the room spun around me, and a bitter taste filled my mouth.

He rested his hand on my arm. Something bulged under the back of his hand and wriggled under his skin.

"No." I struggled against my restraints. "Leave me alone."

Heat warmed under my skin. His grip tightened.

"Leave you alone? I just met you." He tilted his head, then licked his lips. "We never see new people here. What's your name? Anaya, isn't it?"

"A-*maya*," I corrected. "And I asked you to leave me alone."

He leaned so close, I could see the pores in the lumps under his forehead. His breath stank of rotting fish, and his darting eyes bulged.

My skin warmed until searing heat burst free.

The man screamed and jumped back. He held his burned hand with his uninjured one. Bright blisters appeared on his palm. He looked at me with a slacked jaw.

"I told you..." I said, my hands trembling with rage. "Don't touch me."

He cursed and stumbled out of the room, cradling his burned hand.

My heart pounded. Sweat slicked my forehead. Although the man had left, the vial of orange liquid still flowed into me. My only wish was to rip it out of my flesh. My breathing came in gasps, and the nauseous feeling in my stomach got so intense, I thought I might be sick.

People shouted in raised voices outside my room.

I'd gotten their attention. Good. Maybe next, they'd send in someone more important, so I could burn them, too.

My vision swam, and my head spun.

I was tempted to close my eyes and pass out, but how could I?

I practiced breathing deeply, and I imagined how it felt to be on horseback, with a warm breeze on my face, and Khan trotting nearby. My heartrate slowed, and though the ice-cold liquid from the vial still coursed through my veins, my pounding heart slowed.

The door's hinges squeaked as someone entered. Two people approached me. One I recognized.

Yasira Emmerson.

Her electric blue eyes were as sharp as lightning. Red lipstick contrasted her nearly Albino white skin, the color of blood on snow. I was reminded of the coldness I felt while in her presence. Maybe now, I was beginning to understand why I felt that way.

"Yasira," I said, my voice so hoarse, the word came out as a whisper.

"Amaya," she replied, giving me a curt nod.

I attempted to lift my hands, but with the cuffs chaining me to the bed, only managed to raise them a few inches. "You planned this."

"Yes," she answered matter-of-factly. "We did. My husband and I planned this for years. We weren't intending to kidnap you at first. No, we'd had hopes for making Lucian our own. But then things changed when he discovered his true nature, and we had to alter our plans."

She leaned closer. "We were so happy to have found you."

I scrunched my forehead. "You kidnapped me! What kind of monster are you?"

Her eyes narrowed to slits, snake-like, and her mouth curved into a wicked smile. "Interesting choice of words." She gripped my hand and leaned forward. "Just remember, you're not the only person who's different here. Everyone in this facility was chosen for a reason. Genetic differences that can be improved and reshaped. But you may be our most unique specimen yet."

"I'm not a specimen."

Her eyes turned to sharp daggers. "We're all specimens, Amaya. Every person on the planet. We're nothing but strands of DNA in need of improving. What do you think we're here for? After we die, our bodies decompose and become good for nothing but feeding worms. But we're more than that. You'll be more than that."

A cold shiver skimmed down my spine. This woman was more than delusional, she was crazy. "I never asked to come here. You took me against my will. You'll regret it."

"You're wrong. You'll thank us one day. Have you never thought to ask why Lucian is the only one with viridae sangre who lives forever? Why has everyone else died, and he lived?"

"Because his strand of the virus was unique. I thought that was common knowledge." I could hardly believe I was still talking to this woman. I should've refused to cooperate by speaking with her at all. She was completely incapable of rational thought or interactions. Why hadn't I noticed what a creep she was to begin with? I supposed some people were good at hiding it. Still, I had sensed something was wrong. I just hadn't realized how much.

"His strain of the virus was unique, that's true. But it wasn't only unique, his father engineered it to be one-of-a kind."

"How do you know that?"

"Because we've been experimenting for years, doing things that other scientists would deem inhumane. But they don't understand how much knowledge they could've found if they'd only looked past their own inhibitions."

"Yes," I answered darkly. "You're right, in a way. Hitler thought the same." A sickening nausea coursed through me at the images conjured when I spoke of the experiments during the height of Third Reich's rule. "I remember the pictures I saw in books," I said to her. The human suffering was enough to haunt my nightmares. Images of people so thin they looked little more than skeletons, laying on beds of cold metal plates, surrounded by machines that could've passed for torture devices. "Yes. They made discoveries, too. Just like you. But at what cost?"

She smirked. "You fail to see the innovations. We're only as strong as science allows us to be. What's the suffering of a few people when the entire population of a planet benefits?"

"Benefits how? I see nothing that could justify kidnapping and imprisonment."

"But you will see. Soon you'll realize we've made something more of you. Something so much better. You'll see, and you'll understand that what we're doing is not only for your good, it's for the benefit of the entire population of the planet, not just for now, but for thousands of years to come."

My muscles tensed at my mounting frustration. Reasoning with her was impossible. "If that's so, then you need to let me off this table. I'm sure you're a smart person. I'm sure you understand how much being captive is affecting me mentally and physically. I can't function like this. You want to make me something greater than what I am. But this..." I rattled the chains holding my hands. "This is not the way to do it. I don't know exactly what you're doing to people here but taking their minds from them is not making them better. You're warping them. You're weakening them."

A storm brewed in her eyes.

"At least let me get up and walk around. I already know what will happen if I try to escape. You made it clear what's out there, and what happens when I set foot outside of this place."

She crossed her arms. "You're wasting your time trying to convince me. You should know that with the injections we're giving you, they may make you unstable. We've had problems in the past. At least, until you receive the next injection. Then, I'll allow you to move around the facility as you like. With supervision, of course."

I ground my teeth in frustration. Maybe it was a good thing she didn't let me out right now, because I would've most likely strangled her. How could she be such a cold-hearted monster?

I took a deep breath to keep a lid on my anger. At least she'd agreed to let me get off this table at some point.

She patted my arm. "I know this must be terrifying for you," she said, her voice mockingly compassionate. "But you'd be surprised what fear can teach you."

"I've had my fair share of it, thanks," I answered sarcastically. "Why don't you tell me why you're really doing this?" So far, no one had bothered to give me any sort of explanations of why the Emmersons were experimenting on people. Learning about someone's abilities was a lousy excuse. There had to be more to it. What would cause a person to become so desperate that they had no choice but to kidnap people and experiment on them?

"Yasira," I spoke her name in a quiet voice, yet I hoped she heard the intensity. "Why are you taking people against their will? Did something happen to you to make you do it? Or maybe something happened to someone you care about?"

Her eyes narrowed, and it seemed I'd struck a chord.

"Did something happen to you?" I demanded.

"No," she answered finally. "It was my daughter."

I raised an eyebrow. "Your daughter?"

"Yes. Her name is Sasha." Her lips hinted at a smile, one filled with more sadness than happiness. "She was six when they diagnosed her." Yasira's eyes darted to the door. "I—I haven't spoken to many people about her."

"What did they diagnose her with?" I asked, hoping to keep her talking. The more I could find out about Yasira and her motivations, the better.

"Cancer," she answered matter-of-factly. "Very aggressive. They gave her a month to live."

Although Yasira may have been one of the most deranged people I knew, my heart still hurt for her.

"Umber and I were shattered, of course. Nothing prepares you for the death of a child." She hung her head. "We knew we didn't have much time, so we flew to Mexico."

Mexico. Is that where we are?

"We found a doctor experimenting with new treatments." She looked up, and tears shone in her eyes. "He said he could cure her, but he needed blood." She squeezed my hand. "Not just any blood. Viridae sangre."

I recoiled. I didn't like where this conversation was going. "The virus? Why?"

"He said she didn't have cancer, but a rare form of the virus. It was intricately linked to the primary virus. The doctor was able to gain a sample of VS, and he stopped the progression of her symptoms. But only for a while." She paused, staring across the room, as if caught up in another time. "Sasha recovered eventually. But she was never the same person."

"Where is she now?" I asked, dreading the answer.

"She's here, of course. We rarely leave her side."

"May I see her?"

"No," she answered too quickly. "Never. Sasha can never see anyone but us."

"Why?"

Yasira gripped the edge of the table. "Because…" she whispered. "She's not human anymore."

"Not human?" A flicker of fear pinched me. "Then what is she?"

"No." She spoke with authority. "I've already told you too much." She stood straight and took a deep breath. "Your next treatment is tomorrow morning. Get some rest until then. Trust me, you'll want it." She turned to leave, then paused. "Oh, yes, and try not to burn our technicians. Especially Flint. He's so sensitive. We have so little help around here; we don't need someone like you scaring them off."

"I won't make any promises," I said, my tone harsh.

She gave me a smug glare, then her eyes softened. "Well, I can't say I would've been any less defiant at your age, although soon, I think you'll understand everything we're doing here is for your own good." She gave a nod, as if to reassure herself. "Yes, soon, I think."

She left the room, and my vision blurred. I blinked, but it only got worse. The last of the orange fluid had drained from the tube in my arm, and the bitterness I tasted in my mouth had turned to a thick coating that tasted of iron.

When I closed my eyes, I imagined freedom.

And in the state between sleep and wakefulness, I saw Lucian searching for me.

15

LUCIAN

ightning streaked across the sky. Thunder boomed around me and the two officers as we hiked down a winding trail through the forest. A steady rain started to fall, so we pulled up our raincoats' hoods to cover our heads.

"This isn't good," Officer Butler said. "Rain will wash away any footprints we might find."

Officer Foster grunted his agreement, and we continued up the hill. Acorns crunched under our boots. The dampness plastered my clothes to my skin. I kept my hands in my pockets, more a force of habit than anything else. It seemed I'd been hiding my hands and face a lot since Amaya had gone missing. If she never returned, would I hide myself away forever? If I'd really been a vampire, crawling into a coffin seemed a fitting choice of action for me. I was better off dead if she never returned.

Shaking my head, I tried to clear away the negative thoughts. *I'll find her. I have to.*

Briars tore at my jacket, and the steady drizzle turned to a downpour as we climbed higher. The trees thinned, and we crested the hill.

Dead grass filled the area, and the lack of trees was a stark contrast to the rest of the hillside.

Movement caught my eye.

White and red blurred in the trees below, then disappeared, as if smoke.

I pointed. "Did you see that?"

"I didn't see anything," Foster said.

"What was it?" Butler asked.

"Not sure." I scanned the trees, their trunks darkened by the rain, their leaves drooping. I listened for footsteps, but the drumming rain, coupled with the rumble of thunder, masked any sounds.

"Let's keep moving," Foster said.

I hesitated, but the others continued forward, and not seeing anything, I followed. Strange. Usually, my heightened senses made it easy for me to pick out anything hiding in the woods. Maybe being so stressed at Amaya's disappearance was making me see things.

We hiked around the clearing, and I noted the oddness of the absence of the trees, as if they didn't dare to grow here, as if the land were cursed.

"Over here," Butler called. He stood a few yards away, and I moved to stand beside him.

"What have you got?" Foster asked, as he also made his way toward us.

"Look." Butler pointed to the ground. "See how the grass is beaten down? It goes in a straight line."

"Yes, I see it." I scanned the area. "There's a similar pattern beside it. Like two tracks." I looked up at the officers and wiped the water from my face. "Maybe the landing skids from a helicopter?"

Foster rubbed his chin. "Yes. With all the trees around, this is the only place for a helicopter to land, and I'll bet that's precisely what they did. But let's keep searching. See if there's any other evidence left behind." He shook out his raincoat. "It won't be easy to do in this weather."

We continued searching. A damp chill burrowed under my skin. My heartbeat seemed to echo the incessant pounding of the rain. Fear clawed like a phantom under my skin, and it was hard to keep the terror from rising up and choking me. Morbid thoughts flashed through my head, and the dread that we might find Amaya's body lying dead on the rain-soaked hillside left me shaking.

A glint of white flashed from the ground. I knelt to get a better look. A pearl glistened among the debris of grass and leaves.

My breathing stopped for a half second.

I reached for it, but hesitated.

"Over here," I called.

Soggy footsteps plodded over the ground as the officers approached. The rain turned to a slow drizzle as the two men stood over me.

Officer Foster knelt beside me. His eyes widened as he looked at the single pearl.

"Do you think this is hers?" he asked.

"I think so." I nodded. "It's similar to the others I found."

"Then she was most likely up here." Officer Foster frowned.

"Yes," I said. "I think Jayden was right. Someone was up here with a helicopter."

"But, who?" Sergeant Butler asked.

I rubbed my forehead. "We don't have many friends, officers." Breaking sticks echoed behind us, and we spun around to face the forest. The dark chasm of trees formed domes beneath, as if they were dark caves leading into the mouth of hell. A blur of fur dashed through the foliage.

"Khan, is that you?" I called.

"Khan?" Officer Foster questioned, raising an eyebrow.

"Amaya's dog." I reached out my hand. "Here boy. It's okay."

The bushes rustled, and a high-pitched whine came from the shelter of the trees.

"Come here," I repeated. "It's okay. It's just me."

Officer Butler hooked his thumbs in his belt loops. "Is he always so skittish?"

"Not usually. Something has him spooked." I took a step toward the tree line. "Khan. It's okay. Come here, boy!"

A moment ticked past before a dog the size of a wolf moved silently from the bushes.

He shook the water from his coat of white fur. Wolfish yellow eyes spoke of intelligence. Sticks and briars matted his fur. He walked cautiously toward me until he closed the gap between us. Hesitantly, he stuck his cold nose in the palm of my hand.

With his nearness, a lump formed in my throat.

I knelt and hugged him to my chest. "What are you doing out here all alone?"

He yelped, and I scratched behind his ears.

"He's not alone," a female voice came from the forest. Chloe stepped out of the woods. Damp hair hung in limp strands down her face. Her eyes were wild, more animal than Khan's. But she blinked and took a step forward, and her eyes became her own again.

"Chloe," I said, surprise in my voice. "What's going on?"

"I followed him." She pointed at the dog. "He led me here. I think this is the last place Amaya was."

"Yes," Officer Butler said behind me. "We were coming to the same conclusion."

"He stopped here," Chloe continued. "It's like her scent disappeared."

"It did," I answered. "Amaya was taken by someone on a helicopter."

Chloe's face fell. She bit her lip and glanced away. "Who would do that?" she asked quietly.

"We don't know," Butler answered. "At least, not yet."

Chloe brushed damp locks of hair from her face. "We have to find her."

"But how?" I cast a glance at Butler and Foster.

Butler heaved a long, weary sigh. The look he gave me, with his eyebrows furrowed and the tight line of his mouth, told me there was little hope. "Judging by the time she was taken, and the capability of her captors to fly her any place on the planet, she could literally be anywhere."

"So, we're at a dead end?" Chloe asked.

"No." Determination filled my words. "No, there's got to be something."

"Like what?" Chloe asked.

"The airport," Butler answered. He pointed south. "Only thirty miles away. They may have picked up the chopper on their radar. It's the only thing I've got at this point. But if we want those records, we'll have to go in person to get them. They don't give you that kind of thing over the phone."

"Then we'll head to the airport," I said as a gust of wind brought a torrent of rain toward us, nearly drowning my own voice. "And pray we find something."

16

AMAYA

Time blurred. I didn't know how long I'd been in this place, this nightmare. My existence was nothing but a blur of images and sounds and pain. The pain, most of all, kept me closest to reality.

The needle sticks came half-a-dozen times a day now.

I would have succumbed to complete madness if I hadn't switched the bags of saline. And one other thing. Lucian. Thinking of returning to him was the only thing keeping my mind clear. I couldn't succumb to the treatments. I had to stay whole for Lucian.

They'd let me out of my room a few times and escorted me through limited places in the facility. I'd learned of several exit points, and I stored those images to my memory for later use. Not a minute went by that I didn't think of escape.

I'd also learned the name of the young man they were keeping. Blaise. He'd been here for years. They called him "the prototype." Whatever they did to him, they wanted to do to me.

Apprehension quickened my heart as I sat at a table in a

dining area. The room had only a few narrow, horizontal windows at the top of the wall, and grass grew at the window's bottom, which meant this room was partially underground, as was most of the facility. Finding this place in the jungle from above, in a search plane or a helicopter, would be difficult, if not impossible, which was most likely why they'd chosen this location.

The door swung open behind me.

I turned and saw Blaise walking with slow, plodding steps into the room, then he sat on a bench near the back wall.

For the first time that I had seen, he had no one accompanying him. His stare was still vacant, his dark hair sticking up in every direction. Circles shadowed his eyes, and his thin hospital gown hung from a malnourished frame.

Sorrow gripped me at the sight of him. He'd been kidnapped just like me. I'd never been able to talk to him again, since that first time. Now was my chance.

I walked toward him, clutching my hospital gown around me. My bare feet shuffled over the cold linoleum floor. Anxiety quickened my heartbeat. What if he was too far gone to understand anything? What would I say to him in the first place? *Hi, we've both been kidnapped...*

But maybe if I found out more about him, I'd learn more regarding our captors. Any information concerning this place at this point was a help. When I reached the table, I sat across from him. His eyes widened for half-a-second, and it seemed a hint of lucidity lurked in the dark depths of his pupils.

"Hi," I said. "My name is Amaya."

He nodded, though didn't speak.

"You're called Blaise, right?"

His unblinking stare made me wonder if he spoke another language. It had been a while since I'd heard my dad speak his native language, but I'd do my best.

"*Cómo se llama?* Blaise?"

He nodded. "Yes," he said finally.

"You speak English?" I asked.

"Both. Spanish also," he answered.

"Where are you from?" I asked.

"Mexico. Our closest village is Santa Lucia, but my family's home is far from there." His eyes wandered to the sliver of windows. "My home."

"They took you," I said, more of a statement than a question.

"Yes." Anger flashed in his eyes. A good sign. Somewhere in there, emotions still lingered, despite all they had done to him.

"They took me, too," I said. "I live in New York state. They knocked me out, and I don't remember arriving here. Do you know where we are?"

"The jungle. I don't know where."

"Do you remember them taking you? Did you travel far from your home?" If so, at least I've had some idea of what country we were in.

He pointed to his forehead. "No memory."

I sank in my chair. Figuring out where we were was the first step in finding my way home, but how could I make it back home if I didn't know where to start?

Blaise rested his hands on the table. Needle pricks had left his skin bruised in mottled shades of yellow and purple. Just like mine.

"You tried to escape once?" he asked.

I nodded. "I didn't get very far." Wind gusted outside the window, making the weeds beat against the glass. "The guards stopped me, but even if they hadn't, the jungle would've killed me."

"No," he said with a shake of his head. "Not kill you. The jungle is danger, yes. But kill you? No. There are poisons, and there are antidotes."

I shot him a scrutinizing glance. "You're familiar with the jungle?"

He nodded. "I've spent my life in it."

My thoughts spiraled with the possibilities. I'd escaped, but what good had it done me? I would never survive out there. But with Blaise... was it possible? I glanced behind us, to the door that was partially open. A few voices echoed down the hallway, but they were too far away to make out the words. I leaned closer to Blaise, whispering. "Would you know how to survive out there if we escaped?"

Escaped. I could hardly believe I'd uttered the word out loud. It had been the only thing on my mind, but I hadn't dared spoken it out loud.

"I could survive," he said matter-of-factly. "If you got us out."

I thrummed my fingers on the tabletop. The possibilities whirled through my head. Could we do it? Did we have any other choice?

As if out of habit, I glanced over my shoulder again. Someone passed by the doorway, but they didn't even pause.

"It's possible," I admitted, speaking in hushed tones. "They've gotten lax, the longer I've been here." I sorted through my tangled web of thoughts. "If we go at night, there will be less guards on duty. The security isn't great here, because they're confident the jungle will do their job for them, which means getting out of here shouldn't be too hard if we move fast enough. Once we get out, we'll have to make it several miles into the jungle. And we can't leave tracks, which will be nearly impossible in that underbrush." I didn't know a lot about jungle survival, but my cop dad had taught me enough about tracking to understand how to leave minimal trace. Doing that in the jungle wouldn't be easy. "I don't know. Maybe it wouldn't be worth the risk."

"No." Blaise spoke in a clipped tone. "We go soon. The injections..." He rubbed his shoulder, and a shadow passed over his eyes. "They rob my mind soon if we don't act."

I pondered our situation. Wouldn't it be worth the risk? Even if we ended up getting caught, we'd be back in the place we started. What other choice did we have?

"All right," I said. "But we can't go like this." I tugged on my hospital gown. "The thorns are terrible. They tore up my arms and did worse to my feet. We need actual clothes, and we need shoes."

For the first time since I'd seen him, a slight smile curved his mouth. "Shoes." He laughed quietly. "You have soft feet. I have no need to cover my feet."

I eyed him. "Maybe you don't, but I can't walk five steps out there without turning my soles to a bloody, sticky mess." I sighed, nervously thrumming my fingers on the table. "I'll need shoes, different clothes. Food..." I trailed off. Food. Since I'd arrived here, I'd eaten little, and I rarely felt hunger. "Blaise." I turned my gaze on him. "How much have you eaten since you've been here? Have you been hungry?"

"No. I eat nothing. Water. Only a little."

I crossed my arms, unsettled at the implication. "It must be the injections they've been giving us. They haven't given us feeding tubes, so that means they aren't supplying us with the calories we need. They're doing something else to us. Changing us."

Mr. Emmerson mentioned something about making me better, but what had he really meant? What were they doing to us to change our DNA so drastically as to not need food?

Shaking my head, I focused on the present. *Escape.* The thought consumed me.

"We might need food in the jungle," I said. "Once the injections stop, we may start to feel normal again. If that happens, we'll have to find food. We'll have access to berries and wild plants, but many of them will be poisonous."

"Don't worry about that." He gave a smug smile. "I know which ones to eat."

I raised an eyebrow at his comment. "You do?"

"Yes," he answered curtly.

"All right, then." I eyed him. "I guess I'll have to trust you on that. We'll have access to fire, at least."

Blaise tilted his head. "Fire? How?"

I snapped. A flame flickered from my fingertip. His eyes widened. "How is this possible?"

"Vampire virus survivor," I answered. "I thought everyone knew we controlled fire once we got the vaccine." I extinguished the flame with another snap. "Didn't you know?"

"My village is remote. We know little of the outside world."

"Ah." I wrinkled my forehead in confusion. I'd assumed he was another survivor of the vampire virus like me. But there must've been some other reason they'd taken him for experimentation. "Blaise, do you have any unusual abilities? Have you ever had the vampire virus?"

"No."

"Do you know why they took you?"

His eyes darkened. He glanced away.

"Don't want to tell me?" I pried.

"No." He refused to meet my gaze.

"There must have been some reason."

He pursed his lips, refusing to answer. Was it a rare blood disorder? Maybe something that made his body more susceptible to their experiments? Either he didn't know, or more likely, he was too ashamed, or perhaps afraid, to tell me.

"Fair enough." I crossed my arms and decided to change the subject. "They're letting me out of my room tonight for a walk through the facility. I'll try to find shoes for me and clothes for both of us. I'll also look for other supplies and some canteens. We may not need food, but we'll at least need water. If I manage to find everything we need, we'll leave soon. We'll have to meet after midnight when there are the least number of guards out there. And we'll leave from the south entrance. It's the most remote and the least guarded." I'd spent my time memorizing these things.

"When do we go?" he asked.

"I don't know. This is all assuming I'm able to steal some supplies. But we'll go soon. In a few days, I hope."

Too many factors were at play. Most of all, our survival was at risk. One missed step, and we didn't just stumble, we plummeted into the abyss.

17

———

LUCIAN

As the rain continued its incessant soaking, the new facility's log walls darkened somberly against a gray sky. Half-a-dozen lights flashed from police cars as we approached. Red and blue flashes reflected off news vans parked near the building. A bustle of reporters pushed against one another, lights blaring off camera lenses, and raised voices shouting for interviews.

"What are *they* doing here?" Chloe asked, her tone sharp, accusatory. She pushed strands of rain-soaked hair from her forehead. Kahn trotted faithfully beside her. The lights of the police vehicles flashed so brightly, they reflected in his white fur.

I glanced at the two officers walking beside us. "Did you call them here?" I demanded.

Officer Foster spread his hands in a conciliatory gesture. "It couldn't be avoided, Mr. Vidraru. Be surprised they've only shown up now. De la Vega missing is a high-profile case." He chuckled quietly.

I ground my teeth in frustration. "You didn't answer my question. Did you call them?"

"I didn't. You'd be surprised how fast word gets around when a celebrity's involved."

"I've had a little experience with it," I replied in a dry tone.

We approached the new facility, and the few people who lingered outside turned their gazes on us.

A reporter paced near a news van. Her red umbrella stood out among the somber tones of gray surrounding her. Cunning eyes focused on me, and I was reminded of a lioness fixating on a gazelle.

She wore a tawny-colored overcoat spattered in raindrops. The hue of her red stilettos, sinking a bit in the wet ground, matched her lipstick. Her smirk told me so much. I knew her type. I'd seen reporters like her too many times to count. She'd do anything for a story. Nothing was sacred.

"Mr. Vidraru," she called, her voice commanding and edged in a condescending tone. "Macy MacKinnon with KUTV. I have a few questions for you."

I locked my jaw and focused on the porch ahead. She stepped in front of me. Her shrewd gaze pinned me. Good thing about being around reporters for so long—it made me more experienced in dealing with them. Ignoring them was usually the best tactic.

"What happened to Amaya De la Vega? You were still dating, weren't you?"

"No questions, please," I attempted a polite tone, though I wasn't sure it came out that way, and pushed past her.

"What was your relationship like?" she continued. "Were you having problems? Did she run away? Were you abusive, Mr. Vidraru?"

I stopped mid-step, right at the bottom of the stairs leading to the porch. I couldn't let this one go.

"She didn't run away," I said, a growl in my voice. "And I never laid a finger on her in anger." I whipped around and marched up the steps, Chloe and the officers following behind me.

My hands were shaking, so I thrust them in my pockets.

A chasm opened in the pit of my stomach.

This had to be a nightmare. I'd lost so many loved ones before. Each one had torn me apart, taking a piece of myself with them. But I'd healed eventually. Losing Amaya was worse. I would never be the same without her. Not knowing where she was or what was happening to her had filled me with a sense of palpable dread.

When we entered the common room, I landed on a couch. A heavy weight crashed with me.

I had two choices. I could sit here and wallow in my own grief. Or I could get up from this couch and start looking for her again. But I was so drained, how would I be able to start?

Chloe sat beside me, and Khan rested his chin on my knee and whined.

"We'll find her," Chloe said softly.

I couldn't manage to speak with the lump in my throat, so I nodded.

A memory surfaced from lifetimes ago. My mother frequently sat by the fireplace in our one-room hovel, the sound of the spinning wheel rhythmic and calming, the smell of yeasty, rising dough hot in the room. I'd been upset about something, and she'd told me to forget about myself and go help someone else. It had seemed so impossible at the time, but her words had stayed with me. Her memory lingered. Even now, when I was so far away in space and in time, I wondered if she would remember me if I ever returned to her. Would she know how deeply her words had affected me? That even now, more than a hundred years later, her voice still lingered?

I sat up and took a deep breath.

The reporter's question rattled me. But I wasn't the only person suffering.

I patted Khan's head and glanced at Chloe, who I only now noticed had a predatory, wild look in her eyes. What was going on with her?

"Are you okay?" I asked.

She glanced away.

"Chloe," I said. "You haven't been yourself. What's the matter?"

"I'm worried about Amaya," she answered too quickly.

I scrutinized her. "But that's not all, is it?"

She sighed. "I'm okay. Yes, treatment has been hard for me. But I'm managing. Anyway." She scratched behind Kahn's ears. "We need to be focusing on finding Amaya right now."

I eyed her, tempted to press her more on the issue, but she was right. Amaya took precedence. Whatever was happening with Chloe would have to be a conversation for another time.

The two officers came inside and lounged on the sofa across from us. Firelight flickered from the fireplace, reminding me of my mother and her spinning wheel.

"When can we head to the airport?" I asked.

"I talked with the flight radar technician," Foster answered. "They'll be available this afternoon to give us the flight numbers, but they warned that they're a small airport. Some of the information may be missing if the flights were too far away."

"Do you think the flight we're looking for will be on their scanners?"

"No way to know for sure." He hooked his thumbs in his belt loops. "But we'll find out. Until then, get some rest. Get something to eat. I've been on these kinds of cases before, and I've seen people literally collapse from exhaustion. They'll go days without sleeping. Trust me, you need to take care of your health. You know it's what Amaya would want you to do."

There wasn't a chance on this planet I could get any rest. Frustration coiled inside me at Foster's lax attitude. Maybe he was right. Maybe I needed rest. But he wasn't the one who'd lost someone. If he were, he'd understand how desperately I needed to find her.

I paced the room until I stood at the window overlooking the forest. The towers of Crimson Hollow rose above the treetops. The rain-soaked stones made the old facility appear darker, blending in with the gray clouds beyond. The darkness of the walls weren't so different from the rain-drenched logs of the new facility, and I prayed the two weren't becoming one. Without Amaya, perhaps that was our fate.

Hold on Amaya, I whispered to myself. *We'll find you soon. I promise.*

18

———

AMAYA

Night came slowly. I waited in my room, pacing, until I thought I might lose my mind. Maybe I already had. If so, how was I to know? Flora entered and gave me a final injection, then dosed me with the zicanthodine, as least, what she believed was the drug. As the saline dripped into my IV, I lay on my bed, looking at the ceiling, until it had been at least an hour since I'd heard footsteps outside my room.

My heartbeat quickened when I stood. The floor had grown cold as I'd waited on my bed, and the stone chilled my bare feet.

They expected the drug to put me in a deep sleep by now, but with nothing but saline running into my veins, I was wide awake.

I paced to the door, opened it carefully, and peeked into the hallway. Beams of moonlight revealed an empty passage with a few metal doors sealed shut along the corridor. I flexed my fists, allowing warmth to form in my palms. If I needed fire, it would be ready.

Stepping outside, I walked on quiet feet, yet why did my footsteps seem loud enough to wake the dead?

Supplies, I reminded myself. *We need supplies.*

I stepped to a door labeled *Custodio*.

I tried the knob, and it turned. After opening the door, I slipped inside, then I fumbled for a light switch and flipped it on. The small space came into view. Shelves filled with cleaning supplies filled the walls. On the floor sat a mop and bucket. I riffled through the shelves, heart racing, ears alert for any sound. At first glance, the bottles of cleaning solution and rolls of paper towels looked useless, but I had to think outside the box.

Empty water bottles had been discarded in a trash can, so I removed two to use as canteens. I also grabbed a couple rags and tied them together end to end, until I had a rope that I twisted around the bottles. Then, I tied them into a large loop that we'd be able to wear like one-strapped backpacks. It was better than nothing, and we'd need our hands free as we moved through the jungle.

I carefully closed the storage closet, then continued through the facility. The red lights from a sign reading SALIDA glowed above me, but I bypassed the exit and continued down a separate hallway.

The more I wandered from one hallway to the next, the more I realized what a maze this place was. The hallways intersected at odd angles, as if the place were built to resemble a giant spider's web. Dusty signs hung on some of the walls. Although they were written in Spanish, I caught a word here and there. *Habitación.* Room. *Paciente.* Patient.

On one of the walls, a faded illustration on a poster showed a patient smiling from his bed, and a nurse standing nearby. The woman's feathered curls looked like something from the 80s. On a corkboard, I found a calendar. Its pages were curled, so I carefully smoothed the stiff page until I was able to read the date. *March 1991.*

So, this place had been a hospital once upon a time. It must have sat abandoned for more than two decades before the

Emmersons moved in. But how long had they been here? And why?

Spiderwebs crowded the walls, and a thick layer of dust covered the cement floors the deeper I went into the bowels of the hospital. I turned around when I reached a dead end, then continued back the way I came.

In a room with an open door, I found a few rusty landscaping tools and gardening supplies. Some of the blades on the smaller shears were still sharp, so I grabbed them. In the far corner sat a pair of mud-caked boots.

I gingerly stuck my foot into one, doing my best to ignore the scent of sour sweat. The shoe was a size too big, but I could deal with it. I grabbed the boots and held them to my chest, a flicker of hope lighting inside me. The idea of having shoes opened a new path for me. My foot had only recently healed since my last escape attempt. This time, I would be prepared.

As I left the room, a light at the end of the hallway caught my attention. I paced to it, my footsteps whispering over the floor. Rhythmic whirring came from a machine. I followed the sound to a room barred by a metal doorway. Listening, I heard the sound on the other side of the door. *Whir, whir, whir*.

I grabbed the door handle. The cold metal chilled my hands, but the latch opened, and I pushed the door until it swung on silent hinges to reveal a room lit by a blue glow.

The dim lighting shone on a host of machines ringing the walls. A vertical tube filled with blue fluid stood at the room's center, spanning from floor to ceiling. A child floated inside the solution. Black hair fanned out around her face, and a white gown flowed, ethereal and ghostlike, around her. Tubes extended from her mouth, and a mask covered the lower half of her face.

The unnatural bleached whiteness of her skin matched her dress. With her eyes closed, it was hard to tell if she were dead or alive.

The whirring continued, the sound of a breathing machine, in and out, in and out, the machine breathed for her.

I carefully pressed my hand to the glass. The girl remained unmoving in the blue solution.

This must have been the Emmersons' daughter.

My heart broke as I stared at her tiny body. She looked to be seven or eight years old. And how long had she been here floating in this liquid?

Her hand twitched, and my eyes were drawn to her fingers, which weren't fingers at all, but scaled talons.

Just like Lucian's had been.

I swallowed a nervous lump in my throat.

Footsteps echoed in the hallway. I tiptoed to the corner of the room, hiding behind one of the machines.

The man with the beady eyes and bulges under his skin shuffled past, mumbling to himself. What was his name? Flint? I hadn't seen him much since I'd burned him. He walked haltingly, dragging one foot behind him. The bulge under his forehead had grown bigger, and was now tinged green, the skin uneven, like the skin of a toad. He slowed, glancing in one direction and then the other.

I held my breath as his gaze shifted in my direction. He frowned and lumbered to the door.

I stiffened and gripped the blade of the shears. If he came this way, I would be ready.

He grunted, then grabbed the door handle, and pulled it shut.

Exhaling, my grip on the shears relaxed, and I allowed myself to breathe normally. He'd almost seen me. If the Emmersons found out what I was up to, they'd lock me in my room. They'd only allowed me freedom because I hadn't attempted another escape. That—and they knew I would never get far in the jungle. But that was before I'd been able to talk with Blaise.

I glanced back at the girl floating in the blue liquid. Her eyes were still closed, and the machine continued its rhythmic whirring. It seemed as if she must have been there forever, floating. Maybe they were preserving her body in a sort of stasis, where she could never die, but she could never grow either. Who could know how old she really was?

Maybe that's what they were doing with me and the others. This had nothing to do with us, and everything to do with her. Maybe they were changing something in our blood in the hopes to create a cure for her.

Confusion and sadness warred inside me at sight of the girl in the glass. I stepped to the door. Chills crept down my spine as I turned away from her, with the sudden impression that she knew I was here. That she was watching me, and perhaps begging me to set her free.

I glanced over my shoulder, but she remained motionless, only her hair and dress moving, her eyes closed, her forehead wrinkled as if she were in pain. It took a conscious effort to turn away from her and exit the room.

I paced on bare feet through the cold, empty corridors, the reminders of the old hospital all around me, the air musty and smelling of dust. I couldn't shake the image of the girl floating in the glass tube.

If she had been my child, and if I'd found the resources to save her, would I have taken them?

I didn't know the answer. I only knew I never hoped to find out.

It must've have been near three AM by the time I finally returned to my room. I stuffed my supplies inside of the closet, then lay down on my bed.

When I closed my eyes, I still saw the tube with the girl inside, and the whirring of the machines came back to me, as if I were the one inside the glass.

19

Santa Lucia Center for Health and Wellness—
More Than a Hospital

This is an innovative care center. While most care facilities are constructed in the center of overcrowded and polluted metropolitan cities, the founders of Santa Lucia believe a rural setting to be the most beneficial for their patients and their ever-growing needs. Surrounded by lush forests, the patients enjoy a variety of scenery, and are healed by the benefits of fresh air and the surrounding cenotes, for centuries believed to be meccas of healing.

LUCIAN

Bulbs flashed outside the airport, where news vans crowded like vultures outside the terminal. After leaving our car, Foster, Butler, Chloe and I dashed through the crushing slew of reporters. The news of Amaya's disappearance had spread like wildfire. Headlines circulated across the globe. I was used to the attention, of course, but dragging Amaya into this demented circus felt wrong on every level, and disgust filled me as I avoided one reporter after another. I supposed privacy was a thing of fantasy in the world I lived in.

I could blame Victor Warren for that. But I could blame him for many things, which was why I tried not to obsess about him. He couldn't ruin my life. Not anymore.

When we entered the terminal, security guards escorted us through the gaggle of reporters until we bypassed them to an EMPLOYEES ONLY area. The quiet inside came as a welcome respite, and I finally allowed myself to take a deep breath and focus on the present.

We took an escalator to the second level, then walked through a hallway lined with windows on one side, and doors on the other. The sun had finally broken free from the clouds. The warmth on my skin should have brought me some comfort, yet it failed to pierce through the chill in my heart.

We entered a control room through a door at the hallway's end. Several people sat behind desks. Screens filled the walls, and yellow dots labeled with numbers tracked across a map.

"Officer Butler." A woman stood, then crossed to him. Her dark hair fell in curly waves to her shoulders, and her business suit and tight-lipped smile gave her a no-nonsense appearance. "My name is Rebecca Lund. We've been expecting you."

"Good. We don't have time to waste. What can you tell us about that flight?"

"Let me show you." She motioned for us to follow her. We walked past walls of monitors and people sitting behind keyboards, until we entered another smaller room with only one screen and work desk.

Several rolling chairs centered around the screen, and we each took a seat.

"I'm glad you came," Rebecca said, her voice subdued. "This isn't something I wanted to discuss over the phone."

"Why do you say that?" I asked.

"Because." She nodded at the screen. "I don't usually discuss matters of legality with just anyone. That flight you asked about? We recorded it thirty miles south of here on the night of the abduction. Four-fifteen, to be exact. We can learn a few things from that number. One, south and westbound flights are assigned odd numbers, so we know it was headed in one of those directions. Second, it was a private carrier, because it had no airline specified on its flight records. Third, it was a completely bogus flight."

I raised an eyebrow. "What do you mean?"

"I mean that these flight numbers don't check out. I did some digging, and flight four-fifteen is registered to an Augusta Rotorcraft. This helicopter was much faster. You can tell by its flight patterns. A Rotorcraft couldn't have flown from Saratoga to southern New York in forty-five minutes. It just isn't possible. Whatever this helicopter was, it wasn't a Rotorcraft."

"Interesting," Butler said. "Any other information you can gather from this?"

"Yeah," Chloe said. "Like where it went?"

"Our radar doesn't go that far, unfortunately," Rebecca answered. "But you might be able to go to another airport and see if they tracked four-fifteen."

Foster nodded. "We appreciate your help."

"I wish I could do more," she said, looking with a pensive expression at the screen. "Do you really think this was the flight that took Miss De la Vega?"

"We're fairly certain," I answered. "The bogus flight number makes it even more likely that whoever took her didn't want to be found. You said the flight headed to southern New York state?"

"Yes. I can show you." She clicked a few buttons on the keyboard. On one of the screens, a yellow light popped up with the numbers 415 beside it. The light tracked down the screen until it disappeared just south of the New York state border.

Bitter bile thickened in my throat as I watched the moving

dot. Had Amaya been on that flight? If so, what had they done to her? Futile anger turned my blood hot.

They would pay. Whoever had done this to her would regret it.

I would find her captor. Then I would take my revenge.

20

AMAYA

Days passed. How long? One week? Two? I'd only spoken to Blaise on a few occasions, but I'd taken advantage of my time with him, quizzing him on everything he knew about the jungle, like the plants and their properties, which roots to boil to make a poultice, wild edibles and where to find them, and the best ways to sterilize water.

Even with the information, we still had to be prepared before attempting our escape. While I'd been able to gather our supplies, it had been storming for a week straight, and we hadn't yet made our break. But tonight, the rain outside the windows tapered to a slow drizzle, and I couldn't wait any longer.

Night came slowly. The wind gusted, and vines thick with thorns pounded against the slim rectangles of glass. After midnight, I grabbed my makeshift canteens and blades, then pulled on the work boots. Without socks, they would most likely rub blisters, but I had worse things to worry about.

I paced to the doorway and listened before opening the door. With clammy hands, I grabbed the handle and turned. The door swung open, revealing an empty hallway. Red lights glowed from the single *SALIDA* sign. Its promise of escape tempted me, but I couldn't leave yet. This time, I wouldn't go alone.

My footsteps sounded too loud, and my pounding heart sounded even louder. I half-expected Mr. Emmerson to step out from one of the rooms, or one of the staff to find me. But the hallway remained empty until I made it to a door exactly like my own.

I grabbed the knob and turned just as a clap of thunder rumbled outside.

Blaise stood by the window. I had to catch my breath as a shiver ran down my spine. An amber glow shimmered from his pupils. Tilting his head, he smiled slightly, showing the edge of his teeth, and I got the impression he was sizing me up, as if I were his prey.

"Blaise," I said softly. "Are you okay?"

He blinked, and the wild retreated. How much longer would he remain in control of himself? If I took him out in the jungle with me, I had no guarantee he wouldn't turn violent.

But he had a family somewhere. He'd been taken against his will just like me. I couldn't leave him here, no matter how dangerous he had the potential of becoming.

Besides, it wasn't like I couldn't defend myself.

"Let's go," I whispered, impatience in my voice.

He gave a nod, then followed me out of his room. I handed one of the makeshift canteens to him, and one of the blades. He took them without saying a word, his eyes wide and darting.

I continued with him behind me. Our footsteps sounded too loud, and I feared at any moment, one of the guards would appear from the shadows and capture us, tying us to our beds.

It was only because of my cooperation that the Emmersons had allowed me so much freedom. If they caught me escaping this time, I had no doubt they would subdue me until I lost my mind completely.

Footsteps echoed with hollow thuds from up ahead. Blaise and I ducked into a room. We stood as still as possible until the person came into view. Sallow-skinned, cat-eyed Flora shuffled past, mumbling. She opened and closed her hands as she muttered, as if she were arguing with herself. Then her head tilted, and she stopped walking.

My heart pounded. Sweat coated my clammy skin.

After what felt like hours, she shuffled out of earshot. I peeked outside to find an empty hallway.

"It's clear," I whispered to him.

He nodded, then followed me through the hall and to a door at the end.

I cracked it open and peeked outside. The scent of rain lingered. A few drops fell from the roof and gathered in puddles on the ground.

A guard came into view, his flashlight beam illuminating the perimeter.

"Stay back," I whispered to Blaise.

I quietly pulled the door closed. Through the steel panel, I listened to footsteps crunching over gravel outside, my heart still thudding in my chest.

When the silence returned, I peeked outside again. Floodlights illuminated the edge of the forest.

Let's go, I mouthed to him.

He nodded, then followed me outside.

A damp mist coated my skin. My heart pounded with every footstep I took. I breathed deeply to keep the fear from overwhelming me. The boots sounded too loud, and I almost preferred my bare feet to this.

A click echoed behind us.

I spun around to face a guard hefting a rifle, its barrel pointed at us.

As if on instinct, I willed fire into my hands and thrust it at the man. He stumbled back with a gargled scream.

Blaise leaped at him. With a quick jerk of his wrist, he snapped the man's neck, and the guard collapsed to the ground.

I stood with slack jaw and wide eyes. Blaise loomed over the body, his eyes dark and animalistic, full of predatory excitement.

I took a step back, and Blaise stalked toward me.

"Blaise," I whispered, and he blinked.

"Go," was all he said as he jogged around the building.

I debated on following him. He'd so quickly dropped the guard, I didn't know what to think. One thing I knew, the person going into the forest with me wasn't who he seemed, and it would be easy for him to take my life, just as he'd done to the guard.

But I continued forward until we rounded the building and found a path cutting through the trees. Blaise pointed to the trail, and I nodded. We started toward it, careful to keep watch in every direction, until we entered the dome of the forest.

I allowed myself to breathe a sigh of relief once the facility was out of view. But I knew better than to relax.

"Blaise," I said. "Be careful. There are trip wires out here. That's how they caught me last time."

"Then we'll need light."

"Yes," I answered. "But only a little. I don't want to risk alerting anyone." I allowed a tiny flame to flicker from my fingertips. Our footsteps crunched over leaves and sticks, and I returned to feeling thankful that I'd found the boots, imagining what it would be like to have thorns poking into my soles.

Vines snagged at my clothes, but we kept moving. My flame flickered, illuminating the glossy leaves and vibrant jungle flowers. I cupped the flame in my hand.

Shouting came from behind us. An alarm blared.

"They know we escaped," I said to Blaise. "We need to run."

"It's too dense," he said. "We'll trip."

"I don't care. Run!"

He sped ahead, and I sprinted behind him. Adrenaline fueled my movements. My heart raced. The shouts grew closer.

I ran until my lungs screamed for air and sweat drenched my clothes. Trees blurred in my vision. My feet sank in the mud, and

I barely pulled myself free, only to trip over felled trees and dodge thick vines with briars that snagged my sleeves.

When we made it to a clearing, we paused. Moonlight drifted through the rainclouds. Blaise took a step forward, but I stopped him. A thin silver thread reflected ahead, stretching across the grass.

"Do you see it?" I whispered.

He nodded, and we stepped carefully over the trip wire until we made it to the trees. Something clicked under my foot. I froze.

"Blaise," I called. "I stepped on something. Another trip wire, I think."

He whipped around. His eyes widened, and his mouth gaped as he peered behind me.

"Drop your weapons," a man yelled, breaking through the stillness of the forest.

Three guards entered the jungle clearing.

"Drop the weapons," one of the men repeated, his sharp voice making fear crawl down my spine.

I tossed the gardening shears aside. Balling my hands into fists, I extinguished the fire, though I kept the warmth close to the surface.

"Get on the ground," another man yelled.

I glanced at Blaise. His gaze shifted, sizing them up.

Outside the facility, they couldn't keep us contained. Maybe they surrounded us, maybe they had weapons, but they had never seen powers like ours.

"You don't want to make us do that," I said.

"Shut up! I said get on the ground. Now!"

I gave a brief nod to Blaise, and he flexed his jaw, then gave a brief nod.

Opening my fist, I released a blinding fireball. The guards fell back, some dropping their guns to shield their eyes. Blaise launched himself toward one of the guards and snapped the man's neck in a blink.

Shock slapped me. How could he take a person's life with such disregard? Who was this person?

But another guard rushed at me, and I barely had time to react before I shot a ball of flame at him. The impact hit his chest, and he flew backward. Blaise jumped on another man and sent him tumbling to the ground. Gunshots rang out, and Blaise fell back, a spot of red on his shoulder.

Mr. Emmerson entered the clearing. His normally combed hair was disheveled, and he wore rumpled clothes. His eyes widened with surprise as he locked his gaze on me and Blaise.

"What's happening here?" he yelled.

The remaining guards pointed their guns at us. Blaise stood slowly, clutching his wounded shoulder, as the dead guard lay at his feet.

"Time's up," Blaise said through gritted teeth. "You can't contain us any longer. We're leaving."

The jungle rustled around Mr. Emmerson, as if something were out there, watching.

"I'm taking the girl," Blaise seethed. "I'm leaving. Don't try to track me."

Mr. Emmerson took a step toward us. "You'll never survive out there."

"We'll survive better out there than we will here." Blaise tilted his chin at me. "Let's go."

I paced toward the edge of the tree line. Sweat trickled down my face, and my heart pounded with adrenaline. After spending so long inside the facility, the thought of freedom made blood race through my veins and pound through my heart. Still, I couldn't shake the feeling that something was horribly wrong.

"You'll never leave this place." Bitterness dripped from Mr. Emmerson's voice. "I'll study your corpses if I have to." He snapped his fingers.

Behind him, a form emerged. Flint appeared from the jungle, the bulges under his skin weeping pus, though the moonlight revealed green tendrils growing from the bumps. He smiled, baring wicked sharp teeth. The vine-like protrusions shot from his face and hands. Scales covered the growths, and several snake heads tipped the end of each one like some mutated Medusa.

"Kill them," Mr. Emmerson said.

Shock kept me rooted to the spot. Nothing made sense. A creature like this existing seemed to warp reality itself. But adrenaline shunted my fear as the man lunged for me. I leaped to the side, barely escaping a strike from one of the snake's heads.

Flint whipped around, lightning-fast, attacking the younger man. Blaise screamed, a shriek of pain so gut-wrenching, it brought tears to my eyes.

I searched the clearing, but a streak of green lunged for me. Sharp teeth impaled my thigh, burning with icy pinpricks of pain. Numbness spread through my leg. I stepped back and collapsed. Thorns tore at my back and legs. A wave of dizziness disoriented me.

In my blurred vision, Flint stalked toward me. Madness glinted in his eyes. Snakelike vines lengthened and twisted from his head. I scooted back, my pulse pounding. I tried standing, but the numbness spread down to my calf muscle, crippling me.

One of the snakes struck, but I rolled. Balling my fists, I called my fire to the surface. The warmth came slowly, traveling at a snail's pace from my heart and into my arms.

Blaise stalked into the clearing, and Flint's head whipped around to focus on him. I used the distraction to concentrate on creating fire.

"Come on," I urged.

Flint slammed Blaise to the ground, then kicked his head, and Blaise let out a muffled scream.

Sweat streamed down my face. A clammy chill broke out over my skin. Shivers racked my body as I pulled energy from my core organs. A glow encompassed my fists, and I squeezed my hands until my fingernails cut into my flesh.

The venom must have been affecting my powers. The Emmersons had used the virus to manipulate Flint's DNA, warping him into a monster. His powers directly connected to mine, and they were overriding my natural defenses.

Blaise staggered to his feet. Blood from his head soaked his shirt, and his breathing came in ragged gasps. Flint circled him, though he limped, and blood covered one of his legs. Blaise lunged and knocked the shorter man to the ground.

I used the opportunity to catch my breath, allowing oxygen to fuel my muscles. As I attempted to stand, my muscles cramped again, and I remained on the ground, helpless as Flint stood over Blaise. Snakes struck with fierce attacks on his arms and cheeks. Red puffy welts spotted his skin. He attempted to fight off his attacker, but his limbs fell limply to the ground.

Mr. Emmerson paced opposite us, looking on with a dark expression. Hate coiled inside me as I watched the man, too cowardly to fight his own battles.

Blaise cried out. I couldn't imagine what he was going through. I'd been bitten only once and could barely move.

Panic and fear reached up to choke me. But I wouldn't let it. I had to stop Flint, or he would kill Blaise.

I managed to push into a sitting position. My head spun with dizziness, and my muscles ached as if they were being pummeled with a hammer. Still, I was able to lift my arm. I cupped my hand.

Snapping, I created a spark, but it fizzled.

Another snake struck Blaise. His eyes started to swell. Blood dripped down his face.

I snapped again, willing as much energy into it that I could muster.

A flame ignited. This time it stayed alight.

I breathed heavily. My joints ached. My vision grew blurry. Buzzing rang in my ears.

As I climbed to my knees, my energy faded. The flame extinguished, leaving me in darkness but for the light of the moon.

Blaise managed to roll to his side. He coughed violently. His face and hands had grown even more swollen. He gasped, heaving for air.

Still, Flint struck at him, unrelenting, and Mr. Emmerson stood nearby, watching with a calculated expression, his brows knitted, as if he were observing his science experiment come to life.

Flint struck another time, so many times I lost count. Blaise whimpered, and it seemed he would die soon. I knew for a certainty he would never survive the amount of venom flooding his veins. If I didn't stop this now, Blaise would never return to his family, and for my selfish reasons, I wanted him to live so I could survive the jungle. The thought made me unbearably guilty, but I needed him if I wanted to live.

"Fire," I whispered.

Again, I snapped. A spark flicked, then burst into a flame. It warmed my hand, and I drained all my energy into it.

When the fire grew to the size of a baseball, I stretched my senses, reaching its core, and unfurling its wings.

The butterfly rose, growing. It fluttered over me—blue and green, blazing against the deep, still-wet forest in a halo of heat and radiance.

Flint spun around, his gaze fixed on the creation.

With my last ounce of energy, I thrust my arms out, forcing the butterfly to span as large as a vulture. It flew to Flint and hit him in the chest, and then I willed it to explode. The fireball engulfed not only Flint, but Umber Emmerson as well.

Their screams pierced my ears. It was a sound of torment, laced with rage and pain. Something inside me knew I had killed two people with my fire. It changed me; fast as the snap of my fingers, something inside me warped.

Flint and Umber fell to the ground, engulfed in flame. Their skin and hair left a charred, meaty scent to float through the air.

Blaise scooted back, flames reflecting the fear in his eyes.

He looked at me as if I were a witch, a master of the dark arts, some kind of sorceress who would kill him if I took the notion. I knew how he felt, since I'd looked at him the same way less than an hour before.

I realized I was standing with flames bursting from both hands, and I didn't remember how I'd gotten to my feet.

The last I remembered, I hadn't even been able to move. And I had felt as if the last drop of my energy had gone into the flames. But here I was, flames crackling and sputtering. The two men's lifeless corpses lay in a charred heap on the ground. Red coals dropped from their bodies and landed on the grass.

Standing transfixed, I watched the scene with one part amazement and another part disgust.

I'd done this. Nausea twisted my insides. The fire burned until nothing remained but charred skeletons. The air turned still, with only a few crackles to break up the overwhelming silence.

Then my gaze snagged on Blaise, who lay swollen and crumpled on the ground, gasping between sobs. I went to him and grabbed his wrist. His pulse thrummed weakly under my fingertips.

"Blaise. Stay with me." I scanned his wounds. The nausea I'd felt a moment ago came back in full force. Red welts covered his skin. Tiny fang marks drooled red blood that had already started to dry. Bruises mottled his cheeks and hands, and his eyes were nearly swollen shut.

Hopelessness overwhelmed me.

How was I supposed to help him? I had no antivenom. He would never survive unless I got him to a hospital. But we were alone in a foreign jungle. I had nothing.

"Blaise, hang in there. I'm getting help."

Getting help. Right. How did I expect to do that exactly?

I had to calm down and think.

My thoughts went back to Blaise telling me about a flowering plant from the jungle. I couldn't recall its name, but he'd told me how it looked. Blood-red petals and waxy leaves. It stopped swelling and slowed the flow of venom. But what were the chances it would even be out here? Wherever we were. Maybe he would know.

"Blaise, I'm going to look for the flower you told me about—the one that stops venom. Do you have any idea where it grows?" It was a long shot, but what other choice did I have?

"It's an iris. Red petals. Yellow center. Near water."

"Near the water. Got it. I'll be back soon." I pulled enough energy into my hands to create a ball of fire, then I set off toward the forest.

Blaise's moaning stopped me.

I turned around and knelt by him. He managed to push to a sitting position, which shocked me.

"I'm... going with you. Can't stay... They'll find us."

I glanced back the way we came. Blaise was right. It was only a matter of time before Yasira Emmerson realized what had happened to Flint and her husband. She would be inconsolable, filled with an insatiable rage that was fueled by the death of her husband. I imagined revenge would be her only goal. I had no doubt she would set off to find us as soon as she could.

"Can you walk?" I asked.

He nodded. "Just help me up."

I grabbed his arm, and he stood on shaky feet. We walked together, him limping beside me, my free hand still cupping the flame, as we entered the midnight blackness of the jungle.

21

A photograph of Constnatin and Elena Vidraru,
parents of Lucian Vidraru, circa 1870

LUCIAN

Rain pounded unrelentingly. Lightning flashed through the sky outside my window, followed by rumbling thunder. The clock read half past midnight as I paced in my office. I'd given up on sleep hours ago.

A knock came at my door, pulling me from my thoughts.

"Who is it?" I called.

Officer Foster opened the door, and Officer Butler stood behind him.

"It's us," Officer Foster said. "Can we come in?"

"Now?" I asked, glancing at the clock.

"Yes," Officer Butler answered. "We're sorry to bother you so late, but it's important. The night guard let us in. Said you were still awake. Can we talk?"

"Fine." I waved them inside.

The officers entered the room. Rain splattered their

uniforms and dampened their hair. Shadows circled Officer Foster's eyes, and he looked a decade older. His grim expression told me something was wrong.

I frowned. "What's the matter?"

Officer Foster glanced at the window behind me. "The crowd is growing. We barely made it in here. I thought with this weather, they'd go home, but they've taken shelter in the old facility. They rushed at us when they saw the car."

"They're getting angry, too," Butler added.

"Angry?" I questioned.

"They're blaming you, Lucian," he said bluntly. "They think you had something to do with Amaya's disappearance."

I ran my hands down my face. Inside, I felt hollow, as if I were watching things play out from far away, as if I were detached from my own body.

My vision wavered. Dizziness made the room spin. I placed my hands on my desk to keep my balance.

"You all right?" Foster asked.

I took a deep breath. "I will be. Give me a minute." Sweat beaded on my brow, and I had trouble swallowing my rising anger. This whole situation with Amaya had made it harder for me to keep a lid on my emotions. If I weren't careful, I would burst into flames and burn the place down, and probably take out a few protesters with me.

I rose, straightening my jacket, and I paced to the window. In another flash of lightning, the towers of Crimson Hollow loomed as ghostly black structures in an electric glow. I could almost see the gargoyles clinging to the parapets, as if they were keeping the stones from being torn away in the storm.

My blood ran cold as my thoughts turned to Amaya. Was she stranded in this weather? Was she hurt? With a deep inhale, I spun around and faced the officers. "Why are you here?"

Butler wiped the water from his face. "A woman came to the station a few hours ago. Demanded to talk to you. We told her no at first, but she persisted. She's downstairs now." The officers traded a glance. "We think you'll want to hear what she has to say."

I lifted an eyebrow. "Officers, I've dealt with this kind of thing before. She's probably a crazed fan using this crisis as her opportunity to meet me. Chances are she's contacted me before. What's her name?"

"She wouldn't tell us."

"Then that's even more reason to avoid to her."

"But she says she knows you and that you would recognize her. She said it was urgent."

"Urgent?" I questioned. "Does she know anything about Amaya? Because if she doesn't, then I don't want to talk to her."

Again, the officers traded glances.

"What is it?" I asked.

Officer Butler gave me a hardened stare. "She wouldn't tell us anything. Just kept saying she knew you and needed to talk to you. I think you ought to at least talk to her." He paused, then crossed his arms. "Vidraru, the truth is, De la Vega's trail is going cold. We need a new lead. If it's nothing, then we're at the same place we started."

Officer Foster chimed in. "But if this turns out to be legit, it could be the break we're looking for. We've spent countless hours researching leads that turn out to be nothing. We're desperate here."

"Fine." I thrust my finger at him. "But if she turns out to be crazy, I want her out of here. Got it?"

"We got it," they answered.

"Good. Tell her I'll meet her in the lobby. I don't want her anywhere near my room."

"Understood," Butler said. He headed out the door and down the hall, but Butler hesitated. "Vidraru," he said my name with concern. "After you meet with her, get some rest. No one can function under this kind of stress."

"Sure," I answered unenthusiastically. Asking me to sleep right now was like asking me to hike Mt. Everest wearing shackles. Every time I lay down and closed my eyes, all I could see was Amaya's face, and I swore I heard her calling for me, pleading that I find her.

I didn't know why, but I felt she was in danger, as if her pain were linked to mine. She was hurting and afraid, and it killed me inside to think of her that way. No. I couldn't sleep. I wouldn't sleep until I had her safe at my side.

I rubbed at the aching knot in my neck, then followed the officer outside my room and down the hallway. Everything reminded me of Amaya. The paint color on the walls—seafoam green—which she'd picked out. The pictures of scenery from the desert or sunsets on the beaches—she'd picked those. The vases of lavender.

We made it to the staircase, and I followed the officer down until we made it to the parlor.

Officer Butler stood with a woman who faced away from me. She wore a newsboy-style hat and a long gray coat. Dark hair fell to her waist. The officer talked quietly with her, and I couldn't make out their words.

I cleared my throat, and the woman slowly turned to face me.

My heart stopped.

My eyes locked with Sally Anderson's. A sly smile curved her lips.

"Hello, Lucian," she purred demurely. Red lipstick contrasted her chalky white skin. Her makeup was so thick, it caked her face, as if she were trying hard to mask the woman beneath. But I couldn't mistake the madness in her eyes for anyone else's.

My shock turned to terror, then anger punched my chest with the force of a sledgehammer.

I thrust my finger at her face. "Get her out of here!"

"What?" Officer Butler questioned.

"That's Sally Anderson. She nearly killed me and Amaya last year. She belongs in prison. I don't want her anywhere near me."

The two officers grabbed her arms, but she flailed. "Don't touch me. Lucian, you haven't heard what I've got to say."

"Nothing you can say would make me allow you to stay here. Do you hear me? Nothing!" My hands shook, so I stuck them in my pockets. The dizziness I'd felt earlier returned, making the room seem to wobble around me. "I would be a fool to listen to your lies again."

Turning, I marched away.

I couldn't stand to look at her. Everything about her spoke of lies and deception. She'd ruined my life once, and nearly succeeded a second time.

The hallway seemed to close in on me, and I had to lean against the wall to stay upright. My breathing was labored, and a clammy sweat broke out over my skin. I clutched my stomach where nausea welled up, threatening to make me sick.

Behind me, I heard the officers booted feet crossing through the entryway, along with the tapping of Sally's high heels.

"Lucian, listen to me," she called, her voice eerily like the woman I knew from decade's past, as if she'd never aged. "It's about Amaya."

My head snapped up at that.

"Listen to me, Lucian. Please."

Decades of repressed anger rose to choke me. Her words. Her voice. It all sounded too eerily familiar. She'd pleaded with that same voice, those same words, when she'd asked me to bite her.

Stop repressing your true nature...

For all I knew, she was making up information on Amaya to get back in contact with me. She knew I was vulnerable. Probably had seen the news about Amaya on TV or online, and she knew I could be manipulated when I let my guard down at a time like this.

Time had divided us. But my anger had allowed her to create

a noose around my neck, and it killed me to think of her still holding power over me.

But what if she really did know something about Amaya? Wouldn't it be worth my time to at least listen?

The officers dragged her toward the doorway.

"Stop," I said through gritted teeth. "Let her talk."

"Thank you, Lucian," she gushed. "I knew you'd see reason."

The officers released her arms, and she smoothed a hand down her overcoat.

I could hardly believe I was standing here facing Sally Anderson. I'd only caught glimpses of her last year when she'd been with Victor. She'd been so out of-her-mind, she'd looked completely ghostlike and inhuman. The wildness in her eyes had given her the look of insanity.

But now, she stood straight, staring me in the eyes, and it seemed some sanity had returned. Still, she'd aged. Skin sagged from her cheeks and dark spots marred the skin on her neck and backs of her hands. Frizzy gray strands stuck up among the brunette locks.

She crossed her arms as she sized me up.

"Get to the point," I said, impatience clipping my words. "What do you know about Amaya?"

"What?" she asked with mock indignity. "No hello?"

"I don't want to waste my breath."

Her eyes darkened. "Fine. I see how it is. But before you decide to judge me, I'll have you know, Victor used me the same way he used you, Lucian. He drugged me to keep me half-lucid. He robbed more than a decade of my life. He didn't want me telling the world what I knew about him and his con, so he injected me with a serum that robbed my sanity. I was a prisoner. Just like you."

"Cut the pity party. I don't care."

"You should." She pouted. "He manipulated me. It was never my intention to hurt you. All those years ago, I never even got to tell you I was sorry." She clasped her hands. "But I am sorry,

Lucian. I'm sorry for all the pain I put you through. And now, I only want to make it up to you. I may know who took Amaya."

"I'm listening."

She nodded. "These injections I told you about, Victor got them from a supplier who worked out of Argentina."

I raised an eyebrow. "Argentina? Was it Zen-Viro?"

"I never knew their name," she said. "But they supplied him with the serum that took my mind from me."

I scrubbed my knuckles across my stubble-covered chin. Pacing the parlor, I tried connecting the dots. Mr. Emmerson seemed to have an unusual fascination with Amaya's abilities. What if he had taken her to experiment on her?

"What else do you know?" I asked.

"I could tell you what I know," she said. "For a price."

I stopped pacing. Of course, there was price. Should I have been surprised? "What do you want? Money? I have none. Victor took everything."

"No," she said softly. "I want your forgiveness."

Her statement gave me pause. "What?"

"I want your forgiveness, Lucian," she repeated. "For years I've lived with the crushing guilt of what I did to you. I never meant for anything to happen the way it did. Please believe me, Victor manipulated me, just as he did to you. Please, take this burden away from me. Forgive me."

I crossed my arms. "Forgiveness is earned."

"Yes. So let me earn it."

"How?" I demanded.

"Let me help you find Amaya."

"How?" I repeated, steel in my voice. "Do you know where she is?"

"No," she hedged. "But I know where to start looking. The company Warren worked with was in Argentina. But don't waste your time looking there."

"Then where should we look?"

"The Emmersons operate in secrecy. They'll be someplace

remote. There was a young man from a small village called Santa Lucia in the Yucatán peninsula in Mexico. The Emmersons had an unusual interest in him. He went missing three years ago. After that, the villagers started speaking of lights coming from an abandoned hospital in the jungle. Haunted, they say. No one will go near it, not even to look for the missing person."

"How do you know this?" I demanded.

"I have my ways."

I shot her a cold stare. I could hardly believe I was standing here and talking to her. How did I know if she were being truthful? But too much of what she said made sense. The Emmersons had seemed unusually preoccupied with Amaya's powers. And whoever took her would have had the means to afford a helicopter to transport Amaya away.

I rubbed my forehead. Yes, it all sounded true. No one else had any motivation to take Amaya except them.

Pacing the room, my heart raced. "Book a flight," I said to the officers. "We need to get to Santa Lucia as soon as possible."

"May I come?" Sally asked, her voice coy, although I saw the wicked gleam in her eye. I wouldn't take a chance of allowing her anywhere near me, even if she may have helped me.

"I'm not completely crazy. I thank you for your help, but Sally, you must understand why I can't take you with me."

She hung her head. "Yes," she said in a quiet voice. "I understand. But..."

"But what?"

"But I haven't told you everything. Why do you think the Emmersons came to you?"

"Because they wanted to fund us so they could gain access to our patients. Most likely to use them for their experiments."

"No." Her eyes met mine, and the intensity in her gaze sent a shiver down my spine. "There's more."

"Then what is it?" I demanded. "What are you not telling me, Sally?"

Speaking to her so casually made me feel as if I were in my

college dorm again, arguing with her over my supposed vampire abilities. It could have been yesterday.

"Lucian." She stepped toward me, her heels echoing through the room. "It's about Yasira Emmerson. You need to know..." Her voice trailed until she spoke in a whisper. She gently placed one hand on my arm. "She's our daughter."

22

———

AMAYA

A bolt of lightning streaked across the sky. I jumped when the boom of thunder followed. With one arm around Blaise, I limped with him through the dense jungle. Rain pelted in a steady drizzle, its cadence matching the frantic beating of my heart. A thorn tugged at my sleeve, and another brushed my leg. I must have had more than a dozen cuts and scrapes, and they stung like fire, but my pain was nothing compared to the torture Blaise must be enduring.

He walked as if in a trance, his feet dragging, his arms held limply at his sides. His half-closed eyes told me his consciousness was ebbing. How he remained upright was a mystery.

As the sun rose, the storm tapered, leaving a pink-tinged sky streaked with gray clouds. Rainwater dripped from wide jungle leaves into puddles on the muddy ground. The scent of green earth filled my lungs and rejuvenated me. Although we'd endured hell to get here, the jungle was a welcome setting compared to the bleak cinderblock walls of the facility.

The sound of gushing water came from ahead, and we limped into a small clearing. A deep pond overshadowed by a rock outcropping dominated the space. A waterfall poured into the pond, creating a curtain that partially hid a cave. I limped with Blaise around the pond. Droplets splashed my skin as we side-stepped the waterfall. My too-large boots slipped on the rocks, but we managed to make it inside where we took shelter under the dome of rocks.

Cool air washed over me, and I collapsed beside Blaise, only now realizing how exhausted I felt. My leg muscles ached from the exertion, and scratches crisscrossed my arms.

Blaise shifted beside me. Puncture marks covered his skin. Raised welts had formed where some of the bites had gone deep. He moaned, and his eyes closed.

"Stay with me," I whispered to him, staring out at the jungle, a scene that morphed through the wavering lens of the water. I stood slowly, my knotted muscles protesting. If there was any chance to save Blaise, it would be out there somewhere.

I rubbed my forehead, remembering the red flower that slowed venom. I had to find it. If I wanted to save Blaise, I had no other choice.

"Wait..." Blaise moaned weakly as I stepped away from him. Turning, I found him lying with his eyes open, and his eyebrows pinched with pain. "Help me."

I went to him and knelt at his side, then took his hand. His fingers were shockingly cold, and his grip weak. How much time did he have left?

"I have to go find the flower in the jungle—if it's even out there." As I spoke the words, I knew there was little chance of spotting it, and even less chance I would find it in time to save him. I hadn't seen a single plant matching its description as we'd hiked through the dense greenery. But I couldn't just sit here and watch him die. I had to do something. No matter how futile, I had to try.

Blaise squeezed my fingers. "I don't want to die... alone."

"You won't. I promise." Guilt tugged at my heart. I prayed I wasn't lying to him—prayed he wouldn't die alone in the jungle.

His eyes closed, and his breathing turned shallow.

I released his hand and backed away from him. The sun filtered through the veil of water, making his skin look silvery in the light. I kept my hand on the wall for balance as I picked my way over the slippery rocks and left the shelter of the cavern. The sound of rushing water faded as I entered the jungle. Trees as tall as the towers of Crimson Hollow overshadowed me. Crickets chirped and birds cawed in the distance. I brushed past spider webs and ducked under low-hanging vines.

A stream carved its way through the jungle floor, and I followed along the bank, looking for any red irises growing near the water. Remembering how Blaise had described the flower eluded me, and I racked my brain trying to think of anything useful he'd told me. Did it have two leaves or three? A red stamen or yellow?

If I got this wrong and picked the wrong plant, I could possibly poison Blaise and put him into a worse state than he was already in.

Following the stream deeper into the jungle, I was careful to keep track of landmarks—the rotting stump here, the group of orange flowers there—although if I stayed near the stream, making it back shouldn't be too difficult. Up ahead, a spot of crimson stood out against a canvas of green.

My heart leapt as a tall blooming iris came into view, its petals the color of a crimson sunset. Mud squished under my knees as I knelt beside it. The petals of the single bloom fluttered in the wind. I inspected the yellow stamen and glossy green leaves. Worry nagged me. What if this wasn't the one?

But as far as my memory went, it looked identical to the plant Blaise had described.

"Please don't kill him," I muttered as I grasped the stem and dug the roots from the mud until I was able to pull it free.

Cradling the plant to my chest, I turned back the way I'd come.

By the time I made it to the clearing, the sun had reached its zenith overhead. Its blinding rays scorched my skin as I crossed through the open area. Mosquitos buzzed around my ears, but I ignored them as I hiked into the cavern.

Blaise rested in the same position, and a spike of fear shot down my spine as I took in his pale skin, swollen bumps, and faraway gaze. As I drew closer, his eyes blinked, and he focused on the crimson flower I held to my chest.

"You...you found it," he said, gasping.

"Yes." I knelt beside him.

"You'll have to boil its leaves and... and roots together before you can give it to me."

I nodded. "Okay, I'll get a fire started. It shouldn't take long, especially since creating a spark should be a snap."

He only blinked, and I playfully jabbed at his shoulder. "What? Not even a smile for my lame joke? I'm trying to lighten the mood, here."

He gave me a weak smile, although his eyes were filled with pain, and I left the cave and set to work gathering discarded sticks. When my arms were full, I reentered the dome of rocks and arranged the kindling to create a teepee structure. Then, I created a rim around it with the larger logs and sticks.

After I arranged the last of the wood, I snapped my fingers. Energy popped with an electrical spark, and a flame appeared above my fingertips. Cupping the flame, I lowered my hand to the pile. The moisture in the wood worried me. Would I be able to keep a fire going? But after several moments, the flame caught onto a piece of kindling.

When the blaze began spreading, I sat back on my heels and admired my handiwork. Blue and amber flames danced, mesmerizing me, and reminding me of Lucian as he'd taken the form of the phoenix. My heart ached with a deep longing I hadn't expected, and a knot in my throat made it difficult to swallow.

Where was he? What was he doing at this moment? It felt like a lifetime ago when I'd seen him last, when we'd been worried about financing the new facility. Those worries seemed so distant now. All I wanted to do was feel his arms around me and soak in the warmth of his body surrounding mine.

Tears prickled my eyes, but I took a deep breath and managed to swallow that lump stuck in my throat. I wouldn't let his absence overwhelm me. I would have faith that I would see him again. At this point, it was all I could do.

I distracted myself from worrying about Lucian by using three sticks and some rope to create a tripod over the fire, then attached a bottle of water above it, the way Blaise had taught me. When the water heated, I began rinsing the flower's roots. As I stood at the waterfall, allowing the coolness to wash over my hands, I wished I could remove the stains left from my time at the Emmerson's facility. But would I ever truly be free of the trauma they'd caused me to endure?

Flashes of memories shot through me like bullets. The Emmersons daughter trapped inside the glass. Flint, and the snakes coming from his flesh. Burning him and Umber Emmerson alive...

I walked away from the water, my hands cold and damp. I started the task of picking the flower apart, only placing fragments of the petals and roots into the bottle.

When I finished, I sat on a rock and watched the bubbles churn the bits of petals and roots together. Although I had attempted to distract myself, the ache in my chest hadn't lessened. If anything, it had only gotten worse as I watched the boiling water strip the roots and petals to their bare elements.

I rubbed at the bite mark on my thigh, only now resting long enough to examine it. Twin puncture marks left red welts on my skin. Although the pain had subsided, it still tingled and felt numb. What sort of venom had Flint injected into me?

Whatever it was, Blaise had gotten the worst of it, which was why I needed to slow the spread as soon as possible, so I removed the water bottle from over the fire. Perhaps it should have boiled for longer, but I doubted Blaise had time for that. I allowed the liquid to cool, then crossed to Blaise, my footfalls nearly drowned out by the rush of the waterfall.

He opened his eyes as I knelt beside him.

"It's ready," I said, pressing the bottle to his lips, then tipped it and allowed the liquid to trickle into his mouth. He swallowed twice, then laid his head back and closed his eyes.

"Thank you," he whispered.

"Don't thank me yet. I'm not sure if it will slow the poison. Not even sure it's the right flower, to be honest. Let's hope it doesn't kill you."

He nodded weakly. "I would have died already if that were the case. The venom... it can only slow me down. Can't... can't kill me."

"Are you sure about that?" I asked.

"Yes. The doctor couldn't create anything to kill me. He tried."

I narrowed my eyes at him. "He was trying to kill you?"

"At first, yes. Before he tried to use my blood to cure his daughter." He breathed deeply, his eyes still closed. "It never worked."

"How much do you know about their daughter?"

"They call her Sasha." He shook his head. "They keep her sedated. She's too dangerous to be freed."

"Too dangerous? How? What is she capable of?"

"So much..." he said weakly, his voice fading. "So many secrets... they kept."

I patted his shoulder. "Get some rest," I said quietly. "It will take some time before the medicine starts to slow the venom."

He only nodded, his face still pale. "Amaya... thank you. No one has ever been so kind... to me."

I tilted my head. "I did what anyone else would do."

"No." His fingers found mine, and he squeezed them with more force than I anticipated. "You saved me from that place. You healed me."

I pried my fingers from his, unnerved at the closeness. The

gesture was too intimate, and part of me felt as though I were betraying Lucian by having Blaise so near. I stood and took a step away from him. "As I said, anyone else would have done the same."

I glanced behind me, to the world outside the dome of rocks. The sun had already begun to set, and we would need something to eat before that happened. At least, that was the excuse I gave myself as I bade Blaise goodbye and left the cavern behind.

A warning bell rang in my head. Blaise was getting too familiar. I should have known it would happen. Being his nursemaid didn't help the matter. But perhaps I was reading too much into his closeness. I was the first compassionate person he'd contacted in months—years possibly. He must have been craving human connection. Still, I would have to be careful around him. I had no intentions of misleading him and making him think I had romantic feelings for him when the opposite was true.

Wandering through the forest, the light faded more quickly than I anticipated. My boots sank into the soft mud as I continued following along the stream. Crickets chirped and frogs croaked, announcing the arrival of evening.

The wind stirred, brushing strands of dark hair across my cheeks. If Lucian were here, I would hold his hand, feeling the warmth of his skin, and confess how much I missed him. Before I'd been captured, the thought of marriage terrified me. But now, I couldn't imagine spending my life with anyone else.

Maybe it didn't matter if I was ready. Maybe all that mattered was that I'd found the right person—and that would have to be enough. My thoughts turned to the plants surrounding me, and I did my best to recognize anything familiar. A few palms and orchids caught my attention, but nothing looked edible, so I continued down the path.

The landscape sloped until I stood in a bowl-shaped valley filled with vines and greenery. The scent of fresh growth filled my lungs, though the air stilled, and the familiar sounds of chirps and croaks faded. Palms stood like watch towers around the rim of the gorge.

The sun sank behind the forest as I surveyed the area. Trees filled with fruit grew between the larger trees, and I sidestepped the briars to get a closer look. Pink flowers sprouted above the bunches of green fruit about the size of oranges. Knitting my brow, I did my best to remember the plant's name. Sapote, maybe? I gathered a few of the bumpy green fruits, then stopped when I noticed something unusual just beyond the tree.

A square-shaped boulder hid beneath a tangle of vines. I placed the fruit aside, then I pulled at the growth to reveal a stone chiseled with symbols. I ran my fingers over the bumps and rough ridges of the stone's surface.

It was hard to tell what the images depicted, although one image resembled a snake, and on the opposite side, a creature with four legs and a large head. I wandered the area and pulled the vines off four more stones, each carved with images similar to the first one.

Footsteps shifted behind me, and I spun around, my fists flaring with fire.

Flora stumbled back, her cat's eyes wide.

The old woman's gray hair fanned out around her face in greasy strands, and she held her hands up in a defensive gesture, her fingernails resembling claws. "Please," she gasped. "Don't hurt me."

"What are you doing here?" I demanded, and I didn't lower my fists.

23

———

AMAYA

"I escaped," Flora stated as she faced me in the jungle clearing. Ancient Mayan stones sat around us, interspersed in the greenery, and I couldn't help but feel as if they'd drawn me here. Did Flora know anything about them?

"How?" I asked. Suspicions plagued me, and I wasn't sure I could trust her.

"After you left with Blaise," she answered. "Yasira Emmerson lost it when she found out about Umber's death. I warned her not to, but she freed her daughter from the glass chamber, and that's when I ran. I knew better than to stay anywhere near that girl. They caught me and tried to take me with them, but I managed to escape. I've been searching for you ever since. I don't know where they are now, and I don't know their plans, but I want no part of it."

"Why should I believe you?"

"Because." She held out her arms where puncture marks had healed badly, and black spots of blood dried to her wrinkled flesh. "Like you, I was their prisoner. Two years ago, they stole me from my husband, my home, and *mi nietas*—my two granddaughters. I only served the Emmersons because they forced me. But now I've escaped, and I need your help to return home."

I lowered my fists an inch, still unsure if I could trust her, but fairly certain she didn't mean to attack me.

"They changed me," she continued. "Just as they did to Flint and Blaise," she hesitated, "and you..."

As she trailed off, her words struck me. "They melded our DNA with animal DNA sequences, didn't they?"

She nodded. "A simple way of putting it, but yes."

"You." I waved at her. "What did they do to you?"

Her eyes darted around the forest, then went to one of the carved stones. "I... I shouldn't speak here."

"Why?" I questioned. "Are they following you?"

"No." She spoke with a clipped tone. "Yasira was afraid of being discovered, so she left with her daughter and went far away. I don't know where, but I suspect they left the country."

Suspicions nagged at me. What if she were lying? If they were following her, then there was a good chance they would find us soon. But what was I supposed to do? I couldn't kill her, and I couldn't turn her away. Our best option was to make it back to Blaise and hide before they found us.

"Follow me," I told her before collecting the fruit and heading toward the forest, but she placed her claw-tipped hand on my arm, stopping me.

"Wait," she said. "Those stones you were observing, they're the answer to the puzzle you're trying to solve."

"What do you mean?"

She didn't answer, so I mulled over her statement. "I saw a snake carved on one of the stones. They used that for Flint, didn't they? And a cat on another stone. Jaguar, maybe? That's you. But what about Blaise? And me? What did they inject us with? Flora, what are we?"

She flexed her gnarled fingers. Her golden cat's eyes flashed in the light of the setting sun. The wind stirred the wide palm leaves, and a chill went down my spine at the calculating look she gave me.

"The Emmersons researched for years. Every myth. Every legend. They all had a seed of truth. But here in the jungle, they discovered the source of the Mayans' beliefs, and the truth behind the myths."

"Explain what you mean," I said. "Please."

"The source of the powers. Mayans worshipped many gods," she said quietly, almost reverently, as the wind stilled. "But the Emmersons—they chose only the fiercest. Kulkulcán, or Quetzalcoatl, the feathered serpent of war. Xolotl, his twin brother, a soul guide for the dead. The jaguar, the ruler of the underworld, a symbol of the night sun and darkness. And Ixchel..."

Birds cawed overhead, breaking the stillness, and I looked up to see a mass of black bodies crowding the sky. Beyond them, a backdrop of storm clouds dominated the sky. Thunder rumbled with an ominous wail.

"Who's Ix-chel?" I spoke the name haltingly.

"Ix-*shell*," she enunciated. "Does that name mean something to you?"

I rubbed the chill bumps covering my arms. "I've never heard the name until now."

She gave a solemn nod.

"She's a Mayan goddess?" I prodded, hoping to keep her talking.

"Yes, the strongest of them all." She waved her hand dismissively. "But that's all I know."

"Surely you know something else. How long were you with the Emmersons? What else did you see there?"

"Enough questions," she huffed, her cat's eyes narrowing. "I will speak no more of the Emmersons or their experiments."

I took a deep breath to keep a lid on my annoyance. Clutching the fruit to my chest, I started through the forest with Flora lagging. After the sun set, moonlight drifted through the jungle canopy. The milky white light gave an eerie glow to the leaves and vines. It drained the color from the world, and the once vibrant flowers now looked a somber shade of gray.

We walked until the gushing waterfall echoed from ahead. I pushed apart the palm leaves until we entered the clearing where the pool took up the center of the space.

"This way," I called over my shoulder as Flora followed. She stumbled over the uneven ground, and I took her arm, then led her toward the waterfall. Sure, I may have seen her as my enemy not long ago, but not now. We had both escaped the Emmersons, and though she may have worked for them, I couldn't turn her away or mistreat her. I would respect her just as anyone else.

I managed to keep my balance as I climbed up the rocky embankment and entered the shelter of rocks behind the waterfall. Flora followed. Her eyes widened as she entered the cavern. Only a few coals remained of the fire. I found a stick nearby, then used it to stir the coals until a flame appeared, and I stacked more wood on the fire.

Flora shuffled to the fire and sat beside it, reaching her crooked fingers toward the flames. I searched the area, looking for Blaise, but found it empty.

"Where'd he go?" I mumbled to myself, then placed my armful of fruit by the fire.

"Gone, is he?" Flora asked.

I nodded. "It appears that way. He couldn't even stand up on his own when I left. Where could he have gone?"

She shrugged, stringy gray hair swishing around her stooped shoulders. "Not surprising. He managed to sneak off a few times in the facility before the Emmersons sedated him. Dangerous one, that boy. Even before the Emmersons started their experiments."

I sat across from her, letting the flames warm me and chase away my anxiety at Blaise's disappearance. He would be fine. At least, I was fairly certain.

"Tell me about him," I said to break up the silence. "Why do you say he's dangerous?"

"Didn't you know?" She picked up a sapote fruit and starting prying at the green peel.

"Know what?" I asked, grabbing a fruit of my own and began the process of peeling it.

"He's the seventh son of a seventh son."

"Meaning?" I raised an eyebrow.

"You don't know the meaning?"

"No. Should I?" I managed to remove a section of the peel, and citrus-smelling juice spilled onto my fingers.

"The seventh son must come from an unbroken line. No female siblings born between—for his or his father's generation." She nodded toward the forest. "Your friend Blaise is such a person. Rare."

"But what does it mean?" I asked again.

The fire popped. Sparks reflected in her cat's eyes. "Lobo," she whispered. "It means he's a werewolf."

Thunder echoed her words, a long droning sound that overpowered the gurgling of the waterfall. My hands stilled as I held the fruit, and the juice coating my hands turned my fingers cold. Anxiety swirled through my chest.

I didn't believe in werewolves. But not long ago, I hadn't believed in vampires or phoenixes either.

"If he's a werewolf," I said, my voice barely above a whisper, "then what were the Emmersons doing with him?"

She shrugged. "I only know this—the god I spoke of at the ruins, Xolotl, the brother of Kulkulcán, was more than a soul guide for the dead, he was originally the lightning beast of the Mayans, usually depicted with the head of a wolf. The Emmersons take what's already there, and they multiply it."

A spark danced over my knuckles with a brief burst of electric blue. The roaring of the waterfall grew louder in my ears. What did this make me? Flint was the snake, Flora the jaguar, Blaise the wolf, but what was I?

"The goddess you spoke of," I said. "What did you call her?"

"Ixchel," she repeated, firelight dancing in her eyes. "There were those who worshipped her above all others. You can still find her statues in the forests and villages. Some at the bottom of the sea. She brought the storms."

Behind us, heavy footsteps plodded. I spun around to face Blaise. He stood shirtless and soaked. Water dripped from his dark hair and trickled down the sinews and muscles of his defined chest. The wildness had returned to his eyes.

He tossed something toward us. The body of a headless deer tumbled to the ground. Blood leaked from the stump of its neck.

"We have food," was all he said as he stalked around us, circling, keeping his eyes on us as if we were his prey.

"You shouldn't leave," I told him. "You're still recovering. And it's dangerous out there."

"Dangerous?" He laughed. "Do you think I care?" He thrust his finger at Flora. "Why is she here?"

"She found me," I answered, moving to stand in front of her.

"I don't trust her."

"I understand." I spoke with a calm, even tone, afraid even the smallest accusation would provoke him. "She's no longer with the Emmersons. She escaped them. She won't hurt us, Blaise."

"How do you know?" he demanded as he circled us. The flames reflected the water dripping from his face and carved chest. It danced in the dangerous depths of his eyes. "She worked for them. They tricked everyone about who they were. Including her."

"I served them for a time," Flora said from behind me. "Until I found out the truth about the daughter."

I glanced back at her. "What do you mean by that?"

"Sasha," she said. "I know what her purpose is, although the Emmersons refuse to accept it."

I tilted my head. "What's her purpose?"

She shrugged. "To kill," she said matter-of-factly. "There is no creature stronger than that girl. In saving her, they created something wholly unnatural. People fear the fire wielders—those once known as vampire—but there is nothing on this planet more dangerous than Sasha Emmerson. They took every powerful creature they could find and put it into that girl. The snake, the jaguar, and the wolf—she controls them all."

"How do you know all this?" I asked. "Have you seen her outside the glass and not sedated?"

She didn't reply.

"She hasn't," Blaise said, taking a step toward the fire and closing the distance between us. I had to glance up to look into his eyes. Why did he seem so much taller now? "But I have."

"When?"

"I wasn't supposed to see it." The firelight reflected off his damp hair and bare shoulders. "But one night, there was some commotion, and they forgot to sedate me. I snuck outside. I saw her then. She stood in the clearing behind the facility." His gaze grew distant, his tone haunted. "She was so small, so thin. She looked like a ghost as she stood there facing six armed guards, and then she raised her hands. I'll never forget what happened after that." He closed his eyes, as if the memory pained him.

"Why?" I asked, my voice nearly drowned out by the crackling of the fire. "What happened?"

"Their bodies," he answered. "Burned. I've never heard screams like that before. I still hear their screams sometimes, late at night."

Silence pressed in. Disgust shook me to the core, and I sat on a rock near the fire.

"Yasira grabbed her after that, and her father gave her a shot in her arm. They carried her inside the facility. It all happened so quickly, as if they were accustomed to dealing with her escape attempts."

"If she ever does escape," I said, more to myself than to either of them. "Then what?"

"She kills countless thousands. Millions, possibly," Blaise answered.

"No," Flora interjected. "That's not her purpose."

"Then what is?" I asked.

Flora sat opposite me, and Blaise got situated on the rock beside me. "Don't you see?" Flora explained. "The Emmersons have been trying to cure *her* by using *us*, but they've gotten it wrong all along. *She's* the cure. The cure for everyone."

Flora placed her hands in her lap. Her thumbs bent awkwardly, and the claws replacing her fingernails were thick and yellowed. Pus wept from the nailbeds, and blood oozed from cracks in her skin. I was reminded of Lucian when he'd shown me his hands for the first time, which weren't hands at all, but badly scarred talons.

My heart ached again at the thought of Lucian, but I couldn't give in to my pain. I had to hold it together. For him. I focused on the woman sitting across the fire from me.

"Flora, how do you know this?" I asked.

"She doesn't," Blaise butted in. "She's been trying to tell me the same thing for years. It isn't true. The only way to deal with Sasha Emmerson is to kill her." He nodded to the deer's corpse. "Like that animal. She has to be stopped by any means necessary. The Emmersons won't do it because she's their daughter. But I can. I will."

"Blaise," I said flatly, not wanting to mince words. I didn't like his mention of murdering a child, no matter how dangerous she may have been. "That's a little girl you're talking about. Not a monster. Let's consider other options before decided to become her executioners. There may be a way to reverse her powers."

"Not possible," he said with heat in his voice.

"That's not true. I found the phoenix serum last year in Romania. It saved a lot of people. It's possible it could do the same for her. Also, Flora says the Emmersons may have left the country by now." I cast him a sidelong glance. "How could you even find them?"

"They haven't gone anywhere. Believe what you will, but they're still here. They won't leave without us. Our blood keeps their daughter alive. They may go into hiding for some time, especially if they feel their facility is at risk of being discovered, but soon they'll make their move. They'll come after us." He flexed his fists. "This time, I'll be ready."

I almost laughed at his overconfidence. If Sasha was such a capable killer and possessed everyone's combined powers, what possible hope did Blaise have of killing her?

But I didn't voice my concern as he sat beside me, so close I could feel the warmth of his body beside mine. He turned to me, and his eyes were lit with a passion I hadn't expected.

"I'll protect you, Amaya. I promise it."

I didn't make a reply as I tore my gaze from his to stare into the fire. "Blaise, there's no need," I told him.

"But Amaya." His fingertips touched mine as I rested my hands on my knees. "I care about you. More than you know."

The intensity in his eyes shocked me. A wave of anger washed through me at his words. Anger that he was here and not Lucian. Anger that he felt brazen enough to admit feelings for me when all I wanted to do was admit the same to someone else —someone who could have been hundreds of miles away from me.

The unfairness of it all hit me with the force of an avalanche.

My heart ached so badly, I felt as if a bullet had ripped through it. Tears threatened to burst free from the dam I had created—one I feared couldn't hold for much longer.

Blaise's hand was still touching mine when I jerked away from him. "Never say that to me again," I said through clenched teeth. Maybe it was too harsh of a reaction, but my fatigue, hunger, and all-consuming pain had left me raw and vulnerable, and unable to keep a lid on my emotions. Blaise represented everything I was missing, and I hated him for it.

I stood abruptly and marched outside the cavern, leaving the two behind.

24

———

Excerpt from a blog post by BlogDaddy2010

Lucian Vidraru Belongs in Prison—Here's 5 Reasons Why:
1. First, we all know what happened to Sally Anderson, that
woman he bit on a college campus back in the seventies. He
killed her, and why isn't he still serving time for her
murder? Oh yes, because he died in prison. Technically, he
fulfilled his sentence, and there are no laws for what
happens if a person happens to be revived after their death
twenty years prior. What a ridiculous loophole in our
system! We have a criminal walking our streets because of
this.
2. He was known to bite people during the Great Depression
and take their blood. There aren't any recorded deaths from
this incident, but bookkeeping back in the day wasn't great,
and things like that could have been easily swept under
the rug.
3. He's mentally unstable. There's a reason the man was kept
in a former sanitarium. Why do we only see him during
carefully guarded appearances? Why is everything he says

always practiced and coached? Because it's too dangerous to let us see the real Lucian Vidraru.

4. He's over 160 years old. In appearance he looks twenty-something, but someone that old can't be expected to have the greatest mental awareness. He's a danger to himself and others.

5. He kidnapped his girlfriend. Yes, I said it, and this last reason is the biggest doozie of them all. Considering his violent history, it's obvious he kidnapped and most likely murdered his girlfriend, Amaya De la Vega, but of course, he's famous, and—more importantly—he's rich. His crimes will never be discovered. It pays to have money, my friends.

———

LUCIAN

The single-engine plane skidded to a stop over a bumpy ground. Outside the window, a soupy gray sky loomed above the dense jungle. I had to admit, even in a tin can like this, flying gave me a sense of freedom I rarely felt. Maybe being a phoenix had something to do with the feeling. The sprawling village of Santa Lucia punctuated the Yucatán jungle in a collection of one-and two-story cement buildings interspersed with fruit carts and thatched-roof huts. Vibrant paint peeled from the plaster-covered walls. Murals of tropical birds and jungle plants colored the drab concrete structures.

Despite all my fears of losing Amaya, my heart leapt at the sight. We were one step closer to finding her. At least, I prayed it was true. Although Chloe sat beside me, and Sally took the seat up front by the pilot, I was still too close to the woman.

My mind was still reeling from Sally's revelation.

Yasira Emmerson was our daughter. But how? Sally and I had been close, but never intimate. Still, Sally had stolen my DNA before she left me, then she had faked her own death, and Dr. Warren made sure I was blamed for it. After the doctor revived her, he must have used a form of artificial insemination to impregnate her. But for what purpose?

I feared what my own blood would do to a child, and what kind of side effects would come of being born with the vampire virus in her veins.

I went to prison not long after Sally's supposed murder, and I never saw her again. She must have had the baby and raised her while my body was buried in a Colorado prison cemetery. I never got a chance to see my own child be born, or to raise her. I'd had no idea she even existed.

Yasira was so much like her mother; perhaps I should have known instinctually. They both had pale skin and raven black hair, shocking blue eyes, and secretive smiles, but they were more alike than by looks alone. Emotions of betrayal warred within me, heating my blood, and making it hard for me to focus.

Why had Sally waited so long to tell me? Now, it made sense why Yasira had sought me out. She'd wanted to meet her father. Just like her mother, she was too stubborn and too proud to admit the truth. Sally was a master at keeping secretes from me, and so was our daughter.

Daughter.

The word resounded in my head.

I had a daughter, and in appearance, she was double my age. She must have hated me. I had never once been there for her. Was that why they had taken Amaya? As retribution?

No. there must have been more to the story. Or so I hoped. Soon, I hoped to fit all the pieces together.

Chloe stirred beside me. Her blonde hair was disheveled and fell in clumps over her face. Shadows circled her eyes. She'd slept a little on the plane ride from New York to Mexico City, and then to the airport here, but it had been fitful and sporadic. I knew she worried about her friend, which was only more reason to find Amaya and bring her home to us. Did Amaya realize how many people loved and missed her? How many of us needed her?

The pilot spoke from the seat in front of me. "Welcome to Santa Lucia, the hidden jewel of the Yucatán. You may unbuckle and disembark once we've reached the terminal."

The plane moved slowly down the taxiway. I focused on the view outside the window; I couldn't turn my attention to Sally for too long. It was hard to control my fury around her. She'd used me, and every time I looked at her, betrayal punched a hole in my chest at the thought of what she'd done to our daughter—to my flesh and blood.

What sort of childhood had Yasira endured at the hands of someone as mentally unstable as Sally Anderson? It chilled me to the bone to think of the neglect and cruelty the child must have suffered. Willing away the images of my own daughter's abuse, I kept my gaze focused outside, to the lone tower of the airport rising above the jungle, as isolated and bare as the spires of Crimson Hollow.

Imagining being at the new facility with Amaya at my side kept my mind from going to darker places. Had I ever told her how much I loved her? It seemed we spent so much time working on the facility, we had little time for each other. Once I got her back, I vowed things would change. If not—if I had truly lost her—then I would be stuck in the place I had come from, one where my only wish was to find relief in death.

How I would finance our facility was still a mystery, but at this point, money problems were the least of my worries.

The plane slowed, then stopped, and after a few minutes, we disembarked. Bits of broken gravel crunched underfoot, and the air was so dense, I felt as if I were breathing through plastic wrap. The humidity made my T-shirt and jeans stick to my skin. I wore a gray hoodie over my shirt, and I pulled up the hood to cover my head. Not long ago, I used my hood to hide, and now wasn't much different.

When I had Amaya with me, I was a different person—

someone who looked forward to life. Now, heaviness weighed me down, threatening to suffocate me.

Our footsteps echoed as we crossed the blacktop. A few raindrops splattered the ground, and the lightning-sharp scent of ozone filled the air. The wind tousled dried palm fronds across the pavement. An iguana waited under the shade of a tree off in the distance, still as a statue, flakes of skin peeling off its lithe body.

No one spoke as we walked to the terminal and entered the airport through two glass doors covered in fingerprints. Sharp fluorescent lights shone over displays filled with cheap souvenirs. Advisories written in Spanish were posted in intervals along the walls, and when we reached the corridor leading outside, ads littered the cinderblock walls, most of the plastered papers yellowed and curling at the edges.

Chloe fell into step beside me. "Lucian, what's the name of our contact again?"

"Hernandez," I repeated, recalling the instructions Officer Butler had given me before we'd left New York. "Officer Butler said he'd meet us by the taxi terminal."

We exited the airport through another set of glass doors. Taxis and buses waited on the drive outside, and the air reeked of engine exhaust. A group of security officers were stationed outside the exit, and we made our way toward them.

"Vidraru?" One of the men walked forward. His hair was shaved nearly to his scalp. Dark eyes focused on us in a shrewd, calculating gesture.

"Are you Officer Hernandez?" I asked.

"Yes, Lamoni Hernandez. Officer Butler contacted me about the girl. I'm glad you've arrived." The man stretched out his hand to shake. I eyed it, flexing my fingers, remembering it was normal for people to shake skin-to-skin, so I placed my hand in his and shook. His grip was firm, and his gaze confident. He also shook Chloe's hand, although Sally remained behind us, standing aloof with her chin tilted up.

"We're also searching for a missing young man from a local village," Officer Hernandez said. "Like your case, he was visited by the Emmersons shortly before his disappearance."

"We've heard," I said.

"We'll take care of you here, Vidraru," Hernandez said, his tone underscored with determination. "If De la Vega is here, we'll find her."

"Thank you, Officer," I replied. "We'd like to speak to the missing person's family if possible."

His gaze went to Chloe, and then to Sally who was still standing behind us. "I can take you to his family's home, but it's a bit of a drive, and..." He swallowed, as if the subject made him nervous. "I'll just warn you, when we get out in the jungle, you'll need to be cautious."

Chloe spoke up. "Why?"

He pinched his eyebrows to form a severe line. "It may be nothing, but there have been rumors. When they first called me out, I thought it was just the villagers and their superstitions. But now, I believe there may be some truth to their stories of the things they've claimed to see in the jungle."

Sally took a step forward, her heels clicking over cement, mingling with the rumble of engines. "The stories are all true, Officer," she spoke with a soft tone, and the sound of her voice made my skin crawl. I still wasn't comfortable with having her here with us but learning that she was the mother of our daughter changed things. I would do my best to tolerate her presence, but after we found Amaya, my time with her would end, and I never wanted to see her face again—or be anywhere near her.

"Follow me," Officer Hernandez said. "I can escort you there. I've got a Jeep waiting. It will take a few hours before we arrive at the young man's family home. They live deep in the jungle. We'll need to hurry if we want to get there before dark." He turned and took a step toward the doorway, then he paused and looked over his shoulder. "I can take you as far as their home, but I'll go no farther. Just a fair warning—watch your back when we get there. The jungle isn't what you may think."

25

A photograph of a room inside the Santa Lucia Center for Health and Wellness. Once hailed as a groundbreaking and innovative hospital, Santa Lucia suffered financial woes from the offset of its operations, and it was consequently abandoned.

AMAYA

I pushed through the vines and entered a small clearing where the moonlight illuminated a pond. Fireflies danced over the surface and created ripples. The sound of running water mingled with chirping crickets and night creatures inhabiting the jungle. It would have been a peaceful scene if it weren't for the unease warring inside me.

"Amaya," Blaise called from behind, and I spun around. Moonlight revealed his lithe frame moving silently through the jungle leaves. At the sound of Blaise's voice, I stiffened. I didn't really want to have a conversation alone with him in the jungle.

"Amaya," he repeated. "Wait."

I stopped walking and took a deep breath. How had I allowed myself to get into this situation? I had pitied Blaise when I'd first seen him. My heart had hurt for him and for the situation he was in. I'd felt obligated to help him, and if I had to do it all over, I would help him escape again.

But now, I didn't know who he was or understand his capabilities. If he was looking for more than friendship, I would have no choice but to reject him. And then what? Rejecting him meant setting off his anger, which was the last thing I wanted to do right now.

"What do you want?" I asked.

"I just want to talk to you. That's all," he said, his voice soft.

"Talk about what?"

"About you." He took a step closer. "About us."

My muscles tensed. "Blaise, there is no *us*."

"Why not?" he demanded.

I had to choose my words carefully. "Blaise, I don't know you. To be honest, the way you killed those guards without a second thought frightened me." Lucian would have never taken lives so carelessly. Yes, he could seem cold and unfeeling at times, but I had discovered a softer side of Lucian Vidraru—and Blaise was nothing like him. "Plus," I added. "I have someone else."

He slanted his head. "Who?"

I hesitated before answering. I didn't want to drag Lucian into this, but I'd already brought him up.

"It's the vampire, isn't it?"

"He's not a vampire, but yes."

His eyes simmered, and he glanced away, his jaw flexing. "I understand. I've been nothing but a burden since you've met me. When you say you don't know who I am, you're right. You don't know what I can do." Tendons strained as he balled his hands to form fists. "Or how powerful I can be. You only know someone helpless. Someone weak and incompetent. Someone you had to rescue." When he turned to look at me again, anger shone in his eyes. "I'll prove myself to you."

I tilted my head. "Prove yourself how?"

"I don't know yet. But I'll find a way." He continued down the path, but I gently grasped his arm. Blaise had endured so much at the hands of the Emmersons. He didn't deserve more suffering. Although I wouldn't encourage a romantic relationship, I could still be his friend. Plus, his anger bothered me, and I feared what he might do to prove himself to me.

"Blaise, wait," I said. "You don't have to prove anything to me. Just take a walk with me, okay? Tell me about yourself. What is your family like? What do you do for fun?"

His mouth gaped, as if my questions had caught him off guard. "You want to know about me?"

I nodded. "Yes, let's walk back to the cave, and you can tell me."

He glanced back toward the way we'd come. "I suppose that would be okay."

"Good." I kept my hand on his arm as we started hiking through the jungle. "What is your family like?"

"They're okay. Our house was always busy, always something needing to be done. I have so many brothers, and they're all just as stubborn as me."

"Do you get along with them?"

"Mostly, yes. We spent too much time working in the orchards to fight. It was hard work, cutting and pruning in the trees all day. Very hot. Sometimes we would go down to the caves and go swimming to cool off. I miss my brothers. I miss my parents, too. It's been so long since I've seen them. I don't even know how long." His arms tensed, tendons standing out. "I lost all sense of time in the facility. They must have held me as their prisoner for years."

"I can't imagine how hard that must have been for you."

"They'll pay for what they did." He spoke matter-of-factly.

The rushing of the waterfall came from ahead. We stepped into the clearing and made our way around the boulders until we reached the edge of the water. Blaise stared up at the sky where a million stars twinkled.

"This place is so magical," he said, his voice turning soft.

"It's beautiful, yes," I agreed.

"But there's more to it than beauty," he said. "Can't you feel it? In the air? In the plants and in the water? This is why the Emmersons came here. They knew there was magic here. They knew what the magic could do to change us."

"What do you mean by that?"

His gaze locked on me. A chill went down my spine at the intensity of the look, primal and animalistic. A gold sheen glazed his eyes.

"They knew what I was."

"What are you, Blaise?" I asked gently, hoping to keep an even tone so I wouldn't reveal my fear.

He cupped my elbow in his arm. I allowed him to touch me, if only to keep him talking.

"You know already, don't you?"

I managed to nod. "Maybe..." I hedged. "Flora mentioned something... about a..." I couldn't finish. Somehow, saying the word out loud would make it too real.

He leaned in closer and whispered. "Werewolf."

Fear tingled from the top of my head straight to my toes. I wanted to be anywhere but here with him. I managed to break out of his grasp, then take a step backward.

"I-I should probably check on Flora." I turned and marched to the cavern beyond the waterfall, not bothering to glance behind me to see if he followed.

26

AMAYA

The sun sank below the horizon. Mud splattered behind our tires as we drove toward the collection of huts crowded beneath the jungle trees. Officer Hernandez steered the Jeep around water-filled potholes. I rubbed a knot in my neck. We'd been in the cramped confines for more than five hours. When the Jeep finally stopped, I opened my door and climbed from the seat, my muscles sore.

Chickens pecked at the packed ground, and a few goats wandered between the thatch-roofed homes. A collection of beat-up cars sat rotting on the edge of the forest. Despite the movement of the animals around us, the air was still, the area so quiet it was unnerving.

Hinges squealed, and a woman appeared in the shadow of one of the building's doorways. She waited, looking at us, not speaking.

Officer Hernandez stood next to me, and Chloe and Sally crowded around us. "Be careful out here." He nodded at me and Chloe. "Especially you two. Vampire survivors aren't well-liked."

"Thanks for the warning," I said. "But I'm used to it."

"It wouldn't be the first time," Chloe chimed in.

Officer Hernandez nodded, and we walked toward the doorway. The woman didn't move as we approached her. She had a slight build, and large, dark eyes rimmed in thick-framed glasses. Her hair was mostly gray and pulled into a tight bun.

She said something in Spanish to Officer Hernandez. They spoke for a while, and then he pointed to each of us in turn, saying our names as he did.

"*Ingles?*" she asked.

"*Si, por favor*," he answered, then turned to us. "She speaks a little English. She's willing to talk to us, but she doesn't want us inside the house. We'll have to meet her in the back."

"That's fine," I said, and Officer Hernandez led us around the structure. Chickens scurried and goats chewed their cuds, and the scent of their droppings got carried on the wind. A sprawling tree overshadowed a shed comprised of only one wall and a rusted tin roof. Inside, a collection of stools and broken chairs jumbled atop a dirt-packed floor. The shade inside came as welcome relief from the heat.

Family photos had been tacked to the single wall. A makeshift altar had been set up beneath one of the larger pictures—a black-and-white photo of a young man with dark hair and a serious expression. Something in his eyes seemed uncannily familiar. I got the impression he was hiding a deep secret.

Religious candles in various stages of being burned crowded atop the wooden surface beneath. Flames flickered as we moved around the room, and I found a stool and sat on it, as did the others.

The woman and a middle-aged man soon appeared from the house. Wooden chairs creaked as they got situated around us.

"*Mi hijo*." She pointed. "My eldest son, Pedro. He will tell you what he knows about Blaise." She nodded toward the black-and-white picture.

Pedro sat beside his mother, as if to protect her. He folded his arms in a defensive stance before speaking. "My youngest brother was taken more than three years ago." I pondered his words as he continued the story. Like Amaya, the Emmersons had shown interest in him before his disappearance. His father and brothers had searched for the young man. They had found lights in the forest coming from an old hospital that they had thought long abandoned. Any time they got near the place they were attacked by a bizarre creature. His father had nearly been killed, and he had never fully recovered from his injuries. No one would return after that.

"What kind of creature?" I asked.

The man made the sign of the cross. "I will not speak of it."

The woman shifted. "We will not say its name here."

"Can you show us where the hospital is located?" I asked.

The woman and her son traded glances. They spoke in rapid Spanish before the son turned his gaze back on us.

"I am willing to take you near it," he said. "But I will not go to it."

"Fair enough," I answered.

"We will leave at first light in the morning," Pedro said. "No sooner. I will not travel through the jungle at night."

"You're welcome to sleep here," the woman said. "I prepare a meal for you. And I have blankets. Wait." She stood and shuffled away. Her son followed, keeping his arm around her stooped shoulders until they entered the hovel.

As we waited for them to return, I stood and stretched my exhausted muscles, then I left the shelter and took a few steps toward the forest. In those dense trees somewhere, I hoped to find Amaya. My heart leapt with excitement and fear. I wanted to race into the woods and find her right now, on my own, but it would be a foolish thing to do. I could easily get lost, especially since it was nearly sundown.

No, I would bide my time and take my opportunity when it came.

Footsteps shifted behind me, and I turned to see Chloe

approaching. She gave me a brief smile, which surprised me. I hadn't seen her smile in weeks—at least since Amaya had gone missing, and well before that, too.

"Chloe." I nodded.

"Hi," she said weakly, her gaze pinned to the foreboding overgrowth of forest. We stood at its edge, not able to see past the dark palm leaves and vines. It kept its secrets well-hidden and protected. What would we find when we entered?

When Pedro had spoken of a creature, what could he have possibly meant? Someone suffering with viridae sangre could appear as a vampire—at least, that was the popular opinion. If untreated, it wasn't uncommon for someone to become severely reclusive, much like Jayden Black had done. Or was he referring to someone else? Or some*thing* else?

A rush of wind blustered the palm fronds. Behind us, the shelter's tin roof creaked. The air had an unusual scent, of iron and a hint of ash.

Chloe reached out and grasped one of the palm leaves in her hand. Her eyes widened as she felt the waxy surface. "There's something strange about this place."

"What do you mean?"

"I'm not sure." She kept the leaf firmly grasped in her hand, as if she were divining its inner secrets. "It's almost like the forest is trying to talk to me. I know that sounds crazy." She laughed quietly, and her eyes sparkled as she looked at me.

"Chloe, I've been around long enough to know that strange things are a part of life. Plus, it seems as if you've come alive here. I haven't seen you smile in ages; much less heard you laugh."

"Yes," she agreed, looking up at the trees. "I suppose you're right. Maybe I just needed a change of scenery. Or maybe there really is something to this place."

"Either way, I'm glad to see you brightening up. Amaya would too."

At the mention of Amaya, she glanced away and bit her lip. "Do you think she's okay?"

I wanted to comfort her. To tell her without a doubt that yes, Amaya was fine. She had to be. But reality could be harsh and unforgiving. I'd seen too much death and endured too much torture in my lifetime. "I hope so. She's strong and capable. But I can't say for sure. I'm sorry, Chloe."

Chloe only nodded as she fixed her gaze on the forest. "I know."

Behind us, voices murmured. We faced the one-walled structure where Blaise's mother had returned with an armful of blankets. Chloe and I made our way inside and helped arrange the blankets over the hard-packed ground.

"Thank you," I said to the older woman as she placed a threadbare blanket on the ground beside me. "*Gracias*," I repeated.

She smiled, crinkling the wrinkles around her eyes, then she held her hand over her heart. "You will find my Blaise."

"I hope we can," I answered, although I couldn't make any promises. "But he's been lost for many years."

"But he lives," she said. "And you will find him."

She looked at me with hope in her eyes. Telling her the odds of finding him alive seemed like a cruel thing to do. But I didn't want to get her hopes up, either.

She shuffled to me and took my hand in hers. "He is my youngest," she said with tears shining in her eyes. "You understand?"

"Yes." I smiled. "He's your baby."

"He is more than that. Seven sons I had. Seven sons were in his father's family."

"Ah." The light bulb went on. I'd heard of the seventh son superstition. Some said the seventh son had magical powers. Others said he was cursed. There was a more outlandish superstition—one my father had believed, but he had never been able to prove—that the seventh son born to a seventh son became a werewolf.

In the light of who I was, such a myth could have been actual truth. But was there any proof for it?

Perhaps that's why the Emmersons had chosen this place. The countryside brimmed with superstitions, and perhaps more than that. Plus, it was perfectly secluded. It would have been easy for them to hide whatever experiments they were performing.

I placed my hand on top of Blaise's mother's thin fingers. "I'll do my best to bring your son home to you."

"*Gracias*," she sobbed, then pulled my hand from hers and dabbed at her eyes with her sleeve. "Wait for me. Soon, I bring food."

I nodded as she exited the shelter and made her way back to the home.

"This is a horrible place," Sally remarked as she lounged on a blanket behind me. For a few blissful moments, I had nearly forgotten she was with us.

"That's not true," I said. "The family is doing their best to welcome us."

"Are they? Sleeping out in the elements with nothing but blankets?"

I shot her a dark glare. "I suppose you would rather go back to haunting the halls of Crimson Hollow?"

She returned the glare. "You know I wasn't in my right mind. Victor had me on a cocktail of drugs that made it impossible for me to think coherently. Even so." She crossed her arms. "It still beat sleeping in this jungle."

Chloe frowned at the woman. "Why did you want to come so badly if you were just going to hate it?"

"Good point," I chimed in.

"I came because I wanted to make sure Lucian didn't kill our daughter," she answered, her tone dark.

"Why would he kill his own daughter?" Chloe asked.

"Because he doesn't know her like I do," Sally answered. "Nor does he understand her capabilities. Would it surprise you to know you're not the only one with incredible powers?"

"What do you mean by that?" I asked. "What can she do?"

"Take a wild guess. She's your offspring."

"But she's more than that." I flexed my jaw, irritation simmering beneath my skin. "What sort of childhood did she have, Sally? Did you even bother to raise her?"

"Of course, I raised her!" She balled the blanket in her fists. "I wasn't a perfect parent, but who is? I took her everywhere, all over the world. She became a brilliant scientist because of me. And when my health wouldn't allow me to tend to her, Victor was there for her. He was the father you should have been."

"Victor." I spat his name. "So did you create the child in a lab with the doctor using my stolen DNA?"

Her jaw dropped. Her overreaction to my comment made it even more likely. For one thing, the timeline didn't work out. Sally was supposed to have been dead when I went to prison, and her autopsy didn't mention anything about a pregnancy.

What were their intentions for the girl? Whatever it had been, the plan must have backfired, as the two no longer had any control of Yasira Emmerson.

She must have escaped them at some point, then started her own pharmaceutical firm. It must have driven the pair crazy that they couldn't control their creation, which was why they had turned to controlling me instead.

No one spoke as we waited for the boy's mother to return. When she finally arrived from the house, she hefted a pot. Steam rose from the surface, smelling of vegetable broth. I stood and took the load from her, and she smiled and thanked me as I placed the container on a chair.

She brought bowls and spoons from the house, and soon we sat around the room eating and chatting—all except Sally, who took hers to the far corner and ate alone. Good riddance to her.

I didn't have a drop of pity for the woman. She should have been locked in a jail cell for what she'd done to me.

I still remembered lying in the pit in Romania. She'd stood over the opening and dropped a torch on me, then made sure I'd burned. That's when I had discovered my true nature. My body had transformed and risen from the ashes just like a phoenix. I hadn't died, which was most likely the only reason Sally wasn't in prison.

But I hadn't forgotten the crazed look in her eyes as she'd lit me on fire. After we found Amaya and all was said and done, I wanted nothing more to do with the woman.

After we finished eating, Chloe and I helped the boy's mother clean up. I even caught Chloe laughing and smiling as she chatted with the older woman. It seemed Chloe was more at home here than she'd been anyplace else, but it didn't surprise me. Being out in nature, away from the distractions of the world, was the medicine she needed.

Or maybe there was more to her lifted mood than just being away from it all—maybe she was right, and there really was something magical about this place—a world unlike any other, where myths became reality.

27

An Interview with Lucian Vidraru for Reformed Magazine, a
Publication for Reforming Inmates

***"Eventually I forgave my father. I had carried the burden of
hate for too long, and I would no longer allow it to be a
noose around my neck."***

LUCIAN

I slept fitfully until the sun rose. We packed up our things as
Officer Hernandez drove away, and Pedro stood waiting, a
backpack strapped to his back. His expression was appre-
hensive, his eyes dark, as he stared into the jungle.

"My truck will only take us so far," he said to us, nodding
toward a rusting, four-door Bronco parked nearby. "When the
road becomes impassable, we will go on foot."

"I understand," I said.

We crossed dew-covered grass to reach the vehicle. Before
we got inside, the boy's mother came to us. She placed a wrin-

kled hand on my shoulder. Although she didn't speak, I could see the intensity in her eyes. As she squeezed my shoulder, I knew what she was asking. Bring her boy home to her.

I gave a solemn nod. Whether I would be able to follow through with her request was yet to be determined. No one else had been able to recover him. I wasn't sure why she was putting so much faith in me, except that perhaps I was her last hope. No one else would look for him. They feared what lurked in the forest. But I had no reason to fear monsters.

Not when I was one.

We climbed into the Bronco, Chloe and Sally taking the back seat, and I stayed up front by Pedro as he steered us down the road. It only took a few minutes for us to leave all traces of civilization behind and enter the dark canopy of the forest. Cicadas chirped, and birds fluttered overhead as we drove down the dirt road, stirring a cloud of dust behind us. Tree branches scraped over our car's hood, and we bounced as we hit one pothole after another.

Pedro sat stiffly as he gripped the steering wheel. His eyes darted from one tree to another, as if he half expected a demon to jump out at us, which made me curious. What had attacked his father? I decided now was a better time to ask than later. Earlier, he seemed hesitant to speak of it, but perhaps I could coax the truth from him.

"Pedro," I said. "Can you tell me more about this creature? What did it look like?"

He darted a glance at me, and though the look was brief, I saw his gaze linger on my eyes. Not long ago, I'd worn sunglasses to hide the red hue of my pupils. Now, although my eyes had returned to a normal shade of brown, the stories of my appearance remained.

"You want to know what it looked like?" Pedro asked, his accent thick.

"Yes."

"Why?" He tilted his head, his eyes quizzical, as if he thought I might be crazy for wanting to know such a thing.

"I think it would be best for us to know what's out there, and understand what we're up against," I answered.

"Up against?" he repeated. "You do not go 'up against' such creatures as these. Weapons are useless. Evasion…useless. You cannot hide. Only run. Even then, you stand little chance. Although…" he paused to study my hands, which not long ago had been claws, then his gaze returned to studying my face. "Perhaps you would give them a fair fight."

"You called them creatures. Plural. There's more than one?"

He hesitated before answering, his mouth drawn to form a thin line. Beyond him, through the Bronco's windshield, spanned miles and miles of verdant green so thick, I had little chance of spotting anyone—or anything—in such a place. "We do not know how many," he answered. "But there is one more powerful than the others. It only comes at night. It attacks when you least expect. The claws." He held his fingers apart, at least three-inches long. "It…" he trailed off, as if he were stopping himself from revealing too much.

"It what?" I questioned.

"No. I will say no more." He locked his jaw and stared at the road.

"Pedro," Chloe said softly, leaning forward to speak to him. "Please, can't you tell us anything more? Don't be afraid of what we might think. Trust me when I say we've all seen terrifying things. We *are* terrifying things." She glanced at her hands pressed into her lap. "You have nothing to fear."

"Fear?" he barked a cheerless laugh. "You have no idea. You think you're the *diablos*? You know nothing."

"Try me," I challenged, a warning in my voice. My patience was wearing thin. I had no time to debate him over who had been terrorized more, because he would never win the argument. "I've been around for a while, Pedro. I've survived two world wars, the holocaust, torture, and human experiments so chilling, you would never sleep again."

He stared at me with a slack-jawed expression.

"Very well." He cleared his throat. "Maybe you have seen disturbing things, but I am sworn not to speak of the creature."

"You're referring to it as one creature again," I pointed out. "Why?"

Sally leaned forward from her spot in the back seat behind me. "It has something to do with what you're hiding inside your house, doesn't it?"

He shifted, then swallowed, his Adam's apple bobbing.

"What is it?" Sally persisted.

"No." He spat the word, and his cheeks reddened. "I will speak no more of it."

The Bronco slowed, then stopped, as we approached a downed tree across the road. Beyond the fallen log, the jungle loomed, and the road was little more than a path cutting through the dense fortress of trees.

"This is it. From here, we walk," Pedro said. "And pray we survive," he added, his voice haunted as he made the sign of the cross.

28

AMAYA

"We must go."

I opened my eyes to find Flora shaking my shoulder. Only a little light seeped into the cavern as I sat up and rubbed my eyes. I tried to shake the sleep from my head and remember what I was doing here.

I escaped the Emmersons, I reminded myself. *I'm in the jungle with Blaise and Flora.*

"Go where?" I asked.

"Away," she answered. "They're coming for us."

"It's true." Blaise shifted behind Flora. There wasn't enough light to see his facial features, which made him appear as a shadowy figure looming over the elderly woman. "I spotted Yasira and her daughter in the jungle less than an hour ago. They took another trail, but they'll catch up to us soon enough. We've got to run."

"Run where?" I asked.

"I know a place we can hide," Flora said. "There are some ruins not far from here. Come." She motioned, and I nodded, then got to my feet. The roaring of the waterfall drowned out any other sounds as we dashed to the mouth of the cave. Cold droplets splashed my skin. We left the rocky outcropping and entered the jungle.

A gunmetal gray sky spanned above us, although I only caught glimpses through gaps in the thick tree branches. My stomach pinched with hunger pains, and I licked my dry lips. With my hunger returning, whatever experiments the Emmersons had performed must have been wearing off. Maybe that was a good sign, or maybe adding the element of hunger to the situation only complicated matters. Either way, our only concern for now was to escape the Emmersons—and hopefully find our way out of this jungle and get help as soon as we could.

With the thought that the Emmersons were right behind us, my heart raced with the added adrenaline flowing through my veins. We moved with speed through the jungle, although Flora lagged, and I found myself stopping frequently to allow her to catch up. She breathed heavily as she pushed through the thick branches. Blaise stayed several paces ahead, only looking back when Flora pointed the direction to go.

The landscape turned from dense jungle to rocky ground, and formations rose around us, cutting with jagged edges toward the sky. Chirps and caws of jungle creatures filled my ears. As the sun rose higher, the heat made sweat coat my skin, and the humidity turned my hair to a damp mess that stuck to the back of my neck.

Suddenly, behind me, Flora collapsed. I backtracked and knelt beside her.

"Blaise," I called. "Wait."

He came to me as I knelt over the elderly woman. Her skin was ashen, her breathing labored, as I took her cold claw-like hand in mine. Dried blood coated her cheeks, and mud splattered her arms and legs. She tried to speak, but she wheezed and coughed instead.

"We're so close," she managed. "It's just ahead."

Blaise helped me grab Flora's arms and lift her up, although she stumbled as we stepped forward, so he picked her up and carried her as I followed behind. The air quieted, and the only sound came from our labored breathing as we sped through the jungle, past trees and bushes that tore at my skin with their thorny vines.

Ahead, the trees thinned, and soon we entered a clearing. Pyramids of gray stones rose around us, some taller than the trees. A flock of birds took flight as we entered the area. The rain-scented air brushed damp strands of hair across my face. Lightning streaked overhead, its electrical energy buzzing. It raised the fine hairs on the back of my neck.

She is said to bring the storms...

It was hard to believe that the goddess Ixchel really existed. But I couldn't deny the connection I felt to the storms, as if they were calling to me, telling me that a piece of me was connected to them. I was a part of them, just as they were part of me. It was a crazy thought, but one that I couldn't deny.

I stood tall as we faced the pyramids.

"Over there." Flora pointed. "There's an entrance that leads underground."

Blaise nodded. He carried Flora as we crossed the area, thunder rumbling, until we reached the base of the structure.

Carvings of feathered serpents decorated the bottom of the pyramid. As we walked along the perimeter, the image of the jaguar appeared alongside the serpents. Plants grew so thick, it was hard to maneuver around the pyramid's base, but we made it to the far side where broken stones were piled to create a dome.

"Flora, where's the entrance?" I asked.

She pointed to the plants covering the stones, but her breathing was too labored for her to speak. Blaise placed her carefully on the ground, and together, we pulled the vines from the crumbled rocks.

The wet shoots slipped in my hands, but Blaise and I managed to pull away the plants, revealing an opening barely large enough for a person to fit through.

"You crawl inside first," Blaise said. "I'll follow with Flora."

I nodded, hastily glancing over my shoulder before getting to my hands and knees. Mud stuck to my palms as I scooted inside the hole. The scent of damp earth filled the air. I edged forward until the tunnel widened and I was able to stand up.

Blaise followed, cradling Flora to his chest until he was also able to stand.

The darkness swallowed us the deeper we walked, so I snapped my fingers. A brilliant blue flame burst into life, illuminating the stone walls surrounding us. Carvings stood out in detail. Some were so pristine, paint in colors of red and yellow colored their surfaces.

"Beautiful," I whispered as we walked through the narrow, sloping tunnel. "Flora." I glanced at the woman behind me, still in Blaise's arms. "How did you know this was here?"

She mumbled a reply, and the only words I caught were "years ago."

My flame reflected the worry in Blaise's eyes.

"What should we do for her?" he asked.

I cast him a calculating glance. "It wasn't long ago you didn't trust her, and now you want to help her?"

He heaved an exasperated sigh. "Amaya, she was like a mother to me in that place. Besides you, she was the only person who treated me as human. Of course I care for her. Even if she served the Emmersons, it wasn't by choice. I see that now." He looked away. "I'm starting to see things differently now that we've escaped—see people differently."

He pinned his gaze on me once again, and I shuddered at the glance, turning my attention to Flora to keep from reading too much into the exchange.

The elderly woman's face had drained of all color. Her eyes were closed, and her mouth was pinched tight, as if she were in pain.

"She needs help," I said.

"There's nothing we can do for her right now," Blaise admitted. "We'll have to stay hidden until the Emmersons leave the jungle, then we find help."

"Find help where?" I asked.

"My home," Blaise answered. "I didn't recognize where we were until we found the pyramids, but I know my way now. We're not far from my family's village. Maybe five miles. There's a river that will take us right to them."

"Five miles through the jungle could take days," I said.

His shoulders slumped. "Yes. I know. But we have no other choice. We'll hide here until it's safe, then we make our move."

I nodded, and we continued through the tunnel until we reached a dead end. Blaise placed Flora on the ground against a wall, and I sat beside her. Her breathing had evened out a bit, and it seemed as if she were sleeping.

"I'll return," Blaise said to me, then headed toward the exit.

"Where are you going?" I asked.

But either he didn't hear, or he wasn't interested in bothering with an answer. Soon, he left me alone, surrounded by the tomb of the ancient pyramid, with nothing but my thoughts to keep me company.

29

LUCIAN

"I hear the waterfall." Pedro pointed through a gap in the tree branches. "Can you see it?"

"Not yet," I answered. "But I hear it, too." We hiked through the dense jungle. Water roared from up ahead, and we followed a narrow game trail until we reached a clearing. Sunlight sparkled over the water droplets that created a mist over the falls.

"We're getting closer to the hospital," Pedro called.

The others followed, although Chloe stopped, peering at the stream leading away from the waterfall. She pointed, and I followed her line of sight to the body of a beheaded deer lying partially in the stream.

We approached it, and I noticed long, slicing marks covering its neck's stump.

Pedro stopped and stood over the dead animal. He cursed, then rubbed the back of his neck.

"What makes these kinds of marks?" I asked. "A jaguar?"

"Their claws would make smaller markings. This was something else."

"Like what?" I asked.

He gave me a pointed stare, as if to warn me from asking too much. "The creature," he said matter-of-factly.

"You think the creature did this?" Chloe asked.

"I know it did," he answered. "But this was a day ago at least, which means, with any luck, the creature is far away. We should go while we can."

Pedro turned to leave the clearing, but I stood staring at the deer's corpse. Something had done this, and disbelieving Pedro's story of a creature was getting harder to do. Not that I doubted him, but there was always a part of me that wanted to cling to the rational way of thinking—that monsters didn't exist, that we could easily explain everything that happened in our world with tidy scientific principles. But what would explain the claw marks?

If there was such a creature in the jungle, what did that mean for Amaya? If she happened to escape the Emmersons, would she be escaping to somewhere more dangerous? But I couldn't let my mind wander to such a place. Not yet. I would find her and bring her home. That was the only future I was willing to accept.

We moved through the jungle with vines tugging at our clothes, and mud caking our shoes. Squawks and caws surrounded us, and I was sure I had never visited such a vibrant, living place. Trees with roots exposed grew above the bogs, and bright orange flowers gave spots of color to the dense greenery.

Pedro led us to a gravel path partially covered in vines.

"This road will lead you to the old hospital." He pointed down the road. "You'll find it that way. I cannot continue with you."

"We understand," Chloe said.

Pedro turned and left the way we'd come, leaving us alone on the path. We continued down the road without speaking. My mind replayed the image of the dead deer, and I couldn't shake the feeling that something was out there waiting to ambush us.

Anxiety quickened my heartbeats. What would we find when we reached the hospital? Pedro's family had never been able to enter, and the man's father had nearly been killed.

Sunlight dappled the road in front of us, although as we hiked, dark clouds obscured the sky. Wind gusted, bringing the scent of rain. The air turned still, which seemed unnaturally silent in a place with so much life. Chills prickled the back of my neck, and I found myself glancing behind to make sure we weren't being followed.

"Up there." Sally pointed. I followed her line of sight to a gap in the trees. A white structure peeked from the foliage. Excitement raced through my blood. Could Amaya really be so close?

"Move quietly," I said, and we crept toward the structure. As we moved closer, it was hard to tell much about the place. Vines covered most of the building. The hospital was shorter than I expected, as if it were a bunker built half underground, with only a few barred windows peeking from the main floor.

"It looks abandoned," Chloe whispered beside me.

"We should still be careful," I said.

Chloe and Sally followed in a single file line behind me. The sky darkened, and a few drops of rain pelted my skin. The air held a damp chill that hadn't been there before. When we got closer to the structure, I noticed thin, long windows covered in thick layers of grime.

The bushes and grass had been trampled to form a path, and we followed it. White paint peeled from thick concrete walls. Cracks ran along the cement in places. What must have once been a parking lot was now mostly covered in grass, the asphalt broken and nearly unrecognizable.

A deep chill burrowed under my skin as we paced the perimeter of the abandoned hospital. Imagining Amaya trapped in this place was enough to make my blood freeze. She didn't deserve to see life the way I had seen it. I'd been imprisoned on more than one occasion. Some facilities were worse than others. This looked like one of the worst.

I took a deep breath to push away the unbidden images of torture and human experiments.

If anyone had harmed Amaya, they would pay. And then some.

We approached a doorway set deep inside a concrete wall. Green paint peeled from the door's surface. I grabbed the latch and tugged. Rusty hinges squealed, the sound echoing through the forest.

A dark hallway loomed. The scent of antiseptic wafted from the empty corridor. The astringency of the smell meant the place hadn't been abandoned long.

"Anyone else feel super creeped out right now?" Chole asked.

"I'm used to places like this," Sally said with a shrug.

I gave her a sidelong glance. "How much do you know about this place? Honestly."

"Honestly?" She raised an eyebrow. "Absolutely nothing. But I can tell you this, the fact that we weren't attacked yet means something."

"Like what?" I asked.

A spark of apprehension flashed in her eyes. "I'm not sure yet."

I didn't press her, but I knew she wasn't telling us everything.

No one else spoke as we stepped into the hall. We entered the empty shell of the hospital. Our footsteps echoed over scuffed linoleum floors. Light bulbs coated in dust shone weakly, too interspersed to give much light.

A few bulletin boards were tacked to the cinder block walls, but the pages hanging from them had curled from the humidity, making them impossible to read. I felt as if I had stepped back in time two decades. The air smelled musty, the floors coated in grime, although the middle of the corridor gleamed in places, as if someone had walked through recently.

"There's no one here." Chloe's gaze wandering from one open doorway to another.

"They found out we were coming," I suggested. "They left before we could find them."

Sally brushed a hand through the graying strands of her hair. "If that's the case, then where did they go?"

"Good question." Chloe's eyes darted. "And how long ago did they leave?"

"Maybe we can find some clues," I said. "If they left in a rush, they must have left information behind."

"Then we need to find out everything we can." Sally spoke with an authoritative tone. "Just be careful. It wouldn't surprise me if they left this place booby trapped. Our best chance of discovering anything useful is to split up. You two take the corridor to the right. I'll keep to this hallway. We'll regroup here in half an hour."

I almost argued with her suggestion, but I bit my tongue and nodded, and we split up. I was secretly grateful to be separated from Sally. Being in her presence was torture. All I could think about was the way she'd betrayed me. Sure, she claimed to have been manipulated by Dr. Warren, but that didn't make her completely innocent. Plus, the woman should have been sitting in a prison cell, not exploring through the Yucatán. If she meant to betray us by going off on her own, then I was ready for it.

Chloe and I paced to the next room, this one with a metal bed bolted to the center of the floor. Chains hung from the four corners of the frame.

"What's this?" Chloe asked. She paced to the bed and lifted a chain, the links clinking as she held it up for inspection. "They had their patients chained to the beds?"

I stood next to her and examined the metal shackle, but I couldn't look at it for long. My stomach welled with revulsion, and all I could picture was Amaya shackled to this very bed. My nightmares had become reality. My worst fears—of Amaya being imprisoned and tortured—were true.

My nails lengthened until they became claws and punctured the flesh of my palms. Warm blood pooled in my clenched hands, and its sharp scent overpowered the odor of rubbing alcohol.

"Lucian." Chloe's voice called to me, breaking me from the trance.

I looked up and focused on her.

"Lucian, it's okay." She spoke softly, the way Amaya would have done, and the monster in me retreated. I couldn't let it control me. I had to keep fighting it until the time was right—until it was time to take my vengeance.

"Let's keep looking," she said. "We might be able to find out where they went."

I nodded, unable to speak past the lump in my throat, and followed her out of the room. We walked from one hallway to the next until the passages seemed to blur together.

"What's this?" Chloe asked as I followed her inside a space. Vials lined the shelves. Rows of dead animals encased in glass filled the tabletops. I stepped to the shelves, looking at some of the containers, where the deep crimson color glinted in the dim light.

Chloe ran her hand over a piece of paper discarded on one of the tables.

"Look at this," she said.

I walked to her and glanced at the paper. A map was printed on the page. The facility sat at the center of the inked drawing, and a path went from it, past a waterfall, and to a collection of ruins.

The ruins were circled in red.

Chloe tapped the circle. "How much do you want to bet that's where they're headed?"

I nodded. "There's a good chance that's where we'll find them."

Chloe grabbed the map, folded it, and placed it in her pocket. We left the room, and I didn't find it necessary to glance back inside. It reminded me too much of my father's dungeon beneath Castle Bran, too much of the torture and experiments that had left me the way I was.

We continued walking until we met back at the front doorway. Sally was already waiting for us.

"Find anything?" she asked, one eyebrow arching.

"Yes." Chloe pulled the map from her pocket and showed it to her.

"Hmm." Sally bit her bottom lip. "Awfully convenient you found it so easily."

"What do you mean?" Chloe asked.

She shrugged. "Maybe it's nothing, but they could be leading us into a trap."

"A trap?" Chloe asked. "That seems a little over the top."

"I agree with Sally," I chimed in. "For once."

She gave me a snide glare and crossed her arms.

"If anything, we'll have to approach the ruins carefully," I said. "We have no idea what we'll find out there."

"If we find anything at all," Chloe added.

"Maybe," I said. "But it's still worth checking out. What did you find?" I nodded toward the hallway where Sally had come from.

"A broken glass chamber," Sally said. "I fear this isn't good news."

"Why?" Chloe asked.

"Because." She shifted her gaze, her eyes not meeting mine. "They kept the girl, Sasha, in a chamber like that one. If the girl escaped, then we're in more danger than we can imagine."

"Why?" I demanded, standing with squared shoulders to face her. She'd been reluctant to answer our questions, but now, as we were about to face the true evil of this place, we needed answers. "Sally, tell us why she's so dangerous."

She paused before answering, as if she were debating what to say. "Sasha is unlike any other human on our planet. Her genetics give her more than just special abilities. Her powers are so unbelievably strong, no one can control her, which is why her parents locked her up at first, until she learned to get free. Then, they put her under heavy sedation, but even that couldn't stop her, and she broke free from that, too. They finally locked her inside a glass container filled with a concoction of enzymes that kept her unconscious and unable to use her abilities. She had been in that container for years."

"Her parents." I rubbed my forehead, the implication almost too much to comprehend. "Her mother is Yasira, making her..."

"Yes," Sally finished for me. "Our granddaughter. She has your powers flowing through her veins, plus a cocktail of others derived from manipulated DNA."

My head spun. My nightmares had become reality. After what happened with Barb, I'd been so careful to never marry after that—and those women who I allowed near me never got close. I never wanted any children for this very reason, yet Sally and Dr. Warren had stolen my DNA and created a person so powerful no one could control her. What must it be like to be a child with unlimited powers? To have no training and little inhibitions, she could do whatever she pleased without consequence, and with parents like hers, she never had a chance. For a time, they must have encouraged the use of her powers, until it was too late, and they had no choice but to imprison her inside a cage of glass.

"Dr. Warren and I may have had a hand in her creation," Sally said. "Indirectly, of course."

"What do you mean?" Chloe asked with suspicion in her voice.

"Victor Warren had an interest in researching the potential reality of myths and legends, just as Lucian's father. His plan was to create a child with amazing powers, so he used Lucian's DNA to create our child, Yasira."

"But Yasira didn't have any of the abilities," I said. "Which made him believe he had failed."

She nodded. "Yasira's powers may have been dormant, but

her daughter's powers weren't, and that's something Victor never found out."

"How is that possible?" Chloe asked.

"When he found out Yasira had no powers, he cast us both away, leaving me to raise the child on my own. I admit I wasn't a perfect parent. Not even a decent one. I was too distant. At times, when I was lucid enough to care for Yasira, I would take her on extravagant vacations all over the world, give her everything she wanted. But those moments were rare, and she spent most of her time starving in our Brooklyn apartment, or more likely, out on the streets. She learned to be tough and to survive.

"By the time she was sixteen, she found her own way. She left me and never spoke to me again. Then she met Umber."

The hallway became so quiet, I could have heard the whispering of the ghosts of this place.

"I was only able to keep up with her in passing," Sally continued. "I knew they had a child, but I didn't learn much more about the offspring until Victor Warren went to prison and I was freed from the drugs he'd given me. I tried reconnecting with my daughter, only to learn that my granddaughter had become the creature Dr. Warren had envisioned."

She paused. Her gaze went down the hallway, to the door leading outside. "That. And so much more..."

My heart hurt for Yasira—my daughter—who had been raised in such loathsome circumstances. I had suspected Sally was unfit to bring up a child, but now having those fears confirmed left a hole at the bottom of my heart.

Guilt weighed on me. I vowed that if I ever had another opportunity to raise children, I would do more than just be there for them. I would be a mentor and an advocate—someone my own father had never been. Maybe I'd been wronged in the past, but that didn't determine how I chose to live my future. I would make up for all the past wrongs done to me, and if she would have me, I would do it with Amaya at my side.

30

An image of Ixchel, Mayan goddess of storms and lightning. She was also the protector of women and motherhood.

AMAYA

Night fell, and after sleeping all day, Flora finally stirred. The pyramid walls seemed to squeeze us. I had built a small fire to give us light, and the smoke drifted up through cracks in the stones. The air smelled of damp earth mixed with woodsmoke, and as I sat with my knees hugged to my chest, I wondered at the magic of such a place. How long had it been since a human presence had been here?

"Water..." Flora whispered through dry, cracked lips, and I grabbed the plastic bottle.

"Here." I lifted the water bottle to her lips. She took a few sips and nodded. Then, she raised to a sitting position and rested her head against the wall. As I screwed the cap on the bottle, her cat's eyes darted around the room. Her cheeks were sunken, and her skin pale. She looked more like a corpse than a living being.

"How do you feel?"

"Tired," she answered. "So tired. Weary straight to my bones. I'm an old woman, Amaya. Eighty years old come next January. Can you imagine that?"

"But you've made it this far," I encouraged her.

"Yes." She closed her eyes. "Yes, we've made it here."

"Tell me about the ruins," I asked, hoping to keep her talking. I feared if she went to sleep again, she might not wake up. "How did you know they were here?"

"The maps, of course," she answered.

"What maps?"

"The maps the Emmersons collected. When I had spare time in the hospital, I studied the maps. *Someday*, I told myself, *When I escape, I'll need to know my way through the forest.*

"The Emmersons wanted to make sure their location was remote," Flora continued. "So they collected every map they could, drawing circles around all nearby villages, even those not listed on traditional charts. They didn't find many. But they did find the ruins, and they marked them. This was the largest site they found."

I tapped my fingers on my chin, pondering her statement. "Flora, are you saying the Emmersons know where these ruins are?"

She nodded. Her eyes were still closed. "Yes, of course they know. They mapped the whole jungle."

"Then if that's the case, don't you think they might come here to find us?"

"No," she said with a chiding tone. "We're safe here."

I wasn't comfortable with her answer. "But they know exactly where this pyramid is—and they know it's a good place to hide, which means they'll likely realize we've come here."

She waved her hand dismissively. "*Cállate*," she hushed me. "You're overthinking this. We're safe here, and besides that, I couldn't go anywhere else if I wanted. Let an old woman rest."

I sighed in defeat, anxiety quickening my heartbeat, then I

left Flora behind and ventured out of the pyramid. Moonlight revealed tall stone structures covered in vines. A chill bit at my skin, and I rubbed my hands over my arms for warmth. Where was Blaise? He needed to know that we were still in danger here, and that Flora had unwittingly led us to the one place that the Emmersons might search first.

I couldn't understand why Flora thought we would be safe here, but after being held prisoner for so long, I doubted she was able to use sound judgment after so much torment and abuse.

I searched the area for Blaise, but found no signs of human life among the mounds of stones surrounded by trees. The air carried the scent of damp earth, and I breathed it in, thankful to be out of the stuffy confines of the pyramid. I walked to one of the pyramids and peeked around the corner, but I saw only a dark jungle.

I debated on calling Blaise's name, but I decided against it. The sound might carry. But where had he gone? And why hadn't he returned yet? He said his family lived not far away. Perhaps he thought we would slow him down, so he'd left us behind to return to them?

I breathed an exasperated sigh. Like Flora, Blaise was infuriating to deal with. But perhaps I didn't need him. I could wait for Flora's strength to return, and we could make it out of the jungle together. Hadn't Blaise mentioned something about a river leading straight to his home? If I could find the river, then maybe I could follow it and make it out of the forest.

Flora would have to recover before I could go anywhere. Until then, I was stuck here.

Walking around the pyramids, I ran my fingers over the bumpy stones. My fingertips brushed over carvings. In the light of the moon, I pulled away some of the vines and tried inspecting the carvings, but the dim lighting made it impossible to see anything.

I crouched by a pyramid and placed my hand flat against the stonework. A tingle of electricity flowed into my hand, and

Flora's words came back to me. She'd spoken of the goddess Ixchel. I had to admit, there was something about the goddess that felt eerily familiar. I felt it when storms approached, as if I could somehow control the tides of electricity, the wind currents, and the surge of rainwater. The storms filled me with energy and power, and I felt as if I could reach up, touch the clouds, and take a bit of their essence into me.

I shook my head and moved my hand from the stone. Silly thoughts to have at a time like this. But still, did those feelings connect me to the goddess? If so, then how had it happened?

Perhaps the Emmersons' injections had something to do with it.

The bushes rustled, and I spun around to face a tall, shadowy figure walking toward me.

"Blaise," I whispered. "Is that you?"

"It's me," he answered, coming closer so I could see his form in the moonlight.

"Where were you?" I asked. "You've been gone all day."

His eyes darkened. "I don't have time to explain now."

"Why?"

He didn't answer.

"Fine." I said, my frustration building. "But while you've been doing who-knows-what out there, Flora told me the Emmersons know exactly where these ruins are—and since this is the best place to hide, I have no doubt the Emmersons realize it, too. I'll bet they're on their way here to find us."

"If that's true, it's not good." His eyes darkened. "This morning, I spotted Sasha and Yasira near the waterfall where we were last hiding. They're tracking us, but it's slow going." He glanced out into the forest before speaking again, and his voice dropped. "Something's off with Yasira."

I raised an eyebrow. "Off how?"

His dark hair reflected in the moonlight, making the strands look blue. "There's something wrong with her. I don't know how to explain it, but it's almost like her mind is being controlled by her daughter."

"Controlled?"

"Yes. I'm not sure how Sasha is doing it. I tried to lead them off our trail. It's working for now, but they'll find us eventually."

I narrowed my eyes at him. "How is it you've been able to track them all this time without detection?"

"Amaya." His eyes darkened. "I told you—I don't have time to explain."

"Then don't explain. Let me take a wild guess. You've been transforming into a wolf, haven't you?" Saying the words out loud sounded more than a little absurd, although it made sense, too. If he could transform into a wolf, then could he help me discover how to use my own powers?

"It's not that simple. If the Emmersons realize we're hiding here, they'll come for us. They could track us down in an hour. Maybe less."

"Then we'll have to make a run for it. Can we make it to your family's home before they find us? It's only five miles, right?"

"Yes, but as you said, five miles trekking through this jungle would take days."

I crossed my arms, my heart pounding at the thought of the Emmersons confronting us. Glancing up at the sky, a few wispy clouds blocked some of the stars. The gusty wind battered strands of dark hair across my face. A tingle crept across the back of my neck. This place called to me as if I had been here before. In another lifetime, perhaps?

Great. Now I was believing in former lives as well as vampires and werewolves. Still, there was something about this place, and especially these ruins that felt so intimately familiar. Taking a deep breath, I squared my shoulders. Being able to rest all day, plus the intensity of power in this area, meant my fire ability had recharged.

I snapped my fingers, and a fireball ignited in each hand.

Pressing my palms together, I willed the fire to coalesce until the form of wings took shape in the flames.

Blaise's eyes widened. "What are you doing?"

"Testing a theory." I moved my fingers, and the wings fluttered. "Blaise, all we've been doing is running from the Emmersons. But maybe it's time we quit hiding. It's time for us to stop them. If we can't run from them, we can fight them instead."

He nodded, and the firelight reflected in his dark eyes. "Yes, maybe you're right. Although..." his words trailed off, and he glanced toward the forest. "Sasha is more powerful than either of us. I respect your idea, but how will we defeat her?"

"I don't know." I extinguished the flames. Darkness replaced the light, and I had trouble seeing Blaise against the inky backdrop of the forest. "We'll have to prepare for them."

"I can set traps around the perimeter," Blaise said. "They'll be crude, and all they'll do is give us warning that they're approaching and buy us a few seconds of time. If you hear the bushes rustling, you'll know they're here."

I nodded. My gaze wandered up to the tallest pyramid. "We'll be able to see them coming from there. I can take watch from the top of the pyramid."

"Fine. Just be careful. That pyramid is hundreds of years old, and many of the stones are loose."

"I will," I answered.

"I'll try to meet you up there once I set the traps. But I may not have time. I'll use vines to string the branches together on the perimeter and create a trip wire."

I nodded, and we went our separate ways. My stolen combat boots trod over dew-covered grass as I crossed back to the pyramids. When I reached the tallest one, I stood at the base and stared up at the enormous structure, which blocked out half the sky. The pyramid-shaped formation was superimposed over a backdrop of stars. An owl hooted far in the distance, and night insects chirped as I stood looking up.

What if I was wrong in asking Blaise to stand up to the

Emmersons? If we failed at this, we went back to the prison we'd come from—or we died. I wasn't sure which fate was worse. But if we managed to defeat them, did that mean I got to go back to the only home I'd ever known?

My heart ached with a pain worse than any physical discomfort. I missed Lucian more than I could possibly comprehend. Would I be with him again? Where was he? Maybe he'd given up looking for me. Maybe he'd even moved on by now.

But thinking such things felt as if I were betraying him.

I pushed the thoughts from my mind as best as I could, then grabbed the pyramid's stones, found some handholds, and started climbing. My fingertips throbbed by the time I reached halfway. As I caught my breath, sweat ran down my forehead and stung my eyes.

Loose stones clattered to the ground as I started climbing again, the sound ricocheting around the clearing. The noise was barely louder than a quiet conversation, but to me, it seemed more deafening than gunfire, and I cringed at the sound. My heart raced, and I held to the rocks with a death grip, waiting for the echo to die away. Finally, when my heart slowed and my breathing evened out, I climbed an inch higher, then another. Palms slick with sweat, I did my best to not to slip, and grabbed the vines to keep from falling. Several times I slid, and by the time I reached the top, blisters rubbed my fingers raw.

I scooted to the center of the pyramid's top and got a good look at my surroundings. The moonlight leant a little light to the world. Dark forest spread out around us, and I felt as if we were being swallowed by the jungle. As I sat, I tucked my legs to my chest and hugged my arms around my knees.

Sitting here, with the sky so close above, and the sunlight beginning to lighten the horizon, I didn't feel so far from home. I breathed the fresh air, thankful to be free from the confines of the Emmerson's cage.

Since escaping, I'd hardly had time to sit and ponder my situation. But when I really thought about it, it was a miracle that not only I was alive, but Blaise and Flora were as well.

We'd survived the Emmersons once, and we would do it again.

However, remembering the girl floating inside the glass chamber sent a shiver down my spine. There was something so completely unnatural about her. How dangerous must she be if she had to be kept constantly sedated?

Something rustled down below. A shadowy shape on all fours darted between the trees, then disappeared. I sat up taller. The trees on the edge of the clearing shook, and the bushes rustled.

I tensed. My heartbeat quickened. Two forms emerged from the tree line—one tall and thin, and the other much shorter. The young girl's white dress stood out in the somber grays of the false light of the early morning.

It had to be Yasira Emmerson and her daughter Sasha. The mother, Yasira, walked haltingly behind the girl, one foot dragging behind the other, as if she'd been injured. The girl walked with purpose, heading straight for the pyramid where I sat. Her chalky white complexion, stringy dark hair, and expressionless face sent a shiver down my spine. My skin rippled with goosebumps.

I clasped my hands where warmth emanated in my palms. I wouldn't call the fire to life yet, not until they were closer. My hands shook, and a clammy sweat beaded on my skin. Something about the way the girl moved seemed so unnatural, almost as if she floated over the ground like a ghost. She reminded me so much of Sally Anderson—the person I once believed had been a ghost roaming the halls of Crimson Hollow.

The two people stopped walking.

"Blaise," the girl called, her voice eerily childlike. "Come. It's time to go home."

Yasira stepped forward and placed her hand on her daughter's shoulder. I couldn't make sense of the gesture. The woman moved with such jerky, uncoordinated efforts—as if she were being controlled like a puppet.

"We're waiting for you," the girl continued.

A black blur ripped from the forest. It charged the two women, its mouth gaping to reveal rows of serrated teeth.

The animal stopped mid-stride, hanging in the air as if it had hit a wall.

"There you are," the girl said with a giggle. She paced toward the animal, her mother following. "I knew you were here some-where. Now, just show us where the others are, and then we can all go home."

She stood in front of the beast. In the dim lighting, I couldn't get a good look at the creature. It seemed to suck the light from the air around it, and all I could make out was a massive spot of blackness with four legs.

It struck me that this was no wolf.

This was some creature of darkness, something more than a terrestrial being, something born from nightmares. Even so, it had no power compared to the girl. What had she done to him to keep him completely motionless?

The girl paced slowly around the wolf as it hung half-suspended in the air. "Where are Flora and Amaya?" she demanded.

A deep growl rumbled from the creature's chest. Claws lengthened from the area that might have been his front paws, although the monster was shapeless, a blot of inky darkness. Tendrils of wispy smoke curled from the beast's body.

I could hardly comprehend that this *thing* was Blaise. How long had he been this way? Was this the aftereffects of the Emmerson's genetic testing? Or had he always been like this? More likely, he'd started as a wolf, and the Emmersons had warped him.

But now, those questions seemed insignificant as the girl continued her pacing. Her mother stood to the side, unmoving, her gaze vacant, as if she were in a trance. What kind of demented family was this?

"Blaise, you're making me mad," the girl said, placing her hands on her hips. "Where are they? You're hiding them from us, and that's very bad. They need to come home."

The girl stopped walking and stood to face the beast. Beady red eyes focused on the girl, although there were no details to the creature's face other than its eyes.

Sasha reached out and touched what should have been the beast's muzzle. A gargled scream—half-human, half-something demonic—ripped from the creature's throat. The girl flexed her fingers to form a claw shape.

The creature writhed, and the darkness retreated. A humanoid form replaced the dark form. Blaise fell screaming to the ground. Blood streamed from his nose. He gripped clumps of grass as he lay face down. He breathed so heavily, I could hear it from here, and his clothes and hair were drenched in sweat.

The girl lowered her hand, and Blaise laid motionless on the ground.

My heart got caught in my throat. What was she doing to him?

Sasha bent and patted Blaise's cheek. "Take a nap. I'm going to look for your friends. Mommy." She turned to the woman standing behind her. "Go look that way. I'll go this way. Look everywhere. I think he hid them in a tunnel."

My skin crawled with revulsion. Clearly the girl had complete power over her mother, and I had no idea how she'd sedated Blaise, which meant that challenging her would be nearly impossible. Now I could see why the Emmersons had kept the girl locked away. What chance did I have alone against her?

The only choice I had was to attack her before she noticed me. If I could create a fireball powerful enough, I could knock the girl off her feet for a few minutes, just long enough to escape.

But how would I rescue Blaise *and* Flora?

For now, Flora was still safe, and if I could wake Blaise, then perhaps he would be able to escape with me and we could return for Flora later. It was a risky plan, but I had to try something.

Clenching my fists, I called on every bit of strength inside me. Energy drained from my heart, through my blood, and pooled into my fisted hands. Warmth tingled through my fingers until twin fireballs flared to life, lighting the world around me in a dazzling array of light.

The girl looked up, but I didn't allow her a moment to react. With a thrust of my hands, I shot both fireballs straight down at the girl, hitting her square in the chest.

Sasha screamed and fell back, hitting the ground, her gown ignited. I didn't waste time as I scrambled down the side of the pyramid. Time seemed to slow, and I couldn't move fast enough as I half-slid, half-fell down the pyramid's steep outer wall.

By the time I hit the ground, my hands and backs of my thighs were cut and bleeding, although adrenaline masked the pain. I raced for Blaise, who managed to look up as I reached him. He crawled to a sitting position.

With Sasha distracted by the fire, perhaps she'd lost her hold on Blaise. I reached for him, and he took my hand.

"Can you run?" I asked as he got to his feet.

He gave a single nod, and we darted for the forest, Sasha's screams echoing with an eerie childlike wail behind us.

31

Xolotl was commonly depicted as a wolf-headed man and was a soul guide for the dead. He was also a god of monsters, misfortune, and sickness. He is the dark personification of Venus, the evening star.

LUCIAN

We walked through the forest in the gray light of early morning. After spending the night in the old hospital, I was sure I hadn't gotten more than a few hours of sleep. The place reeked of chemicals, and all I could see when I closed my eyes was Amaya strapped to one of the metal tables, ropes cutting into her flesh, her face twisted in pain. The image was enough to drive me mad.

I'd been to some horrific places in my lifetime, but that one would be impossible to forget. It had imprinted on my mind, and I would never be able to shake the fear and agony I'd sensed in that place, as if the spirits of the hospital were begging me to set them free.

When I'd woken, I had a stiff neck and a pounding headache, and I hadn't hesitated to wake everyone else. Even if it was still half dark outside, I had to be free of that place. Fog curled along our path, its tendrils reaching out like claws to catch us. I couldn't shake the feeling that something was horribly wrong with Amaya. What had happened to her? What had caused the Emmersons to move their operation, if that was indeed what had happened? And what about the girl locked inside the glass chamber? Sally thought the girl was dangerous, but I couldn't understand how, and Sally refused to say any more about it.

Sally trailed me and Chloe. Her gaze seemed to peer at nothing in particular, and her red lipstick looked garish against the soft grays of the early morning light illuminating the jungle. I'd done nothing but regretted having her here with us, but what if I were wrong in judging her so harshly? Was it possible she really meant to help and didn't have any ulterior motives?

I shook my head and continued down the path. Perhaps one day I would find it in my heart to forgive her, but that day wasn't now. Was it vain for me to wish that she really had changed? Or was I wasting my time hoping for such a foolish thing? Either way, she had yet to prove she meant to help me.

The path grew more treacherous, with barely enough space for one person to pass. Barbed vines and briars caught our clothes and scratched our skin. Mosquitos buzzed, and I swatted them away as best as I could. Chloe and Sally lagged, and I found myself wanting to go faster, though I had to wait for the other two to catch up.

By mid-morning, we reached a small clearing filled with boulders. The noises of the jungle—birds cawing and insects softly humming—filled the air. Chloe suggested we rest and eat a quick breakfast, so we got situated on the boulders.

Chloe passed out granola bars and bottles of water. We sat and ate, although the food tasted bland to me. I stared out into the forest, wondering how close we were to Amaya—wondering if she were even out there.

If she was still alive, then I still had hope.

After finishing the food, we stood and took the footpath through the forest. Chloe held the map and directed us, and I did my best to concentrate on putting one foot in front of the other, to pace myself and stay with the group.

"Stop," Chloe whispered behind me, and I cast a glance over my shoulder to look at the girl.

"Why?" I whispered as our group paused in walking.

"Listen," she said.

The cacophony of the forest created a dizzying array of sounds around us. What did Chloe hear that I didn't? There were thousands of sounds surrounding us. But as I stood still and paid attention to individual noises, the wail of a crying child carried through the trees from a faraway distance.

"Do you hear that?" Chloe asked, speaking softly.

I nodded.

"Hear what?" Sally asked quietly.

"A child's voice," Chloe answered. "I think she's crying."

"Yes, you're right," Sally said, her eyes widening with fear. "It's her. It's Sasha."

"What do we do?" Chloe asked.

Sally shook her head. "I don't know, but if we confront her, she'll kill us. After the things her mother told her about me, she hates me. She wants me dead. We should turn around now."

"Turn around?" I questioned. "No. We've come too far."

"But you don't understand how dangerous she is!" Sally pleaded.

"Yes, I do," I answered. "Which is precisely why we'll keep going. If that girl is hurting Amaya, then she has to be stopped."

I turned and marched down the path. The others followed. How could Sally suggest turning around? We had come too far, and I was too close to Amaya to even think of going back.

Something dark shadowed the way ahead, and I stopped abruptly, my heart skipping a beat. A chill went down my spine as I stared into the face of a child, although her eyes were anything but innocent, and belonged to something demonic. Blood stained her skin, and blackened patches darkened her cheeks and forehead where chunks of flesh were missing, making her face look skeletal. Singed black hair hung in matted clumps down to her waist. Her dress may have been white at one point, but it was now stained with soot.

She reminded me of a discarded Victorian doll that had been abandoned and left to rot.

Behind her, three people were lying on the ground as if dead.

My heart stopped as I focused on the woman with dark hair fanning around her too-pale skin. That heart-shaped face and almond-brown eyes could belong to no one else but the person I'd traveled so far to find. Amaya.

Amaya! I wanted to scream, but I couldn't seem to do anything but stare in shock. Cold washed over me. How could this be happening? No. No! I refused to let her die. She wasn't dead; I knew it. I only had to get to her, and she would be fine.

I took a step forward, but the girl moved lightning-fast, her form blurring before she stood in front of me.

I could hardly stand to look at the demonic apparition taking the form of a child. Was there anything more disturbing than this? Worse, she was my own offspring. I could do nothing but stare into the cold, unfeeling eyes of my granddaughter.

"Not another step," the girl seethed, her small fists clenched at her sides. "I know who you are. Lucian." Her gaze moved to the woman standing a few paces behind me. "And Sally. My grandparents. Yes." Her gaze wandered back to me. "Mother told me all about you." Then she turned to Sally. "And more about you." She pointed an accusatory finger at the woman. "I'll kill you first. Or should I wait and let you watch as I kill the others? You deserve it. Mother told me what you did her. You deserve a fate worse than death."

Sally's face went so pale, I feared she would pass out. "No..." was all she managed.

Chloe stepped forward and faced the girl. "You won't be killing anyone. Your threats stop here."

"Ha!" The girl's laugh was childlike yet chilling, which seemed so unnatural coming from a creature like her. "Looks like you've got a lot to learn." She moved her arm and thrust her hand out. Chloe flew backward. Her body smacked the trunk of a tree. She groaned before falling in an unconscious heap on the ground, blood oozing from a gash in the back of her head.

Shock tore through me, as if I were the one who had been tossed into the tree. Before I could move toward Chloe, Sasha held up a hand and clenched her fist, and my body froze. I felt as if I'd been wrapped in tight cords. Drawing in a breath was painfully hard to do, and I could do nothing but stand still and look into the face of the demonic child—my own flesh and blood.

I'd imagined my death many times, but since learning I possessed powers similar to a mythical phoenix, of dying and being reborn, I'd assumed death would never be mine to claim.

But now, against a being so powerful and heartless as Sasha Emmerson, a cold dread pierced my heart. Unlike any other moment in my life, now, I knew my own death was imminent.

Amaya, if only we could've had one more moment together…

32

___

AMAYA

I lay frozen on the ground. Grass stuck to the blood drying on my face. My memories came as if from a dream, as I tried to recall how I'd gotten here. I remembered scrambling down the pyramid, then running with Blaise to escape Sasha, but what had happened after that?

We'd been struck by something. All I remembered was a searing pain that hit my back between my shoulder blades. It had hurt so bad, I felt as if every muscle in my body had cramped. The all-engulfing pain had been too much, and I had fallen unconscious after that.

Voices drifted to me from a distance, but I could hardly make sense of them. When the sounds faded, the pain subsided. Was I dying? A light surrounded me. Time drifted until it felt as if it no longer existed.

Mom was sitting beside me, holding my hand. With her other hand, she stroked my hair the way she used to do when I was a little girl. She hummed softly. Tears misted my eyes as a wave of memories engulfed me. Mom felt so close, with her soft fingers gently combing out the tangles in my hair. My hair had always been such a knotted mess, but Mom worked out each snag with gentle precision, until the strands fell in silky waves down my back, and I hardly remembered the tangles being there in the first place.

"You have to go back," Mom said, squeezing my hand, her voice soft and so familiar. "They need you."

Lying here with her, free of the torturous pain of living, the only thing I wanted to tell her was no, I didn't want to go back. I wanted to stay here with her forever and never leave. But something nagged me—it was a name planted deep in the back of my mind.

Lucian.

The name came to me as if from a vast distance, from across oceans and spanning through lifetimes. There was something about the name that meant something so important to me—but what?

"Open your eyes now," Mom said.

But I can't leave you. I wanted to speak the words, but somehow, being in this place, where time had no meaning, I knew she heard my thoughts all the same. Gripping her hand, I wanted to hold on for the rest of eternity.

Please, let me stay.

"I'll be here when you return."

With a great knot lodged in my throat, I released my hand from hers. The light faded. The pain started as a throbbing between my shoulder blades, then bloomed to all-out torture, as if I'd been stabbed through the back with an icepick.

I opened my eyes. Jungle surrounded me, and the damp scent of earth and lingering rain reminded me of everything that had happened up until now—running from the Emmersons, climbing the pyramid, watching as she'd attacked Blaise. We had nearly escaped, when she caught us.

Thunder rumbled in the distance, and Sasha's childlike voice came from a little way off. I focused to find her facing a group of people. My blurry eyes made it hard to tell much about them—a woman with glaring red lipstick who looked oddly familiar, a younger blond woman—Chloe? A tall man.

My heart leapt. Was I only imagining the man standing at the group's center to be Lucian? It was hard to tell, as his hood shaded his face, but he'd always preferred being in the shadows.

Yes, it's Lucian. It has to be!

I wasn't dreaming. It was him. He had found me.

I wanted to call his name, but my throat was raw and hoarse, and I barely managed to lift my head. Someone else lay nearby. Blood streaked his face and matted to his dark hair falling in clumps across his forehead.

Blaise! Was he alive?

I managed to crawl to him. He tilted his face and focused on me. His lips were cracked, and his normally tan face was the color of ash.

"A—Amaya," he managed. "We have to stop her."

I glanced up at the girl who was pacing in front of the group. Lucian stood in front of her. He was so close! I wanted so much to run to Lucian and fall into his arms, but if I did, Sasha would know I was alive. If she got another chance to attack me, I had no doubt she would kill me this time.

Plus, the blonde girl standing beside him had to be Chloe— my only true friend I'd had since arriving at Crimson Hollow. I wanted to rush to her and thank her for coming to find me, but Sasha paced in front of the group, blocking my way.

"Blaise, how do we stop Sasha?" I asked.

"Kill her," he answered. "There's no other way. She must die, or she'll kill everyone in her path. She's powerful, but not invincible. Get her... when she doesn't suspect."

I patted his shoulder. "Will you be okay?" It was a lame question, but what else could I say? What could I possibly do for him out here in the jungle, away from civilization or any kind of medical facility?

"I'm fine, Amaya." He glanced away. "Just stop her. That's all I want."

I only nodded, then focused on the girl.

She had to die. I knew it, yet going through with such a heinous act left me with an unsettled feeling deep inside. To protect my friends, I would do whatever it took. But could I really destroy a child?

Then again, Sasha Emmerson was hardly innocent. If I didn't stop her, and she killed Chloe and Lucian—and I would never be able to live with myself.

With a deep breath, I concentrated on the girl. Sasha still focused on the others, leaving me with the opportunity to attack her when she didn't expect it. I had already hit her with everything I had—and it had hardly done anything.

How could I stop her when my powers were nothing compared to hers?

The girl thrust out her hand and knocked Chloe back. Her body smacked the trunk of a tree, and she fell in a limp heap to the ground. Cold dread pulsed through my blood. I had to help Chloe! But how? The only way to help her was to stop Sasha— and do it before she attacked Lucian.

Now was my chance. Once she attacked them, she would turn to me, and then she would know I had survived. My window of opportunity was shrinking.

She thrust out her fist again and punched toward the two people still standing. A rush of deafening wind blasted from her clenched hand, knocking Lucian and the woman backward.

In a flash of light, someone rushed to Lucian's side. I blinked, hardly comprehending what I saw. Chloe sat at Lucian's side. Hadn't she been unconscious? Her body glowed, and my jaw fell open as the glow spread to encompass Lucian.

The brightness grew so blinding, I was forced to shield my eyes. Sasha fell back as two forms lifted off the ground. Wings fanned from Lucian's back, and a whirlwind of flames spiraled around Chloe.

A flicker of hope sparked as I watched Lucian and Chloe rise into the air. Chloe had hidden her talent for so long, but I'd always known she had the potential to be remarkable. And Lucian—he was the original, the phoenix come to life. If anyone could defeat Sasha, it was them.

Lucian dove toward the girl just as Chloe ignited a fireball in her hand. When Lucian hit Sasha's body, she fell screaming to the ground. Chloe used the opportunity to shoot a glowing orb at Sasha, which hit the girl's chest.

Twisting flames in colors of amber and blue exploded around the three. The intense heat singed my cheeks, although I was dozens of feet away. Ringing filled my ears. I found myself lying on my back, looking up at the sky, although I couldn't remember how I'd gotten there.

When I finally pushed onto my elbows, my head spun, and the overpowering scent of char wafted on the air currents. Screaming came from nearby, and I focused on the sound, to find Chloe and Lucian lying prone on the ground. Blood spilled from cuts on their faces and arms. Their eyes were open but unblinking.

My heart stopped, and I felt as if time had stopped too.

Sasha Emmerson hovered in the air several feet above them. Her dark hair fanned in an unseen breeze around her face, which was now completely restored and unburnt. Her white dress also floated ghostlike.

Fear hit me with the force of a tidal wave.

No! I wanted to scream.

I crawled to my hands and knees when thunder rumbled overhead. Behind me, a figure approached, and I spun around to see Flora limping to my side. Her cat's eyes were wide and feral. A maelstrom of storm clouds loomed behind her just beyond the treetops. Lightning flashed. I tasted its spark of energy on the wind. It raised the fine hairs on the back of my neck.

"Flora," I whispered, pleading. "What do I do? My friends— they're..." I couldn't say the word. Saying it out loud made it real, and I knew it couldn't be true. They were phoenixes. They would never die. Still, if I didn't stop Sasha, she would go on to kill again. She would never stop.

"Use your powers to their full ability." Flora said, her voice raspy, as she reached my side. "Do what you were made for."

"But how?"

She patted my shoulder, the fingers of her clawed hand bent and warped. "You know how. You always have."

I nodded, hoping, *praying*, she was right.

With a deep inhale, I turned to face Sasha, who was hovering toward me. Her eyes were lit with calculated intelligence and a spark of madness.

"I know you..." she spoke with a hardened edge. "Amaya. You came to see me when I was trapped. You didn't even try to set me free!"

Fear washed through me. With a calming breath, I released my pain, my hatred, my torment, and with it, I released my fear.

Sasha would have no control over me.

I raised both hands toward the storm, letting the electricity in the air come to me, as if I were a lightning rod. A spark danced over my knuckles, then trailed down my arms and into my heart.

Thrusting my hands out, I released the full brunt of the power into the girl gliding toward me. A blasting jolt of lightning shook the entire earth. Its boom encompassed the ground, hit the trees with the force of a hurricane. I flew backward and smacked into the ground hard, my teeth rattling inside my skull. Buzzing filled my ears as if a million bees had invaded my head.

The tang of bile mixed with blood swirled in my mouth.

Something red dripped into my eyes, and I wiped it away to find sticky blood smeared onto my fingertips.

This is it, I thought. I used all my power to stop her. *If I die now, I'll have succeeded.*

But had I stopped her?

I couldn't be sure. As I managed to crawl to a sitting position, I was stunned to find every tree and bush leveled, their roots sticking from the ground. Smoke curled from their stumps. Only the pyramids remained standing around us, as if beacons calling to the gods.

Had I done that?

My vision blurred as more blood dripped into my eyes. I did my best to wipe it away, then I pushed into a crouch, and finally managed to stand upright. The world spun around me, but as I took deep breaths, I managed to keep my balance and walk across the scarred, blackened area that had once been jungle.

I counted six people lying motionless on the ground. Among them, Lucian, and I couldn't go another minute without making sure he was alive.

"Lucian," I gasped as I knelt at his side, taking his cold hands in mine. "Can you hear me?" I rested my head on his chest and listened for the sound of his heartbeat.

Seconds stretched into minutes. The scent of spiced amber and dark forests reminded me of all the time we had spent together—the laughter and the smiles and the tears. He'd comforted me during difficult times, calmed me during my anguish.

"Amaya," he whispered, and the sound of his voice saying my name pushed me over the edge.

"Lucian," I gasped. "You're okay."

Tears flowed from my eyes, washing away the blood. Something had broken inside me when he was gone. Listening to the sound of his beating heart filled a chasm inside me—a bottomless pit of hopelessness that had nearly swallowed me whole.

"It's really you?" he asked.

"Yes," I managed between sobs. "Yes. It's me. How did you ever find me?"

He cupped my cheek. His hands, at first cold, were now beginning to warm. "I'll always find you, Amaya. Wherever they take you, wherever they hide you, I'll find you." He leaned forward and gently pressed a kiss to my forehead. "I'll find you no matter what."

I squeezed his hand so tightly, I worried I would break his fingers. But I never ever wanted to let him go, and as long as I lived, I never would.

Someone moved to stand nearby, and I looked up to see Chloe. She knelt beside us as Lucian sat up.

"Amaya," she said, and I let go of Lucian. "You're alive!"

"Yes." I hugged her, and she squeezed me back.

"I missed you so much," she said, her voice hitching. When she pulled away, she brushed the tears from her eyes. "What was that?" She pointed behind me, and I couldn't help but turn and look at the blackened landscape. The thorns and vines which had so violently ripped at me were now gone, and in their place, what would grow? Blaise got to his feet and limped to Flora, who he helped stand, and they walked toward us.

"The Emmersons were experimenting on me," I explained. "As well as several others." I pointed to Blaise and Flora. "Lucian, Chloe, meet Blaise and Flora."

They nodded at one another, although everyone's faces were pale and awestruck, as if we were in a dream and could hardly believe what was happening, as if we could snap our fingers and be back to our lives as they should have been before the Emmersons interfered.

Sasha's body lay in a broken heap, and as I got a good look at what remained of her, I knew I had killed her. The feeling came in a rush of bittersweet emotions. I had stopped a terrible evil from killing my friends and destroying countless others—but I had taken a life as well. It was a feeling I knew I would never be comfortable with, but one I would have to live with all the same.

Lucian threaded his fingers through mine. "What now?"

I turned to Blaise, who sat looking at us with an odd expression, almost as if he couldn't believe Lucian were a real, flesh and blood person.

"We can go back to my home." Blaise squared his shoulders. "I want to see my family. They need to know I'm okay."

"You're Blaise?" Chloe asked, arching an eyebrow. "The one who went missing?"

He nodded, and as their gazed connected, I detected a spark of attraction in the look. Should I mention to Chloe that Blaise was a shapeshifting wolf creature? But that didn't seem important now. Not in present company.

We stood and limped toward the forest, but not before stopping to stand over the body of the child who almost destroyed us all.

Her skin had already turned leathery, and her bones bleached and white, as if she had been dead for a decade and not merely a few minutes.

"What's happening to her?" Chloe asked. "Why does her body look that way?"

Flora knelt at the girl's side. "It's from all the years of being held in stasis inside the glass chamber. The enzyme the Emmersons used to sustain her life is now taking its toll on what remains of her body."

The woman with the red lipstick stepped forward, and as I finally got a good look at her, I knew her. She was the ghost who haunted Crimson Hollow, and who had attempted to kill Lucian. Sally Anderson.

"I never expected to have to live through the death of a grandchild." She knelt at the side of the girl's corpse. Lucian knelt with her, and his eyes filled with sadness—at a life lost, at the pain of experiencing death, of what could have been.

"I never knew her," Lucian said. "Never knew my daughter Yasira, either." He looked up. "Where is she?"

"Yasira?" I echoed. "I don't know."

"If she's alive, then we're still in danger," Flora said, her fears mirroring mine, although I couldn't ponder on it for too long, as our attention was directed back to the girl's body.

I watched in fascination as a tiny green vine sprouted from one of her empty eye sockets. Leaves unfurled, and more vines grew from her face, her shoulders and torso, legs and arms.

Flowers started as purple buds, then they too opened until they were in full bloom. The scent of life and lavender hung in the air, filling me with a calmness and peace I hadn't anticipated. Daisies and roses bloomed, along with a cluster of dandelions.

"What's happening?" Blaise asked.

A moth with lacy white wings flitted past and landed on one of the flowers. A gentle wind blew and tugged the spores from the dandelions. The white seedlings got caught on the wind and twirled through the air, dancing in an unheard symphony, yet one I felt deep in my heart all the same.

Shimmering white light came from the girl's body, like all the life that had been harbored there were now able to be set free. My skin tingled at the light's intensity, as if I had been electrified again. But this time, the feeling came not as overwhelming power, but of peace.

The light glowed around each of us, but it was the brightest over Lucian, Chloe, Blaise, and me.

"It can sense our powers," Chloe said, her voice filled with awe.

"Yes," Blaise answered. "I can feel it too."

I lifted my hand, and a seedling floated above my upturned palm. Its glow encompassed my fingers. My skin tingled with warmth. I caught my breath at the intensity of its power, as if I were holding a ball of electricity. But as the seedling settled on my palm, the intensity faded, and it felt as if the tiny sprout were absorbing all my energy, until dizziness clouded my vision.

The world wavered, and spots danced in my eyes. Around me, the others had fallen unconscious to the ground. I tossed the seed out of my hand, but it was too late.

The pod took all my powers. It was my last coherent thought before the world turned black.

33

LUCIAN

I sat at Amaya's bedside in the new facility. The wind blew a gentle breeze through the gauzy curtains. Cards and flowers took up the shelf space. For the past week, she'd been unconscious. The doctors didn't know what to do with her, and rather than letting her stay trapped in a hospital bed, I'd decided to bring her home.

The air brought the scents of fall, of leaves and a hint of winter. Amaya loved this time of year. I squeezed her hand and glanced at the clock.

They would be here soon.

So much had happened in the last week. After Sasha's death, I'd awoken to find my fire powers gone, and everyone else's powers had faded as well. The genetic mutations in our blood had disappeared, leaving us as average people.

My heart leapt at the joy of knowing I would one day be able to grow old and eventually die. Most people would never wish for such a thing, but it had been my only hope for the majority of my life. Now that it had happened, I didn't want to go on my journey alone.

Amaya, please wake up, I urged her silently, yet her eyes remained closed, her soft lashes motionless except for a twitch now and then.

Yes, I wanted to die eventually, but how could I do it without her?

Footsteps came from the hallway, and I sat up straight. A knock came at the door, then slowly swung open to reveal a group of people. Chloe, Blaise, Sally, and Officer Butler entered. But the person I had expected wasn't with them.

"How is she?" Chloe asked.

"The same," I answered.

She nodded.

"What else can we do for her?" Sally asked, sincerity in her voice, and although I hadn't found it in me yet to forgive her, she'd proven her heart was in the right place. She'd traveled with us to the Yucatán and back, she'd helped us find Amaya and the others, and she hadn't done any of it for nefarious or selfish reasons—at least, not that I could tell. Still, it was hard to trust a person who had nearly killed me, even if she did claim to be coerced by the likes of Dr. Victor Warren.

"I don't know," I answered. "I don't understand why we all woke up and she didn't."

"It could be because of her injections," Blaise suggested. "The Emmersons gave her their most potent formula."

Officer Butler rested his hand on my shoulder. "At least she's home."

Home. Yes. It was what Amaya always wanted. I glanced out the window, where the reds and golds of the leaves stretched toward the horizon, and far beyond, where the towers of Crimson Hollow peeked above the forest canopy.

Squeezing her hand again, I willed her to wake up when Chloe stood beside me. "Let us know if you need anything," she said.

I nodded, knowing Chloe could only offer what she was capable of giving. Blaise and Chole left the room, and after a few more words, Sally and the officer left as well, leaving me alone with Amaya.

She'd sacrificed everything to save me from Sasha, but how could I do the same for her? I would give her my life if I thought it would help her.

Another knock came at the door, and I almost told them to come back later when Sally peeked inside.

"You have a visitor," she said.

"Who?" I asked.

She opened the door wider to reveal Yasira Emmerson standing on the threshold. I almost bolted upright and demanded she leave. My blood boiled at the sight of her—the person who had stolen Amaya away from me.

"What is *she* doing here?" I thrust my finger at her. "Find Officer Butler. Arrest her!"

"Lucian," Sally said softly. "She's here to help."

Yasira's gaze didn't meet mine. Her dark hair was uncombed and reminded me of her daughter's. Her clothes were wrinkled, and shadows circled her eyes, as if she hadn't slept for days.

"Help her?" I demanded. "I don't want her anywhere near her!"

"Lucian, please," Yasira said, her voice verging on tears. "My husband and my daughter are dead. I plan to turn myself into the authorities as soon as I help Amaya. I—I know what I did was wrong. We never should have kidnapped Amaya, or anyone for that matter. We did it to save our daughter, but we never should have done what we did. I know offering my apologies isn't enough, which is why I brought this."

She held up a vial filled with glittering gold liquid. "This is the last of it," she said.

"The last of what?" I crossed my arms.

"The last of the serum Umber and I stole from your father's tomb."

My eyes widened. "What?"

"We visited Bran Castle five years ago, right after Sasha went into a medical coma. This vial was the only one left in your father's lab. It was a prototype to the one you found in his tomb. Inferior. But we managed to manipulate it to be more effective than the serum you found last year in your father's grave. With this, we were able to increase the virus's potency and fuse it with manipulated DNA to increase the powers of VS survivors, among other abilities."

My anger rose as I remembered the metal tables and chains. "You mean VS survivors like Amaya, who you kidnapped and tortured. Why am I bothering to even listen to you!" I wanted to throw her out of the room, yet the thought nagged me that maybe she could save Amaya, so she stayed. For now, at least.

"Yes, we used a version of this serum on Amaya. Our hope, of course, was that we would learn how to save Sasha." Tears misted Yasira's eyes, and she bit her lip and glanced away. "All I ever wanted was a child. I wanted to give her the childhood I never had. I would make sure she had everything she needed—a safe environment, a family who loved her, parents who wanted her, who were thrilled she existed." She sniffed, then her gaze lowered, and although she was a monster for what she had done to Amaya and the others, a drop of pity pinched me. *I* was this person's—Yasira's—father. She was my own flesh and blood. And Sally was her mother. A more twisted family had never existed, yet here we stood together in the same room, talking as if everything were perfectly normal.

"I did what I could to save my daughter," Yasira continued. "I should have stopped when Umber suggested turning the old hospital into a lab and using it for human experiments. But I had already gone so far, turning back seemed impossible."

She gripped the vial with white knuckles, and I feared she would break the delicate glass. "I'm a ruined person. I know I'm irredeemable. In trying to save Sasha, not only did we create a monster, but we took people against their will and turned them to monsters as well. I have no hope left." She held the vial out toward me. "But you can still have hope. When I go to prison, my only comfort will come in knowing you used this to save Amaya, and I hope… to start a family of your own. Please, accept this antidote. It can wake Amaya from her coma, and it will make her as she was before she ever contracted the virus. Also, it will make sure you never have children cursed to become like Sasha."

Emotions warred within me. Should I take the vial from her? What if this were a trick? But the tears glistening in her eyes were genuine.

"You'll have a chance to start the life you always wanted," Sally said quietly, and my eyes met hers.

The life I always wanted?

Yes. Sally knew what kind of life I wanted—one with a family in it, a family I could grow old with. For so long, I had been so angry at her for taking that from me.

"I'm going to prison, Lucian," Yasira said. "I've no doubt I'll be there for the rest of my life. If I get one last act of freedom, I want this to be it."

Outside, leaves bustled and dashed against the window. Afternoon sunlight peeked through the clouds and illuminated the vial sitting on Yasira Emmerson's hand. Could it really be so easy?

I had struggled through lifetimes of pain for this very thing sitting on Yasira's palm. All I had to do was reach out and take it. But I had one final test for Yasira. If she was as benevolent as she wanted me to believe, then she would need to prove it. Her and her mother would have to prove it to me.

"That's not the only reason you came here, is it?" I questioned.

She tilted her head.

"The money you inherited after Umber's death," I explained. "What did you intend to do with it? Were you giving it to your mother?"

I glanced at Sally, who's face remained expressionless.

"You say you're here to redeem yourself," I said. "Do it by

helping more than just Amaya. Promise me your funds will go to helping every single person who walks into the doors of this facility, and then our bargain will be complete."

Yasira closed her eyes and nodded. "You have my word."

I took a deep breath, glanced one more time at Amaya, and I took the vial.

34

AMAYA

I sat on my horse with my dog Khan trailing faithfully behind me, and Lucian riding beside me. He sat easily in the saddle, as if he'd ridden a hundred times before.

"You've had practice at this, haven't you?" I asked.

"I may have ridden a time or two." He winked. "Before cars were invented."

I laughed. It felt so good to laugh. As I stared out at the horizon, the sun was just rising above the hilltops, spreading yellow rays across the land, turning the autumn leaves to fiery gold. After waking from my coma, it had taken some time for me to regain my strength. Lucian had been at my side the whole time, and he had explained everything to me—how Yasira had produced the serum to restore my health, and how he'd bargained to get her approval for the funding for our new facility.

For once, it seemed everything would be okay. I'd spent so long in the Emmerson's facility, then fighting for my survival afterwards, that I'd forgotten what hope felt like. I breathed in the crisp air, letting it fill me with warmth.

We kicked our horses forward and took the trail toward the hilltop. Wildflowers grew along our path, their petals blowing gently in the breeze. I held the reins between my hands. It felt odd not to have the spark of energy usually coursing through my fingertips and waiting to be set free. At first, I had thought losing my powers would be difficult to deal with, but a week had gone by since I'd lost them, and I found myself being silently grateful they were gone.

Not only were my own powers gone, but since Sasha's death, everyone else's had faded as well, returning all the VS survivors to normal, as if we had never been infected. It was strange to think those powers wouldn't be part of me anymore, but maybe they'd never been truly mine to begin with.

"What are you thinking about?" Lucian asked me.

I shrugged. "Just thinking how weird it is not to have my abilities. Calling storms was pretty cool, you have to admit."

"Yes," he agreed. "But I, for one, am glad to be free of that curse."

"Chloe would agree," I added.

"Chloe—yes." He tilted his head. "I haven't seen her lately. Where is she?"

"You didn't know?" I asked.

"Know what?" he questioned with one eyebrow raised.

"After I woke up from my coma, she flew back to Santa Lucia. She's meeting Blaise. Wants to help him recover and reconnect with his family."

"Ah. I should have known." A half-smile lit Lucian's face. "She did seem rather fond of the werewolf, didn't she?"

"Yes, and I think it's good for her to get away. Good for him, too."

Lucian nodded, and a gentle breeze stirred the surrounding stalks of grass.

"Amaya, I need to tell you something," Lucian said.

"Okay." I pushed a strand of hair from my face. "What is it?"

"After Barb, I never wanted to marry anyone again. I was afraid if they ever got pregnant, they would die just like Barb."

"What?" I asked, surprise in my voice. "Lucian, why didn't you say anything?"

"Because I couldn't. I knew I would hurt you if I told you, so I said nothing. But that's all changed since we've lost our powers. Now, I get to live my life how I've always wanted, even if it is more than a century late." A sparkle lit his eyes.

Butterflies flitted through my stomach, and my cheeks heated.

We crested the hilltop and dismounted our horses, allowing them to graze as we sat on the hill and looked toward the horizon. For once, the towers of Crimson Hollow were behind us, and we faced a blank canvas full of potential.

Khan lay by me with his head on his paws. Lucian held me close, then took my hand in his, tracing my fingers with his. Then, he pulled something from his pocket and slid a ring on my finger. Tiny diamonds clustered around a larger stone, glinting in the sun with prismatic beauty.

"What?" I gasped.

He kissed my cheek, and a spark of mischief lit his eyes. "I want you to marry me, Amaya. Will you have me?"

I wanted to tell him that of course I would have him. Thinking of being with him again was the only thing keeping me sane while being imprisoned by the Emmersons. I didn't know how I would live without him.

"Yes," I answered, surer of this than anything else in my life. "I couldn't imagine spending my life with anyone but you."

He kissed me, and in that moment, my fears and worries for the future faded. There was a time I would have struggled over the decision, but my trials had strengthened me, and now I knew without a shadow of a doubt, I had the power to face my future with courage, and I wouldn't do it alone. Lucian squeezed my hand. We faced the rising sun as it chased away the lingering shadows.

S*ocialites* ***expected*** *a large wedding with celebrity guests and a lavish venue. The Vidraru couple declined the spotlight, and instead held a modest wedding situated on the quaint property of the former Crimson Hollow facility. They are calling the ceremony a new beginning, not only for them, but for the tens of thousands of lives impacted by Viridae Sangre.*

ABOUT THE AUTHOR

Tamara Grantham is the award-winning author of more than a dozen books and novellas, including the Olive Kennedy: Fairy World MD series, the Shine novellas, and the Twisted Ever After trilogy. *Dreamthief*, the first book of her Fairy World MD series, won first place for fantasy in INDIEFAB'S Book of the Year Awards, a RONE award for best New Adult Romance of 2016, and is a #1 bestseller on Amazon with over 200 five-star reviews.

Tamara has been a featured speaker at numerous writing conferences and has been a panelist at Comic Con Wizard World. Born and raised in Texas, Tamara now lives with her husband and five children in Wichita, Kansas.

ALSO BY TAMARA GRANTHAM

Legends of Crimson Hollow

Never Call Me Vampire

Dare to Call Me Vampire

The Chronicles of Ithical

The 7th Lie

The End of Never (2023)

The Alderfell Chronicles

The Not-So-Chosen One

Twisted Ever After

The Witch's Tower

Dragon Swan Princess

Rumpel's Redemption

Fairy World MD

Dreamthief

Spellweaver

Bloodthorn

Silverwitch

Goblinwraith (novella)

Deathbringer

Grayghost